The Seed of Gadianton

3rd Novel in the Shaylae Trilogy

J. Antony Miller

authorHOUSE®

AuthorHouse™
1663 Liberty Drive
Bloomington, IN 47403
www.authorhouse.com
Phone: 1 (800) 839-8640

Published by AuthorHouse   12/29/2016

ISBN: 978-1-5246-0751-7 (sc)
ISBN: 978-1-5246-0750-0 (hc)
ISBN: 978-1-5246-0749-4 (e)

Library of Congress Control Number: 2016908245

Print information available on the last page.

Part One
Nashota, the Little Twin

PROLOGUE

Shaylae sat up in bed cross-legged, leaning against three pillows. Asdza and Halona were both asleep, and she was catching up reviewing term papers. "How do these kids even get into DIT?" she said, shaking her head and letting out a huge sigh. "This one," she said flicking her wrist at the screen, "hasn't even grasped the basics of tensor analysis!"

"OK, now you're exaggerating," said Mika. "They wouldn't have gotten past the first round of the application process if that were true."

"Take a look and see if you don't agree with me," she said, sticking her computer under his nose.

Mika grinned. She recognized that grin.

"What?" she said, trying to sound impatient, but his smile was irresistible, pulling her in like a child drawn to a brightly colored carousel. She could not stop her own smile from spreading across her cheeks.

"Oh, I don't know," he said. "In a few minutes you're going to put down that computer, and then I'm going to kiss you until you burst!"

Ten years of marriage really agreed with these two. Only once had angry words passed between them, and that had been four years before their wedding. Now they were joined. Each individual feature of their lives, like strands of silk, braided together into an unbreakable cord.

"You're not *that* good a kisser," she said, closing her laptop.

She half expected him to wrestle her to her back and tickle her—that was his usual response to her jibes—but this time he reached his hand to her cheek with a touch so light it wouldn't have disturbed a snowflake. He leaned up and brought his lips to hers in a kiss that brought tears to her eyes. Her love for him welled up inside her, like magma deep inside a volcano.

3

"OK, so you are," she said trembling, not even breaking the kiss. She sank back on the bed staring into his dark brown eyes, her whole body tingling with anticipation. Nashota had been right; the love they shared was one of the greatest of the Holy Ones' gifts. She closed her eyes as his lips caressed her forehead, her eyelids, her cheeks her nose, and finally engulfed her mouth. With a will of their own, her arms found their way round his broad shoulders, his strong back.

"Mama."

They sat up quickly. Their eight-year-old daughter stood at their doorway, tears in her eyes.

"Mama," she repeated again, using the name she had called her mother since before she could talk.

"What is it, Asdza?"

"She was here again."

Shaylae's heart froze. The first time this had happened she had tried to attribute it to a bad dream, kissed Asdza, and tucked her into her bed, but still, she had had an uneasy feeling about the description of the nightmare: a woman had woken her, stood at the end of the bed and stared, her blue eyes shining with their own inner light. She had said nothing, just stared. "Where is she?"

"She's gone."

"Come here, little one," said Shaylae holding out her arms. She hugged Asdza close to her. The poor little mite was shaking. "It's OK," she said, rubbing her back.

"She laughed at me."

"She laughed? Did she speak to you?"

"She said something, but I don't know what it means."

"What did she say?"

"It sounded like Nashota."

Shaylae brought her hand to her mouth. "Nashota? You're sure she said Nashota?"

"Yes, that's what she said."

Shaylae looked at Mika. He didn't seem concerned, he just shrugged. "Come on, Az, It's probably nothing. I'm sure you'll feel better in the morning," he said. "Let me carry you back to bed."

"No, Mika. I think there's something to this." She reached for her robe and pulled it around her shoulders. "Come on, Asdza, I'll carry you back to bed." She picked up Asdza in her arms, slipped her legs over the side of the bed and stood up. Her left leg folded beneath her and she stumbled, almost dropping Asdza.

"Shaylae!" exclaimed Mika, jumping out of bed. "What happened?"

"I don't know," she said rubbing her knee. "It's never bothered me like this before." Her left leg had never fully recovered from the brutal beating she had received at the hands of Second of the Interstellar Spacecraft *Revenge*, but tonight it felt as if it was on fire.

"Here, I'll take Az back to bed. You lay down."

"You can carry her, but I need to spend some time in her room; find out what's going on."

Mika effortlessly picked up his daughter and carried her to her room, followed by Shaylae, her limp significantly more pronounced. He pushed open the door with his foot, walked over to Asdza's bed, carefully laid her down and pulled the covers over her.

Shaylae's eyes widened as she took a huge breath. "It's so cold."

"What?"

"It's so cold in here. It's got to be close to freezing."

"What are you talking about, hon? It's fine."

"I feel it too," said Asdza, shivering.

Mika looked at them both eyes wide, eyebrows raised.

"I think we need to be alone," she said.

Mika nodded. "You think I should check on Halona?"

Halona was not yet three. She was a daddy's girl if ever there was one, and beautiful almost beyond Shaylae's comprehension.

She thought a moment. "No, she's fine."

Mike leaned down and kissed her. "I'll be right next door," he said as he closed the door behind him.

"Scoot over," said Shaylae as she climbed under the covers with her daughter. "Can I touch your soul, Nituna?" she asked, using the Native American word for daughter. Shaylae could easily move into the mind of any one she wanted, but she never did so uninvited, especially her own children, but to touch another's soul required their willing desire to share; they had to open themselves up to this spiritual kind of embrace.

"Oh yes, Mama. You know I like that." She smiled.

Effortlessly their souls joined as Shaylae sang a lullaby. Asdza's mind was that of a precocious eight-year-old, but it also had the touch of a mature elder. Oh, how she loved this child. As she caressed her with her words and her songs she felt peace returning to Asdza's soul. She stopped shaking and soon fell into a deep, calm sleep.

Shaylae was feeling anything but peace, and she was still shivering. The room became colder still, as an eerie image began to take shape before her.

"Nashota is mine." The voice was harsh, bitter and cold, like a storm of freezing rain. Gradually, at the end of Asdza's bed, the blonde-haired woman materialized. She looked to be about Shaylae's age, and if not for the evil Shaylae sensed emanating from her, she would have been very pretty. Her hair was shoulder length and curly, her eyes blue, but the whites were ruddy. Shaylae shot a glance at Asdza, but thankfully she was still fast asleep. She tried to touch the intruder's mind but all she drew was a blank.

"You can't touch me, or reach me, Shaylae of the Gentle Heart, because when I've disposed of her, this present will cease to exist; no one would have returned to Tal'el'Dine'h; your precious White Cloud would never have been born, and neither would you. Those you call the Dark Ones will destroy your precious Earth."

Shaylae's skin crawled. She felt a primal fear growing within her. "Blessed Ancestors."

"Soon they will no longer have ever existed." She laughed, and her image began to fade.

"Wait, who are you?" Shaylae's voice cracked. Her mouth and throat were dry, her lips so cold they could hardly move, but the terrible apparition was gone. Slowly the room warmed up, but Shaylae would not leave Asdza's bed tonight. She laid her head next to Asdza's and snuggled up to her. For a long time she could not sleep; she just sobbed.

***

"I hardly slept. I kept thinking you'd be coming back to bed," said Mika as he rubbed his weary eyes walking into Asdza's bedroom. Shaylae was still lying next to their daughter, who was peacefully sleeping. The whites of Shaylae's beautiful blue eyes were blood-shot, and her face was blotchy. Mika had only seen his wife cry a few times, and each time it broke his heart.

"Shay, what is it?"

"I'm not sure. But I think it's really bad; terrible."

"What?" He walked over and stood next to her, stroking her hair.

"Could you get me some coffee? I think I need caffeine." She managed the barest of smiles.

"Of course." He didn't move; he just kept staring at her.

"Coffee," she prompted.

"Right," he said as he nodded and turned around. In the kitchen he switched on the coffee maker and watched as the carafe slowly began to fill. He walked over to the window and opened the blinds. Their breakfast room window faced east, with a spectacular view of Millcreek Canyon and the mountains of the Wasatch front.

What could Shaylae have meant when she said something terrible had happened? Why had she been crying? Asdza seemed OK, so what could be wrong? He reached into the cabinet and took out two breakfast mugs. He put two spoonful's of sugar into his. Shaylae would drink hers black and unsweetened.

"You're so good to me," she said.

He turned around. She was standing at the kitchen door, leaning against the wall. Her red silk robe was draped loosely around her, coming to mid-thigh. "How could I not be? You're so beautiful." It was true. Even with her tearstained face, her bloodshot eyes and her disheveled hair her loveliness shone through like Father Sun breaking through the clouds after a storm.

She smiled another half-smile, walked over to the counter and pulled out a barstool. "Is that all you love me for, my beauty?"

Mika was surprised that even in her anxious state she would not let him get away with that minor display of chauvinism. "Here," he said, handing her the coffee mug, shaking his head. He didn't have to answer her charge; he knew she knew better.

"Thanks," she said, cradling the mug, breathing in the aroma. It seemed huge in her tiny hands.

"What happened last night?"

"It was a woman."

"A woman?"

"Yes, maybe the same age as me. She appeared at the end of her bed."

"What did she look like?"

"Well, she should have been pretty. Blonde curly hair, huge bright blue eyes, but there was something distinctly ugly about her."

"Ugly?"

"More evil than ugly."

"Did she say anything?"

"Yes. She said 'Nashota is mine', so I thought she was referring to Matriarch Nashota, but then she said 'this present will cease to exist' and then talking about our ancestors she said 'They will soon no longer ever have existed', so I wondered if she was referring to the Nashota who brought her people back to Tal'el'Dine'h."

"Maybe she meant the Nashota who sent White Cloud back to Earth."

Shaylae frowned. "She might have. I suppose." She took a sip of coffee and stopped. "I've always wondered why they all had the same name. Three different women, all important in the history of the People…"

"Maybe she's the same woman," interrupted Mika with a smile.

Shaylae stopped drinking and looked up at Mika, her eyes wide and her brow furrowed. "Wait a minute, are you suggesting they're the same person?"

"I was kidding."

"But, Mika, what if they are? What if they are all the same person?"

"C'mon, Shay. That's impossible."

"Is it?"

"You're suggesting she's immortal?"

"Maybe. What do you think?"

"But that would make her over five-hundred years old!"

Could it be? Could Nashota really be five-hundred years old? She had said Tal'el'Dine'h was a very special place—holy. Was there something about that planet that kept a person young? Or was it just her? No, it sounded ridiculous, but at the same time it made sense.

"Oh no!" she exclaimed, bringing a hand to her mouth. "What did Nashota tell White Cloud when he came to Earth?"

"That he was to be your great-grandfather."

"No, about growing old?"

"I don't remember."

"I do. I remember it clearly because it bothered me. She said 'you will grow old and die on Earth.'" Shaylae began to cry. "Mika, do you realize what that meant to him? If what we're thinking is true, then White Cloud gave up his life to come to Earth to help me. He would still be alive today on Tal'el'Dine'h if he had stayed there!"

Mika's jaw dropped.

"He did more than just give up his home, Mika, he gave up his life for me." She sat down again. "Mika, it's time to go to visit Nashota. She needs me."

"To Tal'el'Dine'h?"

"No, to the Mesa of Changing Woman, five hundred years ago. I have to learn more about her."

The next morning Shaylae rode off on Snow Lion, and finding a secluded spot, she laid her blanket on the ground and sat cross legged. As she prayed to the blessed ancestors, she felt herself travel across space and time to a small village in mid-winter. Hidden between the folds in space and time she watched …

CHAPTER 1

Long Night, 1584 – Dzil Na'oodilii, Dinetah.

Hastiin took his daughter's hands in his and cradled them against his breast. "Do not worry, my precious Nizhoni, the Blessed Ancestors are with you."

"Father, I feel so near to death."

Hastiin could hardly hear her through her labored breathing.

"No, child, you must not talk so."

She raised her arm weakly and beckoned him to come closer.

"This has been a journey I have traveled in sorrow. I have brought shame upon you and your Hogan, and the Holy Ones have punished me."

"My dearest child, you have done no wrong; in nothing have you offended the Holy Ones. Those who took you captive and lay with you, it is they who offended the Holy Ones and our Blessed Ancestors."

"But, Father, I was weak. I should have been stronger."

Hastiin was weeping now. Even advanced with child and in terrible pain she was still a beauty beyond compare; he had named her well. Her raven hair hung limply, soaked in her sweat, but it was still as fine as the gossamer threads of a spider web. Her eyes were bloodshot her jaw clenched, and her face contorted with pain.

"My daughter, you were but fourteen summers when the Spanish soldiers took you."

She cried out again. She put her hands on her belly and arched her back. "Father, there is something wrong. I can feel it. My child is caught between the worlds."

Matriarch Sahkyo, who had been sitting quietly near the doorway of the Hogan, stood up. "Dear friend, Hastiin, I think you should leave us. Our sisters will attend to your daughter."

Reluctantly Hastiin realized that she was right. This was no place for a man, even the war chief of the Kiiyaa'áanii clan. He stood wearily, his bones stiff from the bitter cold, and let out a great sigh. He pulled his skins closer around his body, and looked sadly at his daughter. "Take care of her," he said. The two young women tending her did not even look up.

"Oh, be off with you old man," said Sahkyo.

Old man! At sixty-five summers, she was almost twice his age, but her smile reached deep into his heart and warmed his body. Her hair was as white as the snow that covered the frozen earth outside of his Hogan but her cheeks were deep red, like the flowers of the desert rose. "Dear daughter, I will not be far. Put your trust in the Blessed Ancestors," he said, as he walked from the Hogan. Father Sun had set about five hands of time before and the sky was dark, echoing his mood.

Sahkyo had followed him out, leaving the younger women to tend to Nizhoni. "Hastiin, my dear friend, I'm sorry," she said, her eyes lowered.

"It does not look good for her, Matriarch?"

Sadly she shook her head. "I'm afraid she may not survive."

Hastiin buried his head in his hands and wept again. "No, the Blessed Ancestors will keep her safe."

She put her hand on his arm. "Perhaps they need her more than we do."

Nizhoni screamed. The sound tore at his soul even more than when his own precious wife had traveled to the Land of the Dead. She screamed again.

"Matriarch, come quickly!"

"Stay here," she said, hurrying back into the Hogan.

Hastiin looked to the south, high in the night sky, where Sister Moon in half face looked on with sadness. He turned his gaze to the east where the Ancient Warrior stood guard just above the horizon, his tomahawk hanging from his belt pointing to Tal'el'Dine'h about four hands diagonally across the sky. Long ago Mother Asdzáán Nádleehé had told The People never to forget this star person, for he was her father. Hastiin did not know what she had meant, or why she had been so insistent that they should never forget, but his people had remembered, and passed the knowledge to each succeeding generation. Five hands above the left foot of the Warrior, diagonally opposite from Tal'el'Dine'h, was another star, a much brighter star. Asdzáán Nádleehé had insisted they never forget him either. "He is the devil," she had said. "His name is Procyon."

Another scream pierced the night.

"Hastiin, come quickly," shouted Sahkyo. "Quickly."

He ran back into the Hogan and rejoiced at the peaceful smile on Nizhoni's face. "I told you the Blessed Ancestors would be with you…"

"They have come for me father."

"No, you are well…"

"Take care of my baby," she said as her eyes misted over, and then closed.

In disbelief he laid his head on his daughter's breast. There was no sound of her breathing soul. The women wept.

"She's gone, dear friend."

"The baby?"

"I'm afraid your granddaughter is also dead." Sahkyo was holding a small bundle, wrapped in a blanket.

"No, she said I was to look after her baby." He stood up and walked toward her and held his arms out toward the bundle but she shook her head and turned away.

"Matriarch," said one of the women. "I think you should see this."

"What is it?" she asked, leaning down next to Nizhoni's bed. "Blessed Ancestors," she exclaimed, "there's another child."

"Another child," said Hastiin incredulously.

"Give me your knife. We must cut it free."

"No, I…"

"Hastiin, the child is yet alive, but will die within the next hair of time unless we free it." Still he stood, transfixed in his sadness. "Hastiin, we don't have time," she said, holding out her hand.

"No, I'll do it," he said, taking out his knife. He knelt down next to his daughter as the women uncovered her belly.

"Cut here," said Sahkyo, indicating a line from Nizhoni's navel to her groin. "Not too deeply. Hurry."

Carefully he cut as Sahkyo had indicated, tears falling from his eyes.

Two of the women used spoon-like wooden tools to spread the wound open, and Sahkyo reached in and carefully took out the unborn baby. There was no sound, no sign of life.

"I'm afraid she too is…"

"No, she is alive," said Hastiin, taking the infant in his arms. He used his hand to wipe away the blood then carefully laid his mouth over hers.

"Gently, gently. Like the breath of a butterfly."

Hastiin breathed into his granddaughter's mouth, once, twice, three times, and then she coughed, and cried.

"Blessed Ancestors," said Sahkyo, holding out her arms.

Hastiin shook his head, and took a blanket from one of the young women. "No, I must show her to Mother Earth, and to Tal'el'Dine'h."

Standing in the doorway were the spirits of two women, shining like the silver moon.

"Take care of her, father," said one of them. "She knows of Tal'el'Dine'h. She knows the way back."

"Nizhoni!"

"Our daughter will find our Blessed Ancestors," said the other. "You need not sing her soul to them, I will take her there."

"Halona, my wife."

The women in the Hogan fell to the floor, heads touching the ground. For a moment all was silent, and then the Matriarch spoke softly. "She has come to us from the Holy Ones."

"Her name is Nashota, the twin," he said, walking outside into the cold night. He held his arms upward, showing her to Tal'el'Dine'h directly in the east. "Her name is Nashota."

***

Shaylae was so moved by this display of love that she could not hold back the tears which trickled down her cheeks.

CHAPTER 2

Shaylae moved forward in time, five years.

***

"Grandfather, what is Tal'el'Dine'h?"

Hastiin laughed. "Five summers old, and already you're asking questions to which I don't know the answer." He stopped, wiping away the wood chips from the eagle he was carving. "Pass me that cloth," he said, pointing to the rag soaked in grease laying on the rock next to Nashota. Taking it from her he rubbed his handiwork vigorously. Father sun shone down on them warmly; it was a beautiful day. Tomorrow would be equal-day and for the next six moons the days would be longer than the nights. It was Hastiin's favorite season when life began anew, the dawn of a new year the Holy Ones had created for them, just as they created a new day each morning.

"Let me see it, Grandfather," she asked holding out her hand.

"Ah, it is not finished, child." She tilted her head to one side and smiled, holding out her hand further. He shook his head. "Oh, but you remind me of her," he said, seeing his own daughter in her mischievous grin. He handed the unfinished eagle to her. It looked huge in her grasp, its wingspan as wide as her body.

"Tal'el'Dine'h," he began, "is Asdzáán Nádleehé's father..."

"You mean like Father Sun?"

"Now that's a silly question," he said. "How could a star in the sky be as great as Father Sun?"

"Why not?"

He looked at her curiously. What could she have meant by that?

15

"When Asdzáán Nádleehé was found on Ch'óol'í'í by First Man…"

"I don't think Tal'el'Dine'h is a star."

"Whatever do you mean, child?"

"I think Tal'el'Dine'h is a world, just like our Glittering World."

"Now that's just foolishness. There is no other Glittering World…"

She smiled and shrugged her shoulders. "I know, grandfather, but I still think Asdzáán Nádleehé was born on Tal'el'Dine'h, the same as we are born into the Glittering World, and that she wants us to go back there."

Hastiin had heard some strange ideas from Nashota's mouth, but none this strange. He was about to say something when as suddenly as she had begun the conversation, it was over.

"Can we go fishing, Grandfather?" she asked, her bright eyes alive with curiosity and intelligence. Curious intelligence may have been a better description. He laughed.

"Of course, child." They began walking back to the Hogan to get his spear.

"I feel the spirit of the eagle," she said, gently running her fingers over the wings of the wooden image.

"Nashota, you are indeed a blessed soul."

"I also feel your spirit in it."

"The Holy Wind is in all things, child, and as we give ourselves to creating something, then our spirit joins with it."

Hand-in hand they walked toward the river, arms swinging happily.

CHAPTER 3

Watching Nashota grow into a lovely young woman filled Shaylae's heart with love for this wonderful blessed ancestor.

***

Nashota was truly a gift from the Holy Ones; smart, beautiful, strong, and healthy. For eleven summers she had brightened Hastiin's life, always happy, smiling all day long, even when doing her chores. The younger children loved her. He watched as she played a game with them. Like a young mother, she had them gathered into a circle. She tied a sash around the eyes of a boy of four summers, turned him around five times and then let him go. The children in the circle called out the sounds of the animals they were pretending to be, scampering away to avoid the boy's clutches. Either he wasn't very good at the game, or the other children were too fleet-footed for him. After a few minutes he was becoming quite frustrated at not being able to catch any of the other squealing children. Nashota must have sensed his discouragement because she deliberately placed herself in his path. He shrieked with delight.

"Got you!" he shouted triumphantly.

"Howl, Howl," said Nashota, making the sound of a captured coyote.

"You're a coyote!" he said.

Nashota made a coyote-whimpering sound.

"And you're Nashota," he cried, pulling off his blindfold.

"Yasi, you're so good at this game," she said, picking him up in her arms and hugging him. She swung him round a few times, both of them laughing.

A child's scream pierced the tranquil afternoon, cut off as suddenly as it began. Hastiin jumped to his feet and ran toward the river, where the horrifying sound had come from. Nashota was already ahead of him, running effortlessly, with graceful strides of her long legs. As he broke through the bush to the clearing by the river bank, Hastiin was horrified to see a full-grown cougar with a little girl of three summers held in his powerful jaws. Nashota was walking toward him, hands outstretched. "Nashota! No! Come back. It's too late," he cried, fearful for his precious granddaughter.

She ignored him. "Brother cougar," she said calmly. "Let little Bluebird go. There's a deer over there," she said, pointing to the east. "He will be a better meal for you."

The cougar dropped the child and growled menacingly. The hair on his back stood up like a line of junipers and he crouched backwards, ready to spring. Hastiin's heart leapt to his mouth, but he could not speak.

"Doli!" Another scream pierced the clearing. It was Dezba, the child's mother.

Nashota held her arm out behind her, palm outward. "Wait, Elder Dezba," she said. She kept walking toward the cougar, all the while speaking softly. The hairs on the cougar's back settled down as he adopted a less threatening posture.

Hastiin was frozen, unsure what to do, unsure if he did anything it would endanger his Nashota's life. "Blessed Ancestors," he whispered. A large crowd of villagers had gathered, all frozen like Hastiin.

Nashota had reached the magnificent creature. She reached out her hand and touched his head. He relaxed and nuzzled against her, rubbing his flanks against her legs. Nashota looked so frail and helpless next to the cougar's rippling, muscular body, yet it was she who was the dominant one. Like a little kitten he purred. Nashota pointed once more to the east, and off the cougar bounded.

Dezba had reached little Doli, who lay motionless on the ground in a widening pool of blood. "Blessed Ancestors, she's dead," she wailed with outstretched hands to the heavens. "She's all I have. Holy Ones, do not take her from me."

Hastiin ran to where the child lay, and placed his arm around Dezba's shoulder. "Come, friend," he said, helping her to her feet. Little Bluebird was motionless, her eyes closed, her face without expression, almost peaceful. A death in the village was always hard, particularly of such a promising young child as this. And for poor Dezba, it would be her second loss in half a sun cycle – her husband had died of the burning blood before the last long night.

Nashota kneeled on the ground in the blood next to Doli. Whispering quietly a prayer to the Holy Ones, she placed her hands on the little ravaged body. Her little tunic was torn open and blood gushed from a huge gaping wound in Doli's stomach, but as Nashota lovingly passed her hands over her, the wounds closed up, and the skin returned to its unblemished perfection. A reverent hush descended upon all present, hardly able to believe, and certainly not understanding what they were witnessing.

Suddenly Doli opened her eyes and whimpered.

"My baby," cried Dezba. "My little Bluebird," she said as she knelt down next to her daughter.

"Mother," was all Doli said as she nestled into her mother's arms.

Nashota said nothing; she stood, returned to her Hogan and changed out of her blood-stained dress. Hastiin followed her to the river and watched silently as she washed the deerskin garment. He had always known his granddaughter was special from the moment he had taken her from his daughter's lifeless body, but this? What was he to make of this? It was almost as if he didn't know her.

She turned and noticed him standing behind her. She waved and smiled. "Grandfather," she called out to him.

He walked over to her, wondering if he was in the presence of one of the Holy Ones, but the closer he got, the more she looked like his little baby. Her fresh, smiling, innocent face held the promise of womanhood, not godhood.

"Would you like salmon tonight?" she asked.

He nodded his head once. She smiled and gestured to the salmon lying on the ground next to her. It was a magnificent fish, the length of his forearm.

"How…" he began, not sure of what to say.

"He came to me, Grandfather."

Later that evening, after they had eaten, Matriarch Sahkyo visited them. Now seventy-six summers she was still an imposing woman.

"Hastiin, I would talk with Little Twin," she said.

Hastiin stood up. "Certainly, Elder," he said, bowing, and taking two steps from her before turning around.

"No, old friend, please stay."

"As you wish, Matriarch," he said, sitting once more next to the fire. "Some fish?" he asked, taking a piece from their evening meal and offering it to her. She took the proffered food and chewed on it thoughtfully.

"Now, little Nashota," she began. "The Holy Ones have truly blessed you."

"Oh, I don't know, Elder..." she began.

"No," said Sahkyo, holding up her hand. "It is true. Never in my memory have I heard of such a one as you; never in the memory of the village." Nashota shrugged nervously, almost uncomfortable at the remarks Elder Sahkyo was making. "Can you tell me what you were thinking; what you saw?"

"I'm not sure I know the answer myself, Elder."

"Did you talk to the cougar's mind?"

"I think so," she said, screwing up her eyes. "It was as if he really was my brother; as if I was connected to him. I sensed his thoughts and he sensed mine." Sahkyo raised her eyebrows and looked at Hastiin, who shrugged. "I saw the deer grazing, and put the picture in his mind," she added.

"And Doli? How did you restore her to life?"

"I'm not sure, Elder," she said. "But she was not quite dead. I could see her body as I would see a rug I was weaving, or a basket I was making. It was just like putting things back in their place, tidying up."

"And what were you feeling?"

"I felt I was part of Mother Earth, the whole world, and I knew there was nothing more important than healing little Bluebird."

For a moment there was silence. Elder Sahkyo reached out toward the fire, warming her hands.

"Hastiin," she said finally. "Our sacred mother, Changing Woman, has a special purpose for this one."

She stood up and left them.

CHAPTER 4

Shaylae knew that today she would visit Nashota. It was her time …

***

Early in the morning, a cold fresh winter morning, not yet one moon after Nashota's fourteenth name-day, she wakened Hastiin, gently shaking his shoulder.

"I've started, Grandfather," she said.

"Started what?" he asked sleepily.

"The cycles of Changing Woman," she said quietly.

He sat up quickly from his bed, pulling the blanket around him. "Oh, my precious granddaughter." He took her in his arms and hugged her. "Let me fetch Dezba. She will know what to do."

Nashota smiled warmly at her grandfather. He was a wonderful man, but not much help in the matters of being a young woman. And since the miracle with little Doli, Dezba had been almost a mother to her. Grandfather was right; she would know what to do. While he was gone she thought how grateful she was for this day the Holy Ones had blessed her with, as they did each new morn. But this day she was especially thankful. Now she was a young woman and could become a bride and mother in the village. She was very late beginning her cycles, but she was happy she had had a few more sun cycles of being a girl. Others her age had started three sun cycles earlier; a few were already married with children.

Dezba came into the Hogan, smiling, and took Nashota into her arms. "Come, young woman, come with me." Dezba showed her how to clean herself, how to dress herself, and how to purify herself. She washed her hair in suds from the yucca root and tied it with a thin strip of deerskin. "For the next four days you will not sleep much, and when you do, you should lie on your back. You will not eat meat or anything with seasoning; sweets and sweetening are especially forbidden. Your diet should be corn foods with no salt added and you should drink very little water."

Nashota nodded. She did not fully understand but she knew the Ceremony of Changing Woman was sacred. It was an announcement made to the People that she was now a woman, ready for courtship and marriage. Runners would be sent to neighboring villages. Hundreds would come to celebrate the new woman among the People; among them would be young men from other clans looking for a bride.

There was a knock at the door of the Hogan. "Where is the young woman?" It was Matriarch Sahkyo.

Nashota opened the door and bowed. Outside her Hogan were all of the woman and girls from the village, each holding a blanket. Behind them, laughing and smiling, some with a touch of embarrassment, were the men and boys, Grandfather among them. While they could watch the proceedings, they could not participate; this was a ceremony for the women.

"Come sister, let us mold you into a woman," said Sahkyo. Dezba and Nashota walked out into the cool morning air. The sun was just rising in a clear blue sky.

"Thank you, blessed Holy Ones, for this new day," said Nashota, touching her hand to her head.

"Lay your blankets here," said Sahkyo, laying hers on the ground. The other girls and women laid their blankets on top of the one Sahkyo had placed. "You may choose any of the women to mold you."

"Then I choose Dezba," said Nashota.

She had seen this part of Kinaalda many times, and she always thought it to be the most beautiful. She lay face down on the blankets, spreading her arms and legs wide. Dezba kneeled next to her.

Whispering precious words of blessing and promise, Dezba molded Nashota's body into a woman. Nashota closed her eyes, lulled by Dezba's soft voice and gentle touch.

"I mold your arms…"

As Dezba spoke, a strange detached feeling came over Nashota, as if she had left her body. She opened her eyes. She was standing on a hillside, overlooking a beautiful valley. Father sun hung low on the horizon but already it was warm. Beautiful birds flew in a clear blue sky as animals, some of whom she did not recognize, grazed peacefully on the grassy slopes. She kicked off her moccasins and wiggled her toes in the lush grass, still damp from the morning dew. The feeling of peace was tangible, almost overwhelming. She took a deep breath of the clean air.

"Where am I?" she asked.

"You are on Tal'el'Dine'h, the home world of Asdzáán Nádleehé."

She whirled around. Behind her stood a young woman, her dark hair hanging below her shoulders. Her face was beautiful, kind and gentle, and her eyes were blue. Nashota had never before seen eyes such a color. She wore a long cloak, green and gold, made of the finest cloth. Surely she was one of the Holy Ones.

"Who are you?" she stammered.

"Like you, I am a daughter of Changing Woman," she said. "My name is Shaylae, but at my Kinaalda Asdzáán Nádleehé came to me and gave me the name Yanaba, 'She Who Meets the Enemy.'" She held out her arms and took Nashota in a warm embrace.

Nashota wasn't sure if she should return the embrace or fall to her knees in worship.

"Asdzáán Nádleehé was born here twenty five hundred sun cycles ago. You were right. Tal'el'Dine'h is not the star you see in your night sky, but a world which calls that star Father Sun."

"Then this is not the Glittering World?"

"We are far from your home, very far."

"Am I really here? How?"

"Yes. I brought you here through time and space. But you will be back at you Kinaalda before any one knows you were gone."

"And Asdzáán Nádleehé was born here? It is so beautiful. Why would she leave, and how did she come to the Glittering World?"

Yanaba smiled sadly. "Dark Ones came to Asdzáán Nádleehé's world and destroyed it. All were killed except her. Her family, her friends, her Elders; all were killed."

Nashota was horrified. "Who would do such a thing? Who are the Dark Ones?"

"They are from the sixth world of the star Procyon."

"The one she calls *The Devil?*"

Yanaba nodded. "Some of her words have become lost in the myths and legends, but yes, it was once an evil place."

Suddenly it was night. A million stars sparkled in the sky. Sister Moon's face was different, and she seemed bigger.

"Tal'el'Dine'h's Sister Moon is not the same as the Glittering World's. And yes, she is bigger because Tal'el'Dine'h is bigger," said Yanaba.

Nashota looked at her curiously. She had read her thoughts.

"See," she said pointing to the east. "The star you call the Sentinel."

"Yes," said Nashota. "I see him."

"Two hands directly above The Sentinel is Procyon."

"The home of the ones you call Dark Ones?"

"Yes."

"And they came to Tal'el'Dine'h many sun cycles ago?"

Once again they were in bright daylight. Yanaba looked eastward and pointed. "There, about four day's journey, stood her city. The Dark One's ship destroyed it. She was standing here, watching, as all that she loved was consumed in a cataclysm."

"She was on her own?"

"She was preparing for her Kinaalda. Like you, it came to her late."

"How did she survive?"

"She was able to shift herself out of the path of destruction."

"Shift?"

Yanaba smiled, but did not explain. "Tal'el'Dine'h would not be able to support life for many generations. Asdzáán Nádleehé searched the heavens and found Earth, the Glittering World. Long Life Man and Happiness Woman found her, and called her their daughter."

"How did she find the Glittering World?"

Once more it was night. "See, three hands to the left of the Sentinel, and slightly above, you see that small dim star?"

"Yes."

"It is the one you call *Father Sun.*"

"He seems so small."

"He is far away, very far away."

"She journeyed to Father Sun? And that is how she came to be the Mother of the People?"

"Yes, it is."

Nashota furrowed her brow. "I don't understand. How can this be?"

"Trust me, dear sister. One day you will understand. Now, I must leave you."

"But there is so much I would ask you."

"In time. For now, enjoy your Kinaalda. It will be wonderful. Be strong and run swiftly. The power of the Holy Wind is within you. You will take great strides in your knowledge and power and you will begin to understand the Universe the Holy Ones created. You will learn how to shift, and one day, not too may sun cycles from now, you will return here to Tal'el'Dine'h with some of Changing Woman's children. Here you will find safety; here you will find knowledge, and here you will find great power. Tal'el'Dine'h is a very special place; it will have the protection of the Holy Ones. Until you are ready to return here, I will continue to watch over you." And she was gone.

"You may arise now, woman of the village and of the People."

Nashota raised her head from the blankets and looked around. All were smiling at her. No one knew anything of her experience with Yanaba, and now would not be the time to tell them.

For the next four days at dawn, at noon, and in the evening, Nashota ran toward the sun, each day running farther. How well she ran would determine how strong a young woman and mother she would be. During the day and into the evening she ground corn into special alkaan batter for the cake she would bake. Dezba coached her in the Blessingway songs she would sing as she became a woman.

Nashota was a little embarrassed by all of the attention she was getting. Each day more people from neighboring villages would arrive to celebrate the Kinaalda. Some of them came on horseback. Nashota was fascinated; no one in the village had a horse. She had seen only a few before, but none this close up. They were magnificent creatures.

Each day more young men would watch her, and cheer her as she raced toward the sun. While she felt self-conscious she also felt a little excitement, thinking that one day soon perhaps she would be the wife of one of these fine young men and bear his children. One in particular had caught her eye. He was a quiet young man, not as boisterous as the others, but extremely handsome and strong. His black hair hung loosely to his broad shoulders, held in place only with a yellow headband. His eyes were piercing, but had a gentle, kind expression. Only once had she been close to him. She had smiled shyly at him, and he had smiled back, but that was all. No words passed between them, but she breathed deeply of his spirit. The scent of him excited her – she did not know why. He stood at least a head taller than her, but then she was only fourteen summers, and he looked to be at least sixteen.

Each day as she ground the corn the young men would stand around and watch her, stare at her was probably a better description, and she had to admit that she didn't mind. But *her* young man was not among them. The grinding was hard work and her knuckles became quite red and sore. Some of them would offer to help her.

"Thank you, but no," she told them. "This is a task I must complete on my own."

On the evening of the fourth day the men dug a shallow pit and lined it with cornhusks in a circular pattern. Nashota and Dezba then poured the batter into the pit. The men covered it with more cornhusks and then lit a fire over it, which burned all night.

"The cake represents Father Sun," Dezba explained. "And the pit represents your womb and your fertility, showing that the power of creation comes through the followers of Changing Woman."

Just before dawn, when the cake was baked, Nashota took it, broke pieces from it and gave to everyone, but she did not eat. The remaining piece of cake was left as a sacrifice to Mother Earth.

As Father Sun rose in the east, Nashota sang the sacred Blessing Way song, handed down from Changing Woman. Everyone was silent, even the little children and the boisterous young men, listening to Nashota's beautiful voice ringing across the valley. When it was over everyone cheered and surrounded her to greet her as the newest young woman of the Dine'h.

As she turned to face her Hogan, she stopped and pointed to the south. "Grandfather, what is that?" she said.

Silence once again descended as everyone stared where Nashota had pointed. About three hundred paces away stood a horse. In the early morning light it appeared to be rider-less.

"Stay here," said Hastiin to Nashota. He beckoned to a few of the warriors. "You men, follow me." They took up a trot as they ran toward the horse. As Hastiin got closer he realized there was a rider hunched over the horse's neck, barely hanging on. Cautiously he approached, not sure what he would find. He recognized the clothes and the jewelry of the rider as Zuni, possibly Acoma. But what would someone from the Sky City be doing this far north? It had to be at least a three-day ride.

Just as they reached the horse the rider began to slip sideways and fell to the ground. He landed awkwardly and did not move. Hastiin covered the last few paces and fell to his knees next to the man. He put his ear to his chest and heard the faintest of heartbeats, but there was no sign of life in his face.

"Let's get him back to the village," said Hastiin. He lifted him up and laid him across the horse's back. The saddle and bridle were Spanish; extravagant, carved leather, jewel encrusted and gold trimmed. "Steady him," he said to one of the men as he took hold of the reins and began leading the horse back to the village, but then he had a darker thought; the horse obviously belonged to an important man and he probably hadn't parted with it willingly. This man was almost certainly being followed.

"Who here has ridden a horse?" he asked.

"I have, War Chief," said a young man of about sixteen summers.

"What is your name, young warrior?"

"I am Niyol, Swift Wind of the Biihyázhí Clan," he said, bowing his head.

"Niyol, ride this horse to the river and then make your way back along the river toward the village. I will send some others on horseback to meet you at the river's edge to disguise his tracks."

He bowed. "War Chief, with respect, I think this is not a good idea."

"And why not, Swift Wind?"

"This horse is unlike any other horse I have seen—a noble horse, a magnificent stallion." Niyol stroked the horse's flanks. "I'm afraid he would be quite noticeable among the horses we rode here."

"I see. And like me, you expect that this man is being followed?"

"Almost certainly." Niyol rubbed the horse's neck. "The man who owns this beautiful animal will not let him go easily."

"Then what do you suggest?"

"That I ride him to the river as you suggest, confusing the tracks, but then ride a half day journey to the east and free him."

Hastiin considered this thoughtfully. "And you would be willing to take this risk?"

"I would, War Chief."

"Then may the Holy Ones be with you."

Niyol leaped effortlessly onto the horse's back and rode slowly toward the river.

Nashota watched as this drama unfolded. One young man had jumped onto the horse and ridden off. Gods, it was *her* young man. Her heart sank. Was he leaving already to go back to his own village?

The others were carrying a body back to the camp. As they came closer it appeared that the man was dead, or very close to death. They laid him at the feet of the Medicine Man who shook his medicine bundle up and down over the man's body, chanting a Blessingway healing song. He then knelt at the man's side. On his left foot he wore a moccasin, but his right foot appeared to be wrapped in some sort of loose, bloody bandage. He carefully unraveled the bandage. A gasp went up from the crowd as the stump where his foot should have been was exposed. It had been cut off at the ankle, and looked as if it had been sealed with fire.

The Medicine Man did not turn around. "Nashota," he said, beckoning her. "Come and see if there is anything you can do for this poor man."

Nashota stepped forward and knelt on the ground. He was barely breathing, and there was a foul stench coming from his right leg. The flesh was gangrenous – he would lose more of his leg, perhaps above the knee. She laid her hands on his chest, and just as she had with Doli two years earlier, she could sense his whole body. She ran her hands down his right leg. Where her hands passed over the flesh it was immediately healed. Cries of amazement went up from the crowd, especially from those not of her village who had not witnessed the miracle of Doli.

The man stirred and cried out in anguish. His breathing became rapid and shallow and he tried to sit up.

"Brother you must rest," said Nashota as she caressed his head and face. "Rest."

He lay back down, his eyes staring up into the sky, breathing calmly.

"Take him to my Hogan," said Hastiin.

Nashota cleaned up the man as best she could, and by noon was even able to feed him a few mouthfuls of soup.

"Who are you?" she asked, when he became more lucid. "And what happened to you?"

"I am Lonan," he answered weakly. "I must speak to your War Chief and Matriarch."

"We are here, brother." Sahkyo and Hastiin stood at the door. "I am Matriarch Sahkyo and this is my War Chief, Hastiin."

"Matriarch, War Chief, I have to leave your village. I will bring a terrible evil to you."

"You think you are being followed?" asked Hastiin. "We had supposed you were. We have covered your tracks and freed your horse a half day's ride from here."

"It won't be enough. These are ruthless men." He coughed raucously. Nashota rubbed his back.

"Tell us what happened, brother," said Sahkyo.

"I am Lonan, from the Sky City. One moon ago, just before Long Night, our city was attacked by the Spanish. In the battle seven of their men were killed, one of them was the nephew of a Nobleman. Five days ago they returned in force, with many men and huge fire sticks on wheels. They killed a thousand of my people: old men, women and children among them." His eyes glazed over. "Some they threw from the cliffs. I hear their cries even now."

Nashota's face creased up in horror. No one killed women and children, even in the most bloody of wars among the warring tribes of the high desert. Who would do such a thing? But then again, it was Spanish men who had raped her mother. Her eyes widened. Her father was Spanish! She had never really thought about it before and the shock of the revelation caused her to shudder. Her father was Spanish!

"And then, they took all of the surviving men over twenty-five summers and did this," he said, pointing to the stump of his right leg.

There was silence in the Hogan, except for Lonan's weeping.

Finally Hastiin spoke. "How did you escape?"

"After they cut off my foot, and sealed it with a fire brand, there was an older man pointing at me, laughing. In my anger and pain I launched myself at him and knocked him off his horse. In the confusion I was somehow able to jump on the horse's back. I rode away as fast as I could. They fired on me with their fire sticks, but they didn't hit me. Others took chase on their horses, but the horse I rode was faster. It wasn't long before I had outrun them. For many hours I looked behind me. I was still getting farther away from them, but they were not going to give up."

"And you think they are still following you?"

"I'm sure of it, which is why you must turn me out of your village. They will take terrible vengeance against you for hiding me. Give me back the horse I rode on, and I will leave you."

"I told you, we let the horse go to confuse those following you," Hastiin reminded him. "Besides, we would never sacrifice you to them. We will hide you, and if necessary fight to protect you."

Lonan looked at Matriarch Sahkyo. She nodded. "Even if it costs us our lives, we will protect you."

"Riders coming in from the South," came the shout from outside.

Hastiin shrugged. "Well, it's too late now," he said. He turned to Nashota. "You stay here, Nashota."

Sahkyo and Hastiin walked outside, leaving Nashota trembling inside the Hogan. She peeked around the door. Seven men on horseback were galloping toward her village. Nothing like this had ever happened to her or to her village before. Was she afraid for herself, for her village, or for Lonan? She didn't know, only that she was terrified.

"Run, little princess, run," whispered Lonan.

Nashota turned to him, smiled, and shook her head. That was one thing she would not do, regardless of how scared she was.

The thundering of horse's hooves and a huge cloud of dust announced the arrival of these strange looking men. There were six Spanish soldiers and an Apache. The soldiers were all wearing some kind of shiny armor and carrying fearsome looking weapons. One of them shouted. Nashota could not understand; presumably they were speaking in Spanish. It was a strange sounding language, musical and smooth, like nothing else she had heard among the people, but as they spoke, it carried anger and hate the like of which she had never sensed before. She was half expecting the Apache to speak, since their languages were similar, but he said nothing.

"Does anyone here speak Spanish?" asked grandfather.

"I do," spoke up one woman. She spat on the ground. "I spent ten years as a slave to these devils."

"Then ask them what they want," said Sahkyo.

An angry conversation followed, and even though the soldiers were in complete command, the woman held her ground. The soldier's voice got louder and louder, until finally he hit the woman across the face with the back of his gloved hand, knocking her a few paces backward onto the ground. Nashota was horrified. She had never seen anyone strike another person before. But this! For a man to strike a woman was unthinkable. A few of the warriors drew their weapons, but before they could retaliate Sahkyo raised her hands.

"Stop," she said. "There will be no fighting here."

Grandfather had helped the woman up from the ground. Sahkyo took her in her arms and wiped the blood from the corner of her mouth.

"What kind of man strikes a woman," said the woman with disgust, glaring at the soldiers. "They want us to turn over the man who stole their master's horse. They say they will leave us in peace if we do."

"Tell them we saw him ride to the west," said Sahkyo.

"I told him but he didn't believe me."

The soldier barked again.

"He says he will search every Hogan and then burn your village to the ground if we don't turn Lonan over to him."

"Tell him…" began Hastiin, but the soldier had already jumped from his horse. He took a long knife from a scabbard at his waist and pointed to the Hogan where Nashota was hiding. She would not let these men take Lonan. Somehow she would stop them. With a show of calmness and poise she was not feeling, she opened the door and stood staring the soldier directly in the eye. He was quite young, and handsome in a strange sort of way. He brandished his sword, pointing it directly at Nashota's throat.

"Step aside," he said.

What was that? She understood him? "The man you are looking for is not in here," she replied in the same language, not sure how she did it. He touched the point of his sword to the side of her neck and she almost fainted as she felt it pierce her flesh.

"Step aside or I will kill you."

"Their minds are weak. They have very little Holy Wind in them. Their Breathing souls will fail them." The voice came to her mind clearly, and at once she knew it was Yanaba.

"The man you seek is not here. You must leave our village. Get back on your horses and leave—now." Her voice was full of authority and power. For a moment the soldier stared at her, unsure of himself. Nashota's heart was beating wildly in her chest, but she felt the power of the Holy Wind welling up inside her. She reached up and grasped the blade of the sword at her throat and took it from the soldier, as she would have taken a stick from a little boy. She threw it to the ground. "Go!" she said with awful finality, pointing to the west.

"The slave is not here," said the soldier, walking back to his horse and mounting. "The girl is right, we must continue looking for him this way." And they galloped off to the west.

The whole village watched in awed silence as the soldiers rode off, not sure what they had just witnessed.

Grandfather was the first to move. "You're hurt," he said reaching for Nashota's hand. She held her right hand to her face. Sure enough there was a nasty cut in her palm and each of her fingers where she had grasped the wicked blade and blood was oozing from the wound on her neck where the soldier had pierced her with his sword. He took the sash from around his waist and was about to bandage her, but by the time he looked back there was no sign of blood, or the cuts that had ravaged his precious granddaughter's hand and throat. She said nothing, as she turned and walked back into the Hogan and closed the door.

Chapter 5

It had gotten a lot colder. A light snow had started falling about two hands of time earlier and it looked as if a more severe storm was coming in. The wind had picked up and the clouds had become much darker. It was about noon when Niyol reached a huge canyon. Realizing he would not be able to ride any further east he decided he had come far enough. He would release the horse here and head back to the village. It would take him until sunset to get back, even if he ran most of the way. He had not regretted volunteering for this mission, but part of him wished he had not. He had not even spoken to the beautiful Nashota; he had never found the courage. Somehow she intimidated him, and it wasn't just her beauty. When she looked at him it was if her eyes could see down to his soul, to the very depths of his being. He had watched, frustrated as other young men had engaged her in conversation, and how so easily and graciously she had returned their attention. He smiled as he thought about her, wondering what she was doing now. He had seen girls become betrothed right after their Kinaalda was over. It was not very often the clans got together, and since it was forbidden to marry within one's own clan, it made sense that betrothals would take place whenever a multi-clan celebration like this took place. Blessed Ancestors! What would he do if she were already betrothed by the time he got back?

He climbed off the horse and slapped its flank as hard as he could. It reared up on its hind legs and took off to the north. He shivered and pulled his blanket tighter around his shoulders. Yes it was definitely getting colder. He could see the horse's tracks in the snow and decided it would be best if he headed south for a while, just in case he had been followed. After running for about a finger of time he turned west. He was not in the least tired. He could keep up this pace for hours, and besides it was keeping him warm. His breath formed clouds of vapor each time he breathed out.

He suddenly came to a dead stop. There were riders to the north about a hundred spear lengths. Spaniards. It had to be. They were following the path he had taken. In a few minutes they would discover where he had freed the horse. Blessed Ancestors! Would they find his tracks? He crouched down, not daring to move, afraid he would give his position away. His heart almost failed him when he saw that the man leading them slowly along his path was not Spanish, he looked like an Apache scout from way to the south of the Land of the Dine'h. How would he escape being caught if they had an experienced Apache scout?

He waited until they were a little further along, and then took off again. This time he was not trotting, he was running; running for his life. He came to a small stream and ran into it. It was not deep, but it was bitterly cold. He waded northward for a half a finger of time before climbing back out and continuing west. Would his little ruse fool his trackers? He doubted it, but maybe it would give him a little more time. As he ran up a small rise he turned. There was no sign of them. For a moment he felt tremendous rush of relief, but it was dashed as he saw them again. They were not walking their horses; they were galloping toward the river, and they had with them the horse he had ridden all this way for nothing.

He ran behind a rock. Exposed as he was on the rise he would stand out like a fire against the white snow. He watched them as they reached the river. Go south, he urged. The Apache jumped from his horse and squatted down in the river. He put his hand in the water. What was he doing? Go south, he prayed. But then, to his horror, the Apache pointed north. It would be but a few moments until they found the spot where he had left the river.

He began running again down the other side of the rise. They would be on him in less than a finger of time. His only hope was to find somewhere to hide. His eyes darted about in panic, looking for a place where he might be able to lose them, but there was nothing, only sparse bushes of the high desert, mocking him with their lack of refuge. Behind him he heard his pursuers galloping toward him. They were gaining on him fast. There was no escape. He knew he was about to die, but he would not die a coward, no he would fight and die like a man. He stopped and turned to face them.

They were almost upon him. He took out his knife, not sure what good it would do him. He had never used it before against a man. The only fighting he had ever done was under the tutelage of his War Chief. He had never even struck another person in anger, let alone used a knife.

They quickly formed a circle around him. He spun around, watching for any movement, passing his knife from hand to hand. The Apache laughed, and slid effortlessly from his horse. "Put away your knife little Dine'h warrior." He walked toward him, not even holding a weapon. "Where did you get this horse? And where is the man who was riding him?"

"I've never seen this horse before," said Niyol, waiting for death.

The Apache laughed again, and turned away slightly. In one quick movement he hit Niyol across the face with the back of his hand, grabbed his wrist and twisted it so hard Niyol heard it crack. The knife fell from his grip. The Apache threw him to the floor and fell on him, one knee in his stomach, the other on his arm, with a much bigger knife at his throat.

"Kill me. I'm not afraid to die," he said defiantly.

"Oh, I'm not going to kill you. Not yet, not until you've told us what we need to know. But by then you'll be begging for death."

One of the soldiers barked an order in Spanish. The last thing Niyol saw before everything went dark was the Apache's fist coming toward his face.

Nashota was weaving her wedding basket. It would be beautiful. She thought once again of her young man, and wondered if she would ever see him again. Oh how she wished it would be he who shared the wedding jar with her, he who would eat from the wedding basket with her. Blessed Ancestors, she did not even know his name.

Grandfather came and sat beside her. "It is beautiful," he said, admiring the basket. He took a deep breath. "Nashota," he began, and then paused.

"Yes, Grandfather, what is it?"

"Five young men have asked permission to court you."

She looked at him and smiled sadly. "But not the one I wish to court me."

"How do you know? Who would that be?"

"He's already left. Left to go back to his village I think."

"Who?"

"The one who took the horse Lonan rode in on."

"Niyol?"

"Is that his name?"

"Yes. Niyol Swift Wind. I sent him to take the horse half a day's ride from here and then free him."

"Niyol. Niyol Swift Wind." The name rolled around her tongue with ease. She smiled. "And he is returning?"

It was grandfather's turn to smile. He looked toward the sun. "He should be back in four or five hands of time."

Nashota suddenly felt a stab of pain, and gasped, as if she had been hit hard in the stomach.

Grandfather put his hand on her shoulder. "Nashota, what is it."

She had felt a cry of pain from Niyol, but she did not want not to mention it to grandfather. "Oh, just a pain here," she said, rubbing her stomach.

Grandfather nodded. "Ah yes, my precious one, they say the cycles of Changing Woman bring with them pain for some of her daughters."

Nashota nodded. It was a convenient explanation. "Perhaps I will go and rest for a while."

"A good idea."

When she arrived back at her Hogan she lay on her bed. Her heart was pounding, and her mind was racing. Something terrible had happened. Niyol Swift Wind was in trouble. Calm yourself, calm, she told herself. She tried to concentrate, to focus her mind, to free it. Why would she have felt his cry of pain so strongly if they were not already connected? She closed her mind and called out to him but there was nothing. She quickly gathered some things together; her warm deerskin skirt, a wolf skin cape with a warm hood, sheepskin gloves and boots. She also took a skin of water and some jerky. Making sure no one was watching, she slipped out of the Hogan and trotted eastward.

"Where is she going?" asked Sahkyo as they watched her leave the village.

"Niyol is in trouble. She heard his cry."

"And you're not going to stop her? You're not going to send any warriors with her?"

"The Wind whispered to me that this is something she must do on her own."

CHAPTER 6

The next few hours were a nightmare of intense pain, screams, questions and confusion.

"Where is the Acoma slave?"

The six Spanish soldiers and the Apache scout punched Niyol repeatedly in the face, breaking his cheekbones and jaw. His left eye completely closed up. They kicked him in the back, the groin, and his face.

"How did you get the horse?"

They cut his face, arms and hands, his calves and feet, his shoulders; deep wounds. They broke his fingers, deliberately, one by one. The pain was unbearable.

"Where is your village?"

They heated their knives in the fire until they were red-hot and held them against his face and against his still bleeding wounds; his blood sizzled and boiled. Through it all he told them nothing, but he was not sure how much more he could take before leaving this life. He knew he was already dead; it was just a matter of time before he succumbed to the wounds already inflicted. One thing he was sure of, he would not tell them anything that could possibly lead them back to Nashota's village. He barely managed a smile as he thought of the beautiful Nashota. He knew now he would never have her, but knowing that she would be safe gave his death purpose.

"What are you smiling at, dog?" sneered the Apache. "Tell us what we want to know, and then I will kill you quickly. If not, you will suffer, and then you will tell us anyway." He hit him in the face once more, and he fell backwards, not quite unconscious, but not conscious either. He was caught in a dream state between life and death. "But now we will leave you to sleep through the night. Tomorrow we begin again."

The sun was beginning to set in the west. Niyol was not sure if he was dead or alive. Nothing seemed real to him anymore. His consciousness faded in and out, but finally he fell into a restless sleep, full of nightmares of pain.

But then his dreams softened. He dreamed a spirit came to him. Her face was radiant, and her countenance was that of the Holy Ones. She spoke kind words to him. He dreamed she touched his face and arms, his back and chest, his legs and feet, and where she touched, soft relief filled him as the pain faded.

Later, in another dream his tormentors stood up, surprised and angry at the spirit. They picked up their weapons and rushed her. Run, he thought, run before they hurt you. But she held up her hands and they fell to the ground.

Still later, the spirit carried him to the fire and lay down next to him. She covered him with blankets and pressed her warm body next to his, whispering kind words and caressing his face.

"I did not tell them anything," he said, his voice like the croak of a raven.

"I know," she said. "You were very brave. Your place with the Blessed Ancestors is assured."

He felt a warm calm settle over him; this Holy Woman had promised him a place with the Blessed Ancestors. His heart was full. His pain had been worth it and now he could die in peace. He had protected the sweet and lovely Nashota and her village. He fell into a deep and peaceful sleep.

It was almost morning when he spoke to the spirit again, asking her the question which had troubled him all night. "Have you come to take me to the next world, to the land of the dead?" His voice sounded hollow, full of echoes, as if he were in a narrow canyon.

Her reply was a sweet melody of warm words filling his breathing soul. "You will not die, Swift Wind," she cooed "for you will be my husband."

He smiled. That this Holy One would say he was to be her husband convinced him that he was indeed dying.

When he awoke he panicked, remembering where he was. Soon they would begin to torture him again. His face creased up, wondering if he could take any more pain, and then the lines deepened, wondering why he was not still in pain. The reality of the beating and torture he had suffered hit him. And yet... He touched his hand to his face. It felt normal; no broken bones. He looked at his hands and arms. Dried, dark blood covered them, evidence that his ordeal had been real, but there were no stab wounds. He flexed his fingers; they were fine. He turned his arms and hands over; no burn marks. How could this be? Was he still dreaming?

He jumped when he saw the six soldiers and the Apache lying on the ground, apparently dead. What had happened here? Had his dreams been real?

The snap of a twig behind him brought him quickly to his feet in a defensive stance. There, in front of him was a vision even more beautiful than the spirit woman sent by the Holy Ones: Nashota! Cradled in her right arm she had a bundle of twigs and in her left hand she held a rabbit.

"You hungry?" she asked, holding up the rabbit like a trophy.

His mouth was wide open. "Nashota," he blurted. And then, as realization hit him, he said, "Last night. That was you?"

She smiled and nodded, bowing her head.

He pointed over to the soldiers. "You?"

"Yes."

"How?"

She shrugged. "I'm still not sure," she said. "I think I have the power of Changing Woman."

"Changing Woman?" Niyol's mouth fell open again.

She laughed. "Close your mouth, Swift Wind. It is not very becoming."

Quickly he clamped his mouth shut. He must appear as a bumbling fool to her.

"Apparently Asdzáán Nádleehé has a mission for me," she said, arranging the twigs into a small stack over the almost dead fire. She blew on it and it burst into life.

Niyol was still struggling for words. "But what about my wounds?"

Again she shrugged. She whispered a prayer of thanks over the rabbit, then expertly skinned and gutted it. "I'm not sure about that either," she said. "Somehow I am able to see things as they are with the Holy Wind, and I can mend them." She used her knife to cut the meat into small strips, fixed them to a stick she had stripped, and began roasting them over the fire. The smell was delicious.

"And that was you last night? You lay next to me to keep me warm?"

She nodded, a little flush came to her face. She handed him some rabbit meat. It was hot, but he gulped it down. Never had anything tasted so sweet.

She took out a piece of cloth and poured some water over it. "Take off your shirt," she said.

"What?"

"Let me wash you."

His heart pounded. That she would perform this act of love for him was almost too much to bear. "Oh, I couldn't let you…"

"It is a blessing for me, Niyol Swift Wind."

He could say nothing once she had uttered those words. He loosened the ties that held his shirt and slipped it off. She gently wiped the cloth over his arms, chest and back. The touch was magic, heaven. And then she bent down to wash his feet. Her soft hair fell around his ankles, caressing him. Perhaps he really had died, and this was his reward for his bravery. But no, he looked at her face. She was real, and she was smiling up at him with such trust.

"Last night you said…"

"I said what?" she asked, when he paused.

"No, it was nothing." Now it was his turn to blush.

"Please. Tell me. What did I say?" she said, as she ran the cloth over his feet.

"You said… you said I was to be your husband."

She stopped washing him and sat up straight. "How impertinent," she said with a look of surprise on her face, and yet, her flush deepened. "That you would suggest that I would say such a thing. It is not the place of a young woman to say such things."

"I'm sorry," he said.

For a while they said nothing. The only sounds were the crackling fire, and a few birds off in the distance.

"Besides," she said. "You would have to ask my grandfather for permission to court me."

"Would that please you?" he asked.

"Now your legs."

"But…"

"Here," she said, handing him a small blanket. "I will turn around while you remove your pants, and then you can cover yourself with this." She turned around.

He removed his pants quickly and covered himself.

She turned back around and continued washing his legs. The intimacy of this act should have driven him wild, but the innocence and purity of Nashota, and the trust she had placed in him, made it into a sacred, holy act.

"Would it please you?" she asked.

"Would what please me?" he said. And then realizing where she had picked up the conversation he said, "Nashota, It would be beyond my wildest dreams."

"Then I suppose it would please me also, Niyol Swift Wind." She turned away from him, her eyes cast down, but her smile was unmistakable and wide. "There, we're done. You can wash up more completely when we get back to the village."

His heart was full. Twelve hours ago he had been prepared to die for her so that she would be free to marry and raise a family. Now, he was overjoyed that he would be living for her, living with her, as her husband for the rest of his life.

"For the rest of eternity," she said tenderly, looking directly into his eyes.

His eyes widened, and his mouth fell open once more.

She leaned over and kissed his cheek, like the beating of a humming bird's wings her lips brushed against his face. Instinctively he reached for her, put his arms around her and brought his face to hers, his lips brushed against hers, but she quickly brought her hand between them. "That is the only kiss you will get from me; we're not betrothed yet."

They finished their meal in silence. Niyol's mind raced. Had she chosen him or had he chosen her? Perhaps they had been chosen for each other by the Holy Ones themselves.

After they had eaten Niyol pointed to the dead men. "What do we do with them?" he asked.

"We will remove the heavy clothing from the Spanish so that the wolves and coyotes will return them to Mother Earth. The Apache we will take with us, and sing his soul to the Land of the Dead."

Even though the Apache had been one of his torturers, he knew that Nashota spoke wisely. He was still a brother, and who could say what road had brought him across this path.

"We will take the horses as a gift to your village," he said.

Nashota nodded in agreement. "You will teach me how to ride?"

"It's easy. You'll find it better than walking." They began removing the armor from the Spanish soldiers. "We should take their weapons too."

Nashota nodded again. "Back in the village I took a sword from their leader." She paused for a moment and then said, "One of my distant daughters will use it in another battle."

Soon they were finished. They tethered the horses together and rode off to the west. Niyol smiled at how easily Nashota took to riding.

CHAPTER 7

Hastiin was worried. His precious Nashota had been gone all night. He sat cross-legged on the ground facing east and sang his morning prayer to Tsisnaasjini', White Shell Mountain. Had he done the right thing, letting her go on her own? The spirit whispered to him that she was safe but it gave him little comfort, so he sat, chanting prayers softly.

Mid-morning Sahkyo joined him. "What do the spirits tell you?"

He turned to face her. "That she is safe."

"And still you worry?"

"She is my only flesh, the only daughter of my only daughter. Her life means more to me than…" He could hardly find the words that would convey his devotion and dedication to Little Twin. "More than the breath I breathe."

Sahkyo patted his shoulder gently, "I know, I know," she said kindly. "May I join you?"

Hastiin was about to say no, but he realized she was giving him this gift of love out of concern for him. "But the ground is so cold."

She shook out the deerskin rug she had brought with her. "Here," she said. This will keep you a little warmer." He stood up and she spread the skin on the ground. Together they sat, Sahkyo saying nothing, Hastiin chanting prayers.

By noon there was still no sign of her. She had been gone a whole day now, but still Hastiin trusted the whisperings of the wind. Suddenly he felt her spirit, strong, happy, and well. "She's here," he said, jumping to his feet. Hastiin held his hand out and helped Sahkyo to stand.

"Where?" she said. "I don't see her."

"Neither can I – yet. But she's just over that rise," he said, pointing to a gentle hill about two thousand paces away. "With your permission, Matriarch…"

"Of course, go meet her," she said, waving her hand toward the east but Hastiin was already running. Now she too could feel Nashota's remarkable spirit coming to her mind, a spirit so full of wonder, hope, and something else. Like a miraculous vision eight horses came over the top of the hill. Two had riders; one had a body draped over it. Her heart leapt with joy. It was them – Nashota and Niyol. She smiled, and chuckled. Even from this distance she could sense how much in love they were.

The riders pushed their mounts almost to a gallop as soon as they saw Hastiin. In a few hairs of time they were on each other. Nashota jumped from her horse. Her cries of joy filled the whole valley as Hastiin picked her up in his arms and swung her around. Sahkyo could not help but reach her hands to the sky and shout at the top of her voice. "Holy Ones, Great Creators, how kind you are to us. You have brought our dear daughter back to our village."

After Nashota and Niyol had cleaned up and eaten, they were called to the council who wanted a full report of all that had happened. Niyol was reluctant at first, but Hastiin insisted. "It is important for us to know what took place."

The villagers and the guests who still remained after the Kinaalda gathered respectfully around. Among them were Niyol's parents who were obviously bursting with pride at his bravery. With well-chosen words, and with the skill of a seasoned Elder, he related the story from the time he had left them. He didn't leave out any details, although Nashota felt he was exaggerating her part and understating his own bravery. She wanted to interrupt him because he deserved all the credit; after all, he had been willing to sacrifice his own life. When he related how Nashota had subdued the Spanish, and healed him there were gasps of surprise, even perhaps unbelief, but Niyol insisted that he told the truth. Even the people of her own village who had seen wondrous things at her hands before were astonished, but the guests seemed to be finding it hard to accept any of this, yet the evidence was before their eyes.

"We left the Spanish to be returned to Mother Earth, but the Apache, with your permission, Nashota suggested we bring him back to sing his soul to the dead," he said, as he finished the tale.

Sahkyo nodded. "A noble gesture indeed young woman, considering what he did to Niyol."

"He is still one of us," she said.

"Then we will respect your wishes." She gestured to some of the men. "Prepare the Apache for his journey to his Ancestors."

They came and lifted his body with respect and carried it away.

"Is there anything else you wish to add, Swift Wind?" said Hastiin. "Or to ask," he added.

He paused a moment. "There is, Elder."

More silence. "Speak, Niyol. Do not be afraid."

"I would talk to you alone, War Chief," he said, looking at the expectant faces around him.

Hastiin laughed. "Niyol, my young brave, there is not a person here who does not know what it is in your heart. And look at Little Twin; anyone who cannot tell what is on both of your minds must have been asleep the last hand of time."

Nashota blushed furiously as the young women and girls turned to her, smiling, giggling. Some of the young men did not look so happy, but it was too bad; she had chosen.

Niyol cleared his throat. "With your permission, and blessing, I would like to court your granddaughter."

Hastiin adopted a serious, fatherly tone. "Granddaughter, is this what you wish also?"

Nashota could not speak. She simply nodded, eyes to the ground.

"Swift Wind, will you honor her virtue?"

"Upon my life I will."

He turned to Niyol's parents. "Is this acceptable to you also."

They nodded. "It is," said his father, still beaming with pride.

"Then you have my permission and my blessing to court her."

A cheer went up from the crowd.

CHAPTER 8

Four moons went by. During the courtship it was customary for the young man to stay at the village of his love, and to act as a servant to her family. Of course Hastiin did not treat him as such, although Niyol certainly had many chores. From dawn to dusk he would work around the village, helping to repair Hogans, building new Hogans, one of which would become home for him and his wife when the time came. They had him tending to the sheep, shearing them when spring began. The women took the wool and spun it into fine yarn. He watched Nashota with fascination as she died the wool a rainbow of different colors and began weaving a beautiful blanket.

"It is beautiful, Nashota."

"I will wear it for the first time when I become your wife," she said, smiling. "And I will make another just like it for you, when you become my husband."

Hastiin continued Niyol's training as a warrior. He was a quick learner, strong, fast, and agile. 'You will make a strong War Chief one day,' Hastiin had told him.

Niyol taught the other warriors how to ride. They went out on hunting trips together, so much more successful than on foot. They were able to round up more of the wild sheep and goats, and even a few more horses. The village began to prosper, as it never had before.

During their courtship, Niyol and Nashota were not permitted to be alone. Mostly they spent time with others in a group. If they wanted to talk just to each other, another had to be within seeing and hearing distance. Niyol struggled a little with this. He wanted to be completely alone with her, to hold her close to him, and to talk of things he did not want others to hear. Still he would wait patiently. One day she would be his betrothed, and then shortly after that they would become husband and wife.

For Nashota the wait was not a problem. She still did not feel quite ready for the marriage bed, although there was no uncertainty about her love for Niyol. Besides she wanted to find out more about the things Yanaba had told her. She still did not know how she was able to heal people, or how she had been able to kill those Spanish soldiers and the Apache with her mind, but as the long nights of winter rolled into the long days of summer she found she was able to sense more and more things with her mind. More than that, she had always had the ability to sense people's feelings but lately she was able to hear their thoughts, especially those of grandfather and Niyol, and others close to her.

There were no special happenings in the village, nothing out of the ordinary, just village life going from day to day. Perhaps these special powers only became evident when she or someone she loved was in trouble. Yanaba had told her that one day she would learn how to shift, and one day, she would return to Tal'el'Dine'h.

"Grandfather," she said one evening as they prepared for bed. "Do you know what it means to shift?"

"No. I've never heard of such a thing. Why do you ask?"

Nashota decided it was time to tell him of Yanaba's visit during her Kinaalda. He listened quietly as she related every detail of what she had seen and heard. He thought about this long and hard before he spoke.

"I cannot imagine what this all means," he said thoughtfully. "She said you would return to this other world."

Nashota nodded. "And she told me that Tal'el'Dine'h was the name of this world, not the star we see in our sky."

"You said she was able to take you from day to night?"

"Yes."

"How can that be? It is either day or night. How could it be both?"

"I have wondered that myself."

"You are more special than I ever imagined. That you would be charged with this mission of which you know so little…" his voice trailed off leaving the thought incomplete.

"Please don't tell Matriarch Sahkyo of this until it is time."

"Of course. But now it's time to sleep. You coming in?"

"Soon, grandfather."

She sat, staring to the west. Father Sun would set in a hand of time, perhaps a little less. It was the evening of Long Day. Tomorrow he would begin his journey back from the northwest to the southwest. But why would he travel in the sky this way? Sister moon also traveled through the sky as she went through her cycles, the cycles governed by Changing Woman. Tonight was when she hid her face. Straining her eyes she could just make out the shadowy disk of Sister Moon. She had not gone away, she was just dark. Nashota had seen this before many times but never really given it much thought. Since she had been a little girl she had watched with fascination as Sister Moon went through her cycles. From glorious full face, gradually shrinking night by night until there was nothing left, and then growing again to her full glory. But now she could see that her face was still there, just dark, and that had to mean it was always there as she went through her cycles. How could this be? How could the light of Sister Moon go away, if she did not?

Following behind Father Sun were two other bright stars. The first was about three hands behind the sun, the second, the brighter of the two, about four hands. A sudden realization hit her: those two stars also moved. She was sure that a few moons ago the brighter star had been alone, and the dimmer star moved closer and closer each day, until it had over taken the brighter star. No other stars did this, did they? There was something very important about this, something she had to figure out. Somehow she knew it had something to do with her mission from Yanaba. She thought long and hard about it, but nothing seemed to make sense. For three hands of time she sat, staring, as those two bright stars continued to follow Father Sun and Sister Moon. Soon they too would set.

"Nashota, time to sleep."

She turned. It was her grandfather calling her from the Hogan. It was quite dark now.

"Grandfather, could you look at the sky with me."

"Certainly." He walked over to where she sat, and joined her on the ground.

"See those two stars?" she said, pointing to the west. "The first is about two fingers above the horizon, the other, the brighter one is following him."

"Yes, I see them."

"They are not always in that position, following Father Sun as he sets."

"I have never really noticed."

"And see how they follow him, in a straight line, almost as if they were his children."

"Yes, they do."

"They do move, Grandfather. Not two moons ago the brighter of the two was ahead of the other."

"Oh, I don't think so. How could that be? All stars move with the sky as it moves around us."

"I know, and it makes my head ache thinking about it." She shrugged and smiled. "Maybe I should sleep now."

Hastiin put his arm around Nashota as they walked back to the Hogan. Before entering she looked once again to the western horizon, holding her hand at arm's length between her and those two bright stars. They were about two fingers apart.

Five nights went by. Each night Nashota watched the progress of Sister Moon and the two bright stars. Each night the two bright stars moved further and further apart; now more than a hand separated them. Sister Moon was three hands behind them, and her crescent was growing bigger each night.

Chapter 9

Midsummer, 1599

Nashota woke up early. She walked out of the Hogan, hoping not to disturb Grandfather. Father Sun would not rise for another two fingers of time, but the eastern sky was a beautiful blanket of color. The majesty of it took her breath away. She walked thirty paces to the east, fell to her knees, and raised her arms high above her head. "Thank you, Holy Ones, for creating this new day for us, this beautiful new day." She took a deep breath of the fresh morning air and reveled in the joy she felt as it filled her body.

"Nashota, you're up early."

She whirled around. "Niyol." Her heart began to beat a little faster. "You shouldn't be here."

"I know. What are you looking at?"

"The beauty of the world – and its mysteries."

"Mysteries?"

"Yes. Like why does Sister Moon go through her cycle?"

"There is only one mystery I wish to understand."

"Yes," she said, still staring eastward.

"It is the mystery of you."

She turned back to him and smiled. "Oh, there's no mystery to me."

"But there is. How could you heal me the way you did? And how could you kill those men?"

"To me it is also…"

"And the biggest mystery of all," he said, interrupting her. "Why would someone like you, someone as wonderful as you, as beautiful as you love me?"

"Niyol, when you left our village that day on the Spanish horse, I thought I would never see you again." She put her hand on his arm. He covered it lovingly with his. "I wanted to follow you, forget my Kinaalda. I wanted to be with only you."

She looked up at him. His head was bent toward hers, their faces almost touching. Should I kiss him, she asked herself, should I? Oh, how she wanted to, but she could not, they were not yet betrothed. She felt herself almost melt as he brought his lips closer to hers. She could not stop herself. She leaned closer to him and kissed his lips.

There was a noise behind them. They turned to see Hastiin coming out of the Hogan. "Well, well, what do we have here?" he demanded.

Nashota was about to speak but Niyol beat her to it,

"Elder Hastiin," he said bowing his head. "Forgive me. This is my fault, not Nashota's. It was not planned. I was out walking and..."

Grandfather held up his hand. "Come inside the Hogan, both of you."

"Grandfather, it was quite innocent," protested Nashota, although she knew that was not completely true.

Again, he held up his hand, walking away from them toward the Hogan. Once inside he turned and faced them. Nashota had never before seen her grandfather angry, not once. Now she felt so ashamed that she had disappointed him, hurt him.

"I have to ask you some very important questions."

They nodded their heads somberly.

"Swift Wind, do you love Nashota?"

"You know I do, Elder, more than my own life."

"Little Twin, do you love Niyol?"

"You know I do, Grandfather. With all my breathing soul I love him."

"Then if you both feel ready, I would be willing, more than that, I would be happy and honored, to give my blessing to your betrothal." His angry face was replaced by a huge, almost mischievous grin.

Niyol's eyes nearly popped out of his head.

"Grandfather!" said Nashota, not sure whether to be angry or relieved at this little charade, but her heart was beating too wildly in her chest. Betrothals were usually quite short, sometimes only one moon, which meant that by the next new moon she and Niyol could be husband and wife. Was she ready?

"You have my permission to spend the day together. Think about it. If it is what you wish, we could announce it at a village council tonight," he said as he turned to walk out of the Hogan.

"Grandfather, wait," she said. She looked at Niyol with a questioning nod. He nodded back, almost bewildered. "I don't think we need any time."

"We already know, War Chief. I have known since the moment I rode into your village."

"As I have known from the first time my eyes beheld him."

He walked back to the young couple and took them in his arms, kissing the crowns of their heads. "May the Holy Ones bless you both."

CHAPTER 10

The large fire at the center of the village burned brightly. The Elders sat in a semi-circle around it, facing east. Nashota and Niyol stood facing them, holding hands. Behind them the dying rays of Father Sun lit up the sky in a blaze of red, purple and pink.

Hastiin stood up and announced the betrothal of the two young lovers. Matriarch Sahkyo and the Elders added their blessing and approval. For the next three hands of time there was dancing and singing of Blessingway prayer-songs. Everyone in the village rejoiced with the young couple as they swore their love for one another.

"When should we get married?"

Nashota shrugged. "Soon, I suppose."

Arm in arm they walked to their new Hogan. They would be able to live together as man and wife even before the wedding. The only difference between betrothal and marriage was that either one of them could change their minds. Once married it would be almost impossible for them to part. Usually when a couple broke up after marriage one, or both of them, would leave the village. Marriage was a matter of the highest code of honor among the People. Nashota knew she would never change her mind, and she was sure Niyol would not change his, but, there was still the question of lying together as man and wife, for which she still did not feel ready.

As they entered the Hogan Niyol took her in his arms and pulled her to him. His lips touched hers, gently. It was the sweetest, purest of kisses. She had never been kissed before, and was unprepared for the reaction her body had to his as he held her close.

"Niyol..." she began nervously.

He held up his hand and gently touched her lips.

"It's alright, my love. I can wait."

"You can?"

"Until you're ready I can wait. Even after we are married, if you're not ready I will wait."

"Oh, Niyol, I love you so much." She kissed him again.

They lay together on their new bed and slept, locked in an innocent embrace.

Nashota woke first. Their embrace had broken during the night as they had settled into deep sleep. Niyol was lying on his side, facing her. His face looked so pure, so strong, and so handsome. She reached over and gently kissed his nose. He twitched a little but did not wake. She looked over to the door of the Hogan. A brilliant beam of sunlight was peeking into the Hogan through a gap. She watched as countless particles of dust danced in the ray. It was almost magical, they were like little spirits. The ray cut through the darkness of the Hogan where it fell upon a large pottery jar. The side facing the door was bright, a crescent of light which followed the curve of the jar, but the side nearest her was so dark she could hardly see it.

She sat up quickly as the realization hit her. "A crescent of light. Blessed Ancestors."

"What is it?" asked Niyol sleepily.

"Look," she said, pointing to the jar.

"You mean the jar? The jar Dezba gave us?"

"Yes. Look at it. What do you see?"

"I see a beautiful jar..."

"No, no," she said. "Look at where it is light and dark. Look at the shadow."

"Yes. I see it. But I don't understand..."

"What does it look like?"

"I don't know, it looks like..." He sat up suddenly. "It looks like Sister Moon."

"Exactly," she said triumphantly, slapping his chest.

"But what does it mean?"

"Come over here," she said, standing up and walking to the door. "Look at it from here."

From the door the jar was in full light, like a full moon. She took his hand and walked slowly around the jar, circling it like a wolf circling its prey. As she did, she saw the same cycles she saw on Sister Moon.

"You know what this means?" she asked Niyol.

"I know what it means, but I don't believe it."

"It means that sometimes Sister Moon is between Father Sun and us, which is not hard to believe. But what is hard to believe is that sometimes we are between Sister Moon and Father Sun."

"I don't see how this can be."

Nashota ran outside of the Hogan. Niyol followed her. She took a stick and drew a short line on the ground. "This," she said, "is Mother Earth." She drew a large circle around the line and drew a small disk on the circle. "This is Father Sun, as he goes around us." Inside the large circle she drew another circle, again drawing a disk on it. "And this is Sister Moon as she goes around us. See, here, she is between us and Father Sun." She moved the stick, following the curve of the larger circle. "And when Father Sun is over here, we are between him and Sister Moon."

"It also means that Sister Moon is a ball, not a circle."

"Why?"

"Because the shadow on the jar is the same as the shadow on Sister Moon."

For a long time they said nothing, just staring at the drawing Nashota had made on the ground. "We need to get started on our chores," she said finally.

Later that evening Nashota and Niyol went for a walk up a small hill about two thousand paces east of the village.

"Everything looks so small from here," said Niyol.

"But you can almost feel the warmth from here."

"From the fires?"

"No, silly, the warmth of home. The love and caring among the families."

"One day, we will have a family of our own. Little boys and girls of our own."

They sat down on the ground. She cuddled close to him and laid her head on his breast.

"I keep thinking about what about what Yanaba told me during my Kinaalda? She told me I had an important mission."

Niyol thought for a moment, and then said, "She said you had power?"

"Yes. You saw some of it around the campfire of the Spanish."

"I did indeed. And she said you were to return to Tal'el'Dine'h? How?"

"I have no idea? But I think it might have something to do with this magic she calls 'shifting'."

"What is 'shifting'?"

Nashota sat bolt upright. "What's that noise?"

"What noise?"

"Hush, listen."

To the south there was a muffled noise, like thunder far off in the distance.

"You think we're in for a storm?" asked Niyol.

"I don't think so," said Nashota slowly, looking up into the clear sky.

The sound was getting louder. "Horses!" said Niyol. "And they're heading this way."

They jumped up, and without saying a word they began running back toward the village. It would take them at least a finger of time. The riders suddenly appeared as they galloped over a hill. By the time Nashota and Niyol were half way the riders reached the village. The village warriors, caught by surprise, were quickly arming themselves, but Nashota knew they would be no match for the twenty Spanish soldiers brandishing swords and shooting fire-sticks. She couldn't believe her eyes. They were slashing with their swords at women, old men, and even children. What kind of warrior would do such a thing?

"No!" she screamed. She stopped, still five hundred paces from the village and held her hands high in the air. In an instant she was in the center of the village. She stood feet apart, head thrown back, arms outstretched. "NO!" she screamed even louder, and the soldiers were suddenly gone. Warriors found themselves fighting empty air. Every last trace of the soldiers and their horses was gone.

Niyol came running in to the camp, breathless. "Nashota! What happened? You disappeared..."

"Bring me the dead and injured, quickly," she said.

Throughout the night Nashota ministered to the injured, the most seriously hurt first. There were seventeen warriors, eight women, and four children hurt, but miraculously no one was killed. As she healed them she wept, not so much for their pain but for the loss of innocence of the village; it would never be the same.

By morning she was exhausted. Niyol carried her back to their Hogan and returned the favor of four moons earlier when she had washed the blood from him. He removed her bloody clothing and gently washed her body. She hardly moved, and her mind seemed to be half a world away as she stared into the distance, tears rolling down her cheeks. When he was finished he wrapped her in a blanket and laid her down on the bed.

"What happened to the soldiers?" asked Niyol finally. "And how did you disappear as we were running back to the village."

She shrugged and shook her head.

"Do you think it was the magic of shifting, of which Yanaba spoke?"

"Perhaps. I don't know." She turned to him. "We have to leave here."

"You and I?"

"All of us. The whole village."

He was looking directly into her eyes with such devotion. Oh, how she loved him. Why couldn't they be just an ordinary couple? Why did she have to be burdened with this mission?

"You should rest," he said, and with a final brush of his hand against her cheek, he left her to sleep.

CHAPTER 11

"Nashota." The voice was quiet and gentle.

She sat up in bed. At the doorway stood a woman. She couldn't see her very well – it was too dark. "Who are you?"

"Come, walk with me." She turned and walked from the Hogan.

Nashota got up from her bed and followed the mysterious young woman. A week had passed since the Spanish soldiers had invaded her village. Sister Moon was full, but she was not bright yellow, she was a ruddy brown. The dim moonlight lit up the woman's face as she turned to face Nashota.

"Yanaba."

Once again, Nashota was unsure of what to do. She began to fall to her knees, to worship her?

"No, please. Only the Holy Ones are worthy of our worship. I am one of their children, like you."

Nashota was speechless, but Yanaba smiled and took her hand. "I have something to show you." She pointed to Sister Moon. "What do you see?"

"I see Sister Moon, showing her full face," she said. She frowned as she looked a little harder. "But she is darker than she should be. Still, she is quite beautiful."

"She is. The Universe the Holy Ones created for us is glorious and beautiful."

"I have some questions..."

"Please," she said, extending her hands.

"I still don't understand how there can be many worlds, each with its own Father Sun. I have tried to picture this in my mind, but I cannot."

"Draw for me once again the picture you drew for Niyol. The one showing Mother Earth, Sister Moon, and Father Sun."

Nashota picked up a stick and drew a short line. "This is Mother Earth."

Yanaba nodded. "Show me Sister Moon and Father Sun as they are now."

Nashota drew a circle on one side of the line. "This is Sister Moon." She then drew another circle on the other side of the line, further away that the one she had drawn for Sister Moon. "And Father Sun."

Yanaba pointed up in the sky. "Look once again at Sister Moon."

Nashota gasped. Sister Moon had moved into about three-quarter face. "How can this be? Her cycles take one moon to complete."

"Keep looking. Have patience. This will take a while." She sat on the ground. "Join me."

Part of Nashota felt awkward sitting in the presence of Yanaba, but part of her also felt comfortable, as she would have felt sitting next to the twin sister she had never known.

"She still lives."

Nashota turned suddenly to look at Yanaba.

"Your sister. She is with the Holy Ones. She is looking down at you right now. She cannot show herself, or make herself known to you, but one day you will embrace her."

Nashota was suddenly overcome with emotion. Tears began to stream from her eyes. "My twin. My own sister."

Yanaba smiled, put her arm around her, and cradled Nashota's head against her shoulder. After a long time she pointed once again to Sister Moon. "Look, what do you see now?"

"She is in quarter face. How can this be?"

"But is that how she normally looks when she is in quarter face?"

"I don't know what you mean."

Yanaba went back to the drawing Nashota had made in the sand. She drew another Sister Moon one quarter of the way around her circle-path. "This is when you see her in half-face. And this," she said, drawing yet another one even closer to Father Sun, "is how you see her in quarter-face."

Nashota nodded.

"You know that you are the only one of the People who realized how this is so." Yanaba looked at her. "That makes you a very unusual young woman. You are also the only one to realize that Sister Moon is a ball, not a circle."

"That was Niyol who figured that one out."

Yanaba smiled. "You are very blessed, Nashota. He also is a very unusual young man."

She lowered her eyes. "I know."

"Now, if Sister moon is here," she said, pointing back to the original one Nashota had drawn, "How can she look like this now?" she asked, pointing to the quarter-face moon.

"Something is casting a shadow on her?"

"And what could that be? What do you see that is between Father Sun and Sister Moon?"

With a look of surprise on her face she said, "Our Glittering World."

Yanaba nodded her head, looking quite pleased. She looked at Nashota as Nashota would look at a child she was teaching to weave. "Then that," she said, pointing to Sister Moon, "is the shadow of the Glittering World?"

"Yes, I suppose it must be. But why does this not happen every time Sister Moon is in full face?"

"A good question; a question for another time. But for now, look at that shadow. What shape is it?"

For a long time Nashota strained her eyes. It should have been a straight line if it was the shadow of the Glittering World, but it was not. It had a curve to it, but it was a bigger curve than the shadows on Sister Moon's face as she went through her cycles.

"Keep watching."

Nashota watched as that shadow totally consumed Sister Moon's face, although she could still see her very faintly. Then, about three fingers of time later, the shadow began to recede. "She is passing out of our shadow."

"She is."

Again Nashota saw the curve of the shadow. "The Glittering World is also a circle.?" It was both a question and a statement.

"Not a circle, Nashota."

Nashota's mouth fell open when the realization hit her. "She is a ball?"

"Yes."

"Then, we are on the top of that ball? Else we'd fall off."

Yanaba shook her head. "No, but that also is a question for another day. For now, let us just say that Mother Earth holds you close to her, no matter where you are on her."

"Why do I not see the curve of her shape? The horizon is flat."

"It is because she is so much bigger than you can imagine." Yanaba picked up a round rock, about the half the size of her fist. "If this rock were Mother Earth, then the journey you made to rescue Niyol is smaller than the breadth of a hair." She bent down to pick up another rock, a smaller one, about a quarter of the size of the first. "This is how big Sister Moon is compared to Mother Earth," she said, weighing both rocks, one in each hand. She put the larger rock on the ground and handed the other to Nashota. "How far away do you think Sister Moon would be?"

Nashota took the rock, and placed it about a man's pace from the first.

Yanaba looked really pleased. "That's good. Just about right. Now, how far away do you think Father Sun is from Mother Earth?"

Nashota walked about ten paces, stopped and turned. Yanaba shook her head. She walked another ten paces. Yanaba shook her head again and pointed. "See that juniper tree in the distance?"

Nashota turned. About four hundred paces away was a lone juniper atop a small hill. "No! Not that far, surely"

Yanaba nodded. "And his size would be four good paces."

Nashota was completely taken aback. This was too much, all at once. Yet, somehow it made sense – except for one thing. "Then he has to move really fast to move around us in one day."

Yanaba smiled, and raised her eyebrows.

"Unless..." said Nashota. "No, that's impossible."

"Unless what?"

"No, it's too silly."

"Go on. What are you thinking?"

"No, because if we went around him, we too would be moving really fast."

"We don't go around him in one day. It takes a whole sun-cycle for us to travel around Father Sun."

"Then, how does he give us day and night?"

"As we circle Father Sun, Sister Moon circles us. She follows us, as we follow Father Sun. And..."

"Do we turn, as we move around Father Sun?"

Yanaba clapped her hands together. "Nashota, you are the brightest of all of the Holy One's children."

"How far away is Tal'el'Dine'h?"

Yanaba scratched her chin. "Let me see. How can I show you?" She took the stick and made a small dot in the sand. "This is Father Sun." She drew a small circle around it, about a hands width. "This is the path around him which we take in one sun-cycle." She looked off into the distance. "Tal'el'Dine'h is a long way away. About four times the distance you traveled to rescue Niyol. About two or three day's journey."

Nashota's eyes widened.

"It is a lot for you to learn in but a few hands of time."

"Why are you telling me this?"

"Because soon, you will take your people on a journey, back to Tal'el'Dine'h. You will soon be able to shift there. Just as you shifted when you saved your village, one day you will shift to Tal'el'Dine'h,"

"Nashota." It was Niyol calling her from the Hogan.

"He cannot see me. I must leave you."

Nashota whirled around and saw Niyol coming toward her.

"Please, stay." But it was too late; she had disappeared.

Niyol reached her and took her in his arms and held her tightly. "I woke and you were not next to me." He sounded worried and hurt. "I thought you had already decided to leave me

She leaned up and kissed his lips. "I will never leave you, my betrothed." The kiss lasted longer than she had expected, and it was sweet, so sweet. "I told you a long time ago that you would be my husband."

Niyol smiled as they walked back to their Hogan, arms around each other.

CHAPTER 12

Each day Nashota pondered what she had learned from Yanaba. Sister moon was once again new, following as a tiny crescent behind Father Sun. The dimmer of the two stars she had been watching had finally caught up with Father Sun and was no longer visible. Gradually the brighter of the two had moved further away. And what was even stranger was that a new star had moved into line, following Father Sun. He had been ten hands behind Father Sun when she had first noticed him, but tonight he was a hand closer. Yes, there was definitely another star following Father Sun.

She sensed Niyol coming toward her, even though he was obviously trying to sneak up on her. She smiled. They had been living together now for almost a moon, and she found she was becoming more and more comfortable being with him. He still respected her wishes, but as each day passed the surer she was that they were meant for each other. When the time came they would become lovers, as there had never been lovers before in the history of the Glittering World.

"Got you," he said, putting his arms around her waist and hugging her closely. She leaned her head back and kissed his neck. "What are you doing?" he asked.

She pointed high in the sky. "There, a new star following Father Sun."

"Yes, I see it."

"Don't you think it is strange that these stars would wander in the sky so?" She broke of the embrace and turned to him. "And why would these stars that move always follow Father Sun?"

Niyol frowned, as he always did when he thought deeply.

She giggled.

"What?" he said, grabbing her again.

"Oh, nothing," she said. "It's just I love you so much."

"As I love you."

They kissed again. Nashota trembled as they shared this most intimate of moments.

Suddenly, Niyol broke the embrace. "What if they're not stars?"

"What do you mean, of course they're stars…"

"Draw that picture of Father Sun, Sister Moon, and Mother Earth again for me."

Nashota picked up a twig and drew in the dust. "This is Father Sun, in the middle. He doesn't move. This is us," she said, pointing to a spot on the large circle she had drawn around Father Sun. "And this," she said pointing to the small circle around Mother Earth, "is Sister Moon."

He stared at drawing. "It's very strange, but it all makes sense." He looked up into the night sky. "You said all of those other stars are just like Father Sun, only much further away."

"Yes," she answered.

"And Tal'el'Dine'h is a world, like ours, circling her own Father Sun." She nodded.

"Why would Father Sun only have one child?"

"I don't know…"

"What if," interrupted Niyol, "those other stars, the ones that follow him, are not stars at all, but other worlds circling Father Sun, just as we do?"

She slapped him on the arm. "Wait. I think you may be right. Yanaba said that Tal'el'Dine'h was the fourth world around her Father Sun, and that the home world of the Dark Ones was the sixth world around their star. I didn't even think about it at the time. That has to be it."

Niyol took the twig from her. "If this is the path Mother Earth takes around Father Sun," he said, as he drew three more larger circles, "then these could be the paths of those other stars… worlds"

"That would explain why they appear to move in the sky," said Nashota with sudden realization. "Niyol, you are wiser than any Elder."

CHAPTER 13

The moons came and went. Equal day came and went, and another winter was upon them. In less than a moon it would be Long Night, Nashota would be fifteen summers, and still she wasn't married to her betrothed. People in the village smiled, and one or two would mention good-naturedly that they should be married by now, but something was holding her back. She still didn't feel quite ready, but their love blossomed and grew like wildfire. It was as firm and sure as the mountains that surrounded them. In the spring she would marry him, perhaps on Equal Day.

She had taken a walk and found herself sitting under the lone juniper, the one Yanaba had pointed out when she showed her how far away Father Sun was. She sat staring south, looking at Father Sun. She still could not figure out why he moved lower and lower in the sky as winter came upon them. What would cause that? But as hard as she thought about it no answer came to her.

She also thought long and hard about shifting. Yanaba had said it was how she would take her people back to Tal'el'Dine'h. Shifting was a way to move through space and time; she had learned that when she had shifted back to the village the night the Spanish attacked. She stared back toward the village. She could see people going about their daily chores, but could not make out anyone in particular. Wait, was that Niyol tending the horses? He spent more time with them than anyone else in the village. She closed her eyes and her heart swelled as she pictured him in her mind. She couldn't help but smile as she saw him; tall, handsome, powerful muscles, strong back. Oh, he was going to make a wonderful father for her children.

"It is time."

She whirled around, but there was no one with her; she was quite alone.

"*Why wait until spring? You should marry him soon.*"

"*Yanaba?*"

"*You need to be gone from here by spring, by equal day.*"

"But still have no idea how I can travel to Tal'el'Dine'h."

"*This is why you should marry.*"

"I don't understand…"

"*When you and Niyol become husband and wife, when you and he become one, you will understand. Your power will grow as you and Niyol become lovers.*"

Nashota thought about this. She wasn't sure what Yanaba meant, but she was right about one thing: she was ready to become Niyol's lover and wife.

"*It has been hard for him.*"

"What has? Waiting?"

"*Yes, but you were right to wait. I tell you of a surety, Nashota, no man has ever earned the right to be a husband more than he. You are a very fortunate woman; he is a fine man. He is like my own husband: strong and virtuous, kind and loving, and a wonderful lover.*"

"Then I will marry him. On my name day I will marry him."

"*Talk to him; tell him.*"

Nashota stood up and began walking toward him, an excitement building within her, almost consuming her.

"*No. With your mind, with the power of your feelings for him, talk to him.*"

And then Yanaba was gone.

Nashota cast her eyes upon him once more, and then she closed them.

"*Niyol Swift Wind. I want to become your wife. I am ready.*"

"*Nashota!*"

She was almost surprised, not only that he had heard her, but that he had been able to respond to her.

"*Niyol, I love you more than anything else in the Glittering World; more than my own soul.*"

"*As I love you Nashota.*" He paused a moment. "*But… you're sure…*"

"*Yes, my love, yes.*"

CHAPTER 14

Father sun shone brightly as if he too was rejoicing. He seemed larger today. A few cloud people, brilliant white, fluffy and delicate, like wool from a newborn lamb, wandered lazily across the sky. The bitter wind that had howled across the valley for days had finally quieted, replaced by a warmer breeze that had blown in from the south. In the distance the far horizon, at least one day's journey, was crystal clear. No summer haze to blur the dazzling clear view; it was still too cold for that. The trees swayed majestically as if caught in the splendor of the occasion they witnessed. Birds circled above, happy to have the freedom of the clear blue skies once more, but never flying far from the wedding party.

"She's beautiful. She looks just like you did at fifteen," said Mika.

"She is very pretty, mommy," said Asdza.

"She is, my sweet."

Shaylae had brought Mika, Asdza and Halona to witness the wedding. They were peering across time and space, without completing the shift.

"She doesn't need me anymore," said Shaylae, knowing that Nashota had learned enough from her to make the rest of her journey to the old knowledge on her own. "She is more powerful than me, more intelligent."

"How…"

"Hush," she said, touching his lips with her fingers. "See," she said, pointing to a young girl about Asdza's age dancing happily in front of Nashota, casting flowers before her feet as they made their way to the center of the village. "She is the one I told you about, the one Nashota rescued from the cougar."

From the other side of the village they watched as Niyol made his way with his family toward the center of the village.

"He reminds me of you, my love."

Mika put his arm around her shoulder and pulled her close. As she looked into his eyes he kissed her tenderly. Nashota had across her shoulders a brilliantly colored blanket; Niyol wore a similar blanket across his shoulders. "They are a perfect couple."

Shaylae nodded and smiled. They watched in silence as Nashota poured water from a wooden ladle into Niyol's hands, took his hands in hers and washed them. He repeated the gesture for her. Nashota handed her wedding basket to Matriarch Sahkyo who sprinkled the corn pollen on the taa'niil. Niyol and Nashota fed each other from the basket.

Suddenly the silence was broken by whoops of joy. The wedding guests cheered and clapped as the young couple shared their first kiss as man and wife.

Mika turned to Shaylae; a tear fell down her cheeks, sparkling with the radiance in her eyes. But the precious moment was broken as a look of horror filled his eyes. "Who's that?" he said, pointing across the village.

Shaylae turned quickly. She stopped breathing, her heart pounding. Standing on the other side of the wedding party was a young woman with curly blonde hair. It seemed that no one except them could see her, as the wedding continued uninterrupted.

Shaylae turned to Mika, panic in her eyes. "Mika, what should I do?"

He was about to speak, when the woman raised her hands.

Instinctively Shaylae joined souls with Mika and drew on his strength. She gritted her teeth, and with fire in their eyes, they reached out to the girl. She stumbled and fell. Had she been unaware of Shaylae and Mika's presence? If so, she was aware now as she looked directly at them, hate and anger in her eyes. She too reached toward Shaylae, but it was too late. Before she had time to retaliate, Shaylae shifted her, to where she did not know, and hardly cared. All she knew was that she had to remove her from Nashota's village.

Shaylae fell to her knees, gasping for breath, holding her hand over her chest. "Mommy, are you alright?" said Halona.

"I'm fine," she said. Then very softly she added, "Soon, Nashota, when the night and day are the same, you will take your people back to the home from which Asdzáán Nádleehé was driven. May the Holy Ones be with you as you learn what you must know." She turned to Mika. "I was wrong. I must watch over her until they are safely returned to Tal'el'Dine'h. She will be safe once they get there, but I must protect her from the evil woman." She shook with fear and trembling.

CHAPTER 15

Nashota lay awake, staring at the roof of their Hogan. Yanaba had said that her powers would increase when she became a wife and she could definitely feel it. When they had made love she immediately felt more at one with the world, as if she was beginning to sense its unimaginable complexity. She had tasted of this before, but only under very unusual circumstances, like when she had rescued little Bluebird from the cougar, or Niyol from the Apache. But now the feeling remained with her, filling her.

Niyol stirred in his sleep. She could not help but smile as she listened to the comforting sounds of his breathing soul; it filled her with a warm sense of completeness and belonging.

"My husband," she said to herself quietly. "You are my husband, and I adore you." She ran her hands across his bare chest. The feel of his warm skin and his strong muscles made her shiver with pleasure.

The night had passed quickly even though they hadn't slept much. It was a few hands before dawn when she got up as quietly as she could, put on her dress, and went outside. The sky was clear and thousands of stars still glittered in the dark blanket of the night. She breathed deeply of the cool air, and rejoiced as it filled her lungs. Her heart pounded taking the life-bringing wind from the top of her head to the ends of her toes.

She looked up at Sister Moon and wondered if her new powers would take her there. She closed her eyes, concentrated, and breathed deeply, letting the wind fill her breathing soul. She willed herself to Sister Moon. She opened her eyes and found herself looking back at Mother Earth. She did not expect it would have been that easy. Oh, but how beautiful Mother Earth was.

Niyol turned in bed and reached out to touch Nashota, but she was not there. "Nashota?"

"*I am out here my beloved. And it is cold.*"

He stood up, wrapped a blanket around himself, picked up another for his wife and went outside.

"No wonder you're cold," he said, covering her with the warm blanket and putting his arms around her.

She turned to him, smiled, and kissed his cheek. "Niyol, I think I know how I will take us back to Tal'el'Dine'h."

"How?"

"I understand now what Yanaba meant. Come with me, hold my hand."

Niyol took Nashota's hand and squeezed.

"*Join with me, husband.*"

He felt their minds touch, much as they had done last night, but this time something even more powerful was happening: he could see into her soul. He felt her intense love for him, not exactly like his own, but in its own feminine way, just as strong. He felt her wisdom and intelligence, her courage, and strength, but above all he felt her gentleness and kindness.

"*Nashota, what is happening?*"

"*We are joined, soul to soul, just as our ancestors on Tal'el'Dine'h were able to. My power has increased now that I have become wife to my husband. I adore you, Niyol Swift Wind.*"

"*And I you, Nashota. I love you so that it almost gives me pain.*"

They turned to face each other and kissed. It was a kiss full of hope, promise, eternity, but above all it was a kiss of infinite passion.

"*Open your eyes, Niyol.*"

More stars than he had ever seen filled the heavens. They seemed clearer too. Beneath their feet was yellow, almost white dusty sand, yet it was if his feet were not touching the ground. The horizon seemed much closer. Strange mountains loomed before them, reaching higher than any mountains he knew.

"Where are we?"

"We are on Sister Moon."

"How?"

"We are not really standing on Sister Moon, not our bodies at least. We are only here in spirit."

"Then this is the magic Yanaba called shifting."

"Almost. To shift we would have to step across that distance, the same as we can now see across it."

Niyol Looked around. Above them was a brilliant, blue and white ball. He pointed to it.

"Mother Earth?" he asked.

"Yes. Isn't she beautiful?"

"Can you take us to Tal'el'Dine'h? Right now I mean?"

She smiled. "You think I should?"

"Yes. I do. Where is he anyway?"

Nashota pointed. "See the Ancient Warrior?"

Niyol nodded. There stood, the Ancient Warrior, the most spectacular star person in the sky.

"Follow the line from his tomahawk… about four hands. You see Tal'el'Dine'h?"

"Yes, I see him."

The scene changed. The rugged barren mountains were replaced by lush green rolling hills. In the distance they saw water, blue water stretching to the horizon. The sky was blue, not a cloud in sight.

Niyol took in a deep breath. "She is beautiful."

"She will be our new home. We will raise our children here."

"What will become of those left behind?"

"I don't know, but I fear for them, Niyol Swift Wind."

He nodded sadly.

"Let us complete the shift. Step across with me, husband."

Beneath his feet Niyol felt the soft, cool grass of Tal'el'Dine'h. He bent down and touched it, pulled out a handful and held it to his nose, breathing deeply of the aroma. "The land is good," he said. "It will provide well for us and our family."

"Yanaba said we need to leave before equal-day."

"Did she say why?"

"No. All she said was that we needed to be gone from here by spring."

"How many people should we take with us? And how will you decide?"

"I think we need to talk to Matriarch Sahkyo."

"Can we stay here a while?"

Nashota smiled, and sat down on the grass. Niyol joined her and they lay back and kissed.

CHAPTER 16

"Matriarch Sahkyo, we would talk with you," said Nashota, as she and Niyol stood outside her Hogan. "And could we also talk to Hastiin?"

"Certainly, children. Niyol why don't you go and get Hastiin, and, Nashota, you come on in." She sat on a rug and motioned Nashota to join her.

"Is everything alright? Niyol is treating you well?" she asked after Niyol had left.

"Oh yes, Matriarch, he couldn't be better; things couldn't be better."

"So, marriage agrees with you?"

Nashota blushed, and nodded.

Niyol and Hastiin knocked at the door of the Hogan. "Come on in, you old dog," she called out, laughing. Hastiin and Niyol joined them on the rug.

"Now, what is troubling you?" asked Sahkyo.

"There's nothing troubling us," said Nashota. "Well, not really."

"Nashota, I've known you long enough to know that you are carrying a burden. Now, please, share it with me so it may be lightened."

"Grandfather already knows much of what I must tell you, Matriarch, but I begged him to keep silent until I was ready to tell you; until the time approached when I must carry out the mission I was given."

Nashota paused; Sahkyo raised her eyebrows. "Please go on, Nashota."

"First I must tell you that I was visited by a beautiful woman at my Kinaalda; during the molding."

"A Holy One?" asked Sahkyo, not sounding surprised at all.

"I thought so at first, but she told me she was a daughter of Changing Woman, that she was my sister."

"Did she tell you her name?"

"She told me the name given to her at her molding by Asdzáán Nádleehé: Yanaba."

"'She Who Meets The Enemy,'" said Sahkyo, nodding her head.

"Yes, that's what she told me."

"But what enemy?" asked Sahkyo.

"The Dark Ones."

Sahkyo was silent for a while. "The Dark Ones. Yes, the legend speaks of them."

"Yanaba took me to Asdzáán Nádleehé's home world."

"Her home world? Not the Glittering World?"

"No."

"You told me when you were but five summers that Tal'el'Dine'h was Asdzáán Nádleehé's home world," said Hastiin. "I've thought about that often, and somehow, it always seemed to make sense."

Nashota and Niyol told them all that they had learned about Father Sun, Mother Earth, and the other stars in the heavens. They told them how Asdzáán Nádleehé had been born on Tal'el'Dine'h, how the Dark Ones who destroyed her world, and how in anger she had destroyed theirs. They told them that Yanaba had instructed them to return to Tal'el'Dine'h.

"How will you travel that far?" she asked.

"We will shift. It is the power by which Asdzáán Nádleehé traveled here when her world was destroyed by the Dark Ones."

"You asked me about shifting once before. And you know how to 'shift'?" asked Hastiin.

"Yes, Grandfather. We have already visited Tal'el'Dine'h. She is a beautiful world."

"And you must leave the Glittering World, and return to Tal'el'Dine'h? You will not return?"

"We, Matriarch; we will return to Tal'el'Dine'h. Yanaba told me to take many of the People with us. I intend to take our whole village."

Sahkyo leaned over and touched her arm. "That you cannot do."

Nashota was taken aback. "But, Matriarch, why?"

"No, you will take with you young couples and their families. It will be hard establishing yourselves on a new world. Old people like me would be a burden to you."

"Matriarch! You're not old, and you could certainly never be a burden."

"Tsk!" she said.

"The Matriarch is right," said Hastiin. "Besides, you will need young couples from different clans."

There was no arguing with this. If they were to populate a new world they would need to have many clans within which the next generation could marry.

"Perhaps you should take three or four couples from the first four clans created from the skin of Changing Woman: our own clan – the Kiiyaa'áanii, the Honágháahnii, the Todich'ii'nii, and the Hashtl'ishnii."

"But how could I leave you both? And Dezba, and…"

"Hush, child. This is how it must be," said Hastiin. "We must carry on the legacy of Changing Woman here on the Glittering World. Tal'el'Dine'h is for the young."

"We must send runners to the other three clans and have a council of the elders," said Sahkyo as she stood.

CHAPTER 17

The realization that tomorrow she would be leaving her precious Dinetah hit Nashota like an unexpected cold wind blowing in from the North. The last moon she had been busy, too busy to think about the path she had chosen, where it would take her, and what it would take her from. Working with the Elders to select the couples who would accompany her and return to Tal'el'Dine'h was hard. Families whom she thought would be wonderful additions to their new life, the elders rejected; others she thought might not be suitable, the elders chose. But finally fifty couples and their families, young and strong like Nashota and Niyol, were ready to embark on a journey none of them understood, and most of them feared, yet they had all agreed to follow this wondrous young woman called Nashota. Most were older than her; many had small families of their own with children ranging in age from new born to young men and women almost ready to choose spouses of their own, but all of them looked to her as an Elder, readily accepting her as their new Matriarch.

Niyol was sitting on a rug in their Hogan and she had her head in his lap as he tenderly stroked her hair. "This is our last night in our Hogan, my husband," she said. A tear came to her eye, followed by another, and soon she could no longer hold back as she broke down sobbing.

"Oh, Nashota," he said, wiping away her tears. "I know how you feel. You will never see your grandfather again, or Sahkyo, or Dezba or Doli. And I will never see my parents again. But this is what Asdzáán Nádleehé wants us to do. I'm sure of it, and I believe you are the only one who can do this thing."

She nodded her head. "I know, and I also know that when we reach the land of the dead we will all be together again, but I will miss them, and I will miss this wonderful home." She wiped her eyes and stood up. "Do you mind if I spend some time on my own?"

"Of course not, my love."

She stood up and walked out into the cool night air. Not a single cloud person obscured the view of the thousands of stars that filled the clear night sky. The ancient warrior dominated her view to the west, but soon he would set. To his west a waning Sister Moon, in quarter face, was also dipping toward the horizon. Higher in the sky Tal'el'Dine'h twinkled dimly. This time tomorrow he would be her new home, he would be her new Father Sun. Oh, what will become of me, she thought. Am I doing the right thing?

A rustling of leaves behind her brought her back to earth. "Grandfather," she said. "Shouldn't you be asleep?"

"Nashota, I couldn't sleep either."

She grabbed him tightly as he came closer. "Oh, Grandfather, I can't go through with this. I can't leave you; I can't leave my home." She stretched her arms above her. "And I can't leave all of this."

"Nashota, you must be brave. I will miss you too, more than you can possibly know. My life has been so blessed to have had the joy of raising you, watching you grow from infant, to child, to young woman, and to a wife. These precious memories will never leave me." Hastiin placed his hand over his heart. "And as long as they remain with me, you will always be in my heart." He leaned forward and kissed her forehead. "I love you, my precious Little Twin, but this is something you must do."

Nashota buried her head in his chest, and sobbed. "What will become of me? What will become of you?" The last few days Nashota had dreamed of terrible things that would happen to the people and she feared for her family and friends in the village and the other clans.

"I don't know. These are things we must leave in the hands of the Holy Ones. Even if we do not see where the path we must tread leads we must trust them."

She hugged him even closer.

"Grandfather," she said at last. "The sword I took from the Spanish soldier..."

"Yes," he said.

"Keep it safe. Hand it down through the generations. One day Yanaba will need it."

The village was full. The parents and relatives of those chosen to return to Asdzáán Nádleehé's home world were gathered to bid final farewell to their loved ones, knowing they would never see them again in this life. Nashota held up her hands and everyone fell silent. "To those who are left behind, do not grieve for your loved ones. Remember, when we all return to the land of the dead, to the Holy Ones, we will rejoice once more as we share each other's company." She turned to those who would make the journey with her. "To you who have agreed to follow me, I cannot tell you what challenges we will face, or what dangers await us. All I can promise you is that we are fulfilling the will of our blessed and sacred mother, Asdzáán Nádleehé."

Shaylae breathed a sigh of relief. Soon her ordeal would be over and she would be able to return to her children and to her husband. She was sure that once Nashota and her people reached Tal'el'Dine'h that they would be safe from the evil woman who had tried to destroy them. She had returned many times these last few weeks. Shaylae had been able to hold her from doing any harm to Nashota; but with each encounter, she felt a little more of her life drain away. She was never sure how she would be able to repel the next attack, only that she must. Miraculously it seemed, she always found strength, from where she did not know. She had hidden this awful threat from Nashota, in fact she had never shown herself to her again. So, for the first time in two months she felt herself relaxing. She wondered if she should tell Nashota that one day she would be her mentor. She smiled. The paradoxes of shifting through time and space certainly created some interesting situations, but she decided she should probably not tell Nashota anything; let her figure it out for herself. After all, Nashota had not said anything to her when she was younger and Nashota was older.

Nashota raised her arms, ready to make the shift. There was a scream. And then another. The whole crowd was in panic, fear radiated from them, fear that filled Shaylae. Then she saw her. The blonde-haired woman stood in their midst, only her hair was not blonde; it looked to be on fire, standing out from her head like an evil halo. Her eyes flamed, blood red. Her skin shone with evil luminescence, her dress billowed all around her, and the foul smoke of hell surrounded her.

She felt the awful power radiating from the woman, power she knew she was not equal to. Was she about to succeed? Was she about to destroy Nashota and her followers? Shaylae felt her will failing her, felt her life slipping away, helpless and hopeless. Was she destined to fail at the last moment?

"Be gone from here, you spirit from hell!"

Shaylae looked up again. It was Nashota, standing her ground against the evil incarnation. She looked magnificent. She was surrounded by her people, still in the depths of horrific fear.

"Yanaba, come to my aid."

"Yanaba cannot help you. She no longer exists. Once I have killed you, none of your descendants will have ever existed." She stretched forth her hands and Nashota fell, coughing, holding her chest, her face contorted in agony.

Shaylae felt a hand on her shoulder. She turned but there was no one.

"Get up child. Cross the time and space. She needs you."

"White Cloud?"

"Get up. Step across!"

She stood up, feeling strength returning to her body. "Yes, White Cloud, stay with me."

"As I promised I would."

Shaylae stepped across time and space. Immediately the evil one saw her.

"You!" she screamed. "You cannot be here!"

"But I am," Shaylae faced her enemy.

She laughed. "You fool," you are no match for me."

"No, child, you are not. Her spirit can destroy you but physically she is only a woman..."

Not stopping to think for a moment, she launched herself at her. She felt a shock through her whole body as they hit the ground together.

"No!" she screamed. "You cannot stop me. She clawed at Shaylae, scratching, biting, kicking, but Shaylae was stronger and held her fast.

"Now, Nashota, now, you must leave."

Still the woman fought with her. Still she felt her skin being raked, but she held her down.

"You will not succeed. Whatever you are, you cannot stop the will of the Holy Ones."

"The Holy Ones don't exist," she shouted.

Shaylae could feel the woman weakening. Her spiritual power was being spent in her physical struggle, and Nashota was released from the pain that had struck her to the ground.

"Yanaba…"

"Go! You must leave now; else it will be too late. Go!"

Nashota looked lost for a moment, not knowing what to do, but then resolve filled her eyes.

"Come, my people. It is time."

They formed up around her. She raised her arms and they were gone.

"NO!" screamed the woman. "NO!"

She stopped her struggling; Shaylae felt her body go limp beneath her. She turned and looked Shaylae in the eye. Shaylae could hardly bear to look at those eyes, so filled with hatred.

"You have not won; you have merely shifted the battle ground. We will meet again, witch!" And she disappeared. Shaylae was left holding empty space.

She looked up at the villagers who surrounded her; they looked stunned. One of them stepped forward, and took her in his arms.

"Yanaba," he said. "Whoever you are, I thank you."

"Did she call me *witch?*" said Shaylae.

If the man responded she did not hear. Her consciousness drifted away, like a rock sinking in the depths of the sea.

In her dreams a woman bathed her wounds. In her dreams a man sat by her comforting her with soothing words. In her dreams an old woman stood over her, praying. In her dreams, a shaman danced around her bed, waving his medicine bundle. In her dreams she felt the love of a village, a village of the People.

"Hastiin," said the woman, as she bathed Shaylae with cool, healing water. "I think she is waking up."

Shaylae opened her eyes. Sitting by her cot was a woman.

"I am Dezba, Yanaba," she said.

Shaylae smiled. "I know. I watched as Nashota saved your child."

"Then it was you who showed her what to do?" asked the man.

"Oh no," said Shaylae. "Nashota is full of power, more than I will ever have. She did all things on her own."

He shed a few tears. "My precious Nashota, how I miss her already."

"She is fulfilling a marvelous, wondrous, and holy destiny," said Shaylae. "And you will see her again, Hastiin."

"You know who I am?"

She tried to sit up, but the pain was too great. Every muscle ached. She had cuts on her hands and arms. She raised her hand to her face. She felt cuts and swellings there too. She lay back down again. "I have watched as you nurtured and raised Little Twin. I watched as you loved and cared for her. Your place with the Holy Ones and the Blessed Ancestors is assured."

"You watched?"

"But even if I had not, I would have recognized you as a Blessed Ancestor."

He put his hand on his chest, and raised his eyebrows.

Shaylae took his hand. "In a little over four hundred years, one of Nashota's descendants will return to the Glittering World from Tal'el'Dine'h; he will be my great grandfather. So you see, you are also my grandfather."

"Then, where are you from? And when?"

"I have come to you from five hundred years in your future. I live with my husband and two children not too far from where we are right now."

Hastiin took her hand, and held it to his breast. Shaylae forced herself to sit up and embrace this great man.

"Oh, my blessed child."

"My Blessed Ancestor."

Shaylae basked in the warmth of the man who had raised, nurtured, and loved the great Matriarch Nashota.

"What will you do now, Yanaba?"

She could not tell Hastiin that his grand-daughter still lived, five-hundred years in his future; he would not understand. But she knew the time was very close when she would have to go to Tal'el'Dine'h; Nashota had told her she would know when it was time. "Soon, I too must travel to Tal'el'Dine'h. The evil one has shifted the battle ground there."

"Will my Little Twin be safe?"

"The Holy Ones have granted Tal'el'Dine'h their protection. For five hundred years, Nashota's people will live in peace. They will come to know the old powers. They will grow and prosper as no other people have prospered. They will be safe and happy. No, when the evil one said the battle ground has moved, she was talking about the distant future. That is where I will find her. That is where I must go."

"Then go, Yanaba. Go with my blessing, and go with the Holy Ones."

Part Two
Delta Pavonis

CHAPTER 18

Sigmun breathed a sigh of relief as he flopped himself down on the luxurious couch in the family room. "Finally! It's over and I can relax."

Luci jumped up on his lap, hugged him and kissed his face over and over. "Oh, Daddy, where have you been? You've been gone for ages."

"You think they'll leave you alone at last?" said Ayanna, as she sat next to him, threw her arms around his shoulders and hugged him.

"I think so. I hope so."

"You want to go out and celebrate?"

"I think I'd like to relax. Tomorrow I'll feel more like celebrating. Right now, all I feel like doing is sleeping."

Ayanna laughed. "OK. But you're not going to go to bed right now. You can at least eat with us, and tell me everything."

"Yes, Daddy. You have to eat. I helped mommy cook your favorite dinner."

"You did?" said Sigmun as he rolled Luci over on her back and started to tickle her.

Luci barely managed a "Yes," through her hysterical laughter.

"Not Navajo taco's again, little pixie?"

"I'll smack you!" said Ayanna with a snort. "You'll get bean soup and corn bread if you make another crack like that."

Sigmun wasn't paying attention. He was too busy making up for lost time with his cuter-than-cute daughter. She looked nothing like her mom, they were complete opposites, but they were the two most beautiful girls in the three worlds. Luci's curly blonde hair was a mess of tangles, and her blue eyes were streaming with tears, she was laughing so hard.

Tokala ran full speed into the family room and launched himself at his dad, knocking the wind out of him. "Dad, you're home." At seven years old, he was solid and very strong. He was already skilled fighter, Chulukua-Ryu—Ayanna had seen to that. His hair was jet black, his skin olive, and he definitely had the look of his mother in his strong featured face, but like Shaylae, and his little sister, his eyes were bright blue. Tokala had already saved his mom's life once, even before he was born. If not for him, she would have succumbed to Denab. Sigmun hugged him extra hard.

"OK, that's enough of that," said Ayanna, as she rescued her husband from the boisterous affections of the kids. "Go wash up for dinner, rugrats."

Luci scampered off toward the bathroom; Tokala followed, in not so much of a hurry.

Later that evening, after the kids were in bed, Ayanna asked Sigmun, "So, how was your last day of government?"

"It was my last day. How bad could it have been?"

Ayanna tucked her knees under herself, and laid her head on his shoulder. He put his arm around her and held her tightly, tenderly kissing her forehead.

He was relieved. For almost eight years, he had been right hand to Governor Seri, the same woman who had been elected Governor of *Reconciliation*. By acclamation, the people of Yurob had accepted her as interim governor until a new constitution could be drawn up, and a new government elected. She was a natural choice, the best possible choice. For twenty-three years she had worked in the administration section of *Reconciliation*, in the days when it was still called *Revenge*, the last eight of those years as head of the section. She was not a Dark One, but had been chosen for her organizational and diplomatic skills to take care of the day-to-day running of the interstellar craft, something the Dark Ones on board did not want to bother themselves with. Since there was no one on Yurob left who knew the first thing about government once all the Dark Ones were deposed, she was a good choice.

It had been a struggle. It was an enormous task to get representatives from every continent, every region, and every city, to meet and come to agreement as to how they wanted to be governed. A logistical nightmare, Sigmun said, but somehow, Seri took it all in her stride. Then, once the constitution had been accepted, it took another six months to set up the electoral process, to make sure there were acceptable candidates for each position, and that every citizen over five sun-cycles of age would be able to vote. It was a time of great excitement; never before in the history of Yurob had there been an election. Seri was elected governor in a landslide.

Seri had tried to persuade Sigmun to run for office as her Lieutenant Governor. The people certainly loved and trusted him. The media organized an immensely responsive grass-roots campaign to try to convince him, but he decided that government was not where he wanted to spend the rest of his life. So, two sun-cycles after *Reconciliation* had liberated Yurob, they were now self-governing, and Sigmun was free to pursue his dream. He had been itching to get out and travel space, but the tasks of government had forced him to put that goal on hold. Now, he was determined to pursue it, convinced he would do so for the rest of his mortal life. If only the folks at the Interplanetary Space Agency would go along…

He breathed deeply, inhaling the intoxicating aroma of his wife's skin and hair.

"Have you decided where you want to go?"

He held his hand up and waved it in no particular direction. "Out there somewhere; but I'm not holding my breath. I doubt we'll ever get through the bureaucratic tangle at ISA."

Ayanna was an enthusiastic party to this hankering of Sigmun's and she too was looking forward to doing some exploration. It wasn't going to be as easy as jumping into their own personal hyper-ship, picking a star and hitting the *go* button. For one thing, the computer programs which set the hyper-course were extremely complex, and still in development. To even be able to use the programs you had to be a math whiz. Fortunately, both Ayanna and Sigmun qualified on that score. The ISA problem was a much more significant issue.

Ayanna smiled and casually said, "Oh yes, I almost forgot, we got a hyper-com from ISA today."

Sigmun rolled his eyes, and shook his head. "Shut UP! You didn't forget, you little minx." Sigmun was used to Ayanna teasing him like this. "What did it say?"

"Minx! I'm not sure I want to tell you now."

"Ayanna!" he said threateningly.

She laughed. The governments of Yurob and Earth had made a pact that effectively put a moratorium on hyper-travel until various protocols could be worked out. The ISA, still based in the United States, had taken on the responsibility to administer the policy, and was staffed with people from many countries on Earth, as well as people from Yurob. Sigmun had submitted his request six months earlier, in the hope that the moratorium would be lifted soon, but was not hopeful that he would receive any kind of permit.

"It'll be on your PID anyway. Just pull it up."

He quickly found the communiqué.

To: Sigmun, Second of the Eleven, and Lady Ayanna Hale of Yurob
From: Rear Admiral Harley Davidson Tacoma, Acting Director, ISA
Re: Your Request for Authorized Hyper-Travel

Excellencies:

> *Unfortunately at this time we are unable to issue any permits for private Hyper-Travel. However, we are pleased to offer you both commissions in the ISA, as Lieutenant Commanders. If you are willing to accept these commissions, you will report to ISA headquarters in Lafayette, Colorado by May 15th, 2116. You will be expected to complete a four-week training course on ISA protocol regarding contact with intelligent life and a two-week orientation on the latest developments in hyper-analysis and hyper-navigation. Upon successful completion you will be assigned as team leaders of a mission to one of ten local star-systems which have been selected by the ISA. LCDR Hale will assume the role of Mission Commander. Unfortunately, due to the experimental nature of this mission, we cannot honor your request to have your children accompany you.*

"Well, I didn't expect to be able to take the kids. Still, they can at least be with us for the training and orientation." He turned to Ayanna with mock anger. "And just how long were you planning to keep this from me?"

"As long as I could," she said, sauntering sexily into the bedroom, and looking back at him with one of those oh-so-enticing looks in her eyes.

He jumped up and ran after her. It had been a long time since they had seen each other for more than just a few fleeting moments.

***

They took the next hyper-transport to Earth; it took just over a week to make the journey, but once they landed they headed directly via sub-orbital to Denver, where the ISA was headquartered. Mika met them at the airport. He didn't look so great.

"Mika, what's up?" said Sigmun.

"And where's Shay and the kids?" asked Ayanna.

"The kids are with Rey."

"And Shay?"

"She's off gallivanting space-time somewhere." He appeared to be quite distracted.

"And…" prompted Ayanna.

"I'm sorry. She asked me not to tell anyone, other than she's off on some sort of mission."

"Not even me?" said Ayanna, a little surprised.

"Sorry. I don't even know much about what's going on."

Ayanna felt a little put out by this. Through all of Shaylae's confrontations with the Dark Ones, with the councils on Yurob, and with Rolling Darkness she had been at Shaylae's side. Still, she was sure Shaylae had a good reason. She had to have.

"The ISA has put us up at the new Hilton Interplanetary, Lafayette, which is right next to the campus."

"And you're here to welcome us?"

"Yes. Mat and Rey are back at Fort Douglas. I'll be going back to Salt Lake tomorrow, but I'll return in a month to bring you up to speed on HyperNav."

Ayanna was feeling more and more uncomfortable. There was something definitely bothering Mika. He was undeniably not himself.

"Are you sure you're OK?" she asked him. "Everything OK between you and Shay?"

Mika smiled, his first since they arrived. "Ayanna!" he said, shaking his head. Of course things were OK between them. "It's just I'm a little…" he paused.

"Worried about her?"

He nodded. "But enough of that," he said with a visible effort to perk up. "Let's get you settled and we can talk some more about what's been happening on Yurob."

Ayanna bent down to pick up her luggage.

"I'll get that," said Mika. "You take care of Luci and Tokala."

The next four weeks were frankly a bore. Yes, Ayanna understood the need to have protocols, but since she was a kid, protocols and diplomacy had not been her favorite pursuits. Her dad had wanted her to follow in his footsteps as a lawyer, but advanced math and physics were her first love, certainly not politics. Most of it was repetitive anyway, saying the same things over and over again. And since their mission was observational, they were not going to be making any kind of contact with other intelligent life, even if there was such in the systems they would be visiting. So, she endured with patience, trying her hardest not to fall asleep.

Sigmun faired better. After all, he had been a leading diplomat on Yurob for the last eight years. "You really should try harder, Anna," he told her. "Some of this stuff is important."

"If you say so, honey, but as long as one of us is soaking it up…"

Evenings were much more fun. They traveled to the tops of some of the local peaks, some of the highest in the lower 48. They took in the local nightlife, and delicious dining. Lafayette had become *the* hangout, since the ISA had set up headquarters here. Luci and Tok were having a ball; this was much better than school.

Once Mika returned the interesting stuff began. Ayanna had started out a little cocky, again hinting that she didn't really need a refresher course in advanced Hyper-Analysis. But as it turned out, she was a little rusty, and there had been a great deal of progress made in the accuracy, reducing the number of interim steps to reach distant stars.

"OK, so we've been able to speed up the process of local calibration significantly," said Mika, pointing to a formula which filled a large screen, covering one wall of the classroom. "What this means is two things: first, the legs themselves can be much further. Second, the delay between each leg is reduced to about two hours. We're estimating two-to-three light-years per leg, although until we have more confidence in the equipment, we're still recommending that the penultimate leg take you no closer than 10 A.U. on the z-axis of the star. It should be fairly safe from that distance to make a final jump to take you within one million kilometers of a planet."

"I'm assuming we'll be stationary after the jump," said Sigmun.

"Insofar as anything is stationary in space, but given that there is no inertia or momentum in hyper-travel, your motion will be relative to the starting point of the leg; which is one of the many reasons we have to keep the legs short."

"So, at one gee acceleration, we should be able to make planetary orbit in about six hours," said Ayanna.

"Yes, total travel time should be twenty to twenty-four hours. A huge improvement since *Reconciliation* made its journey from Sol to Procyon which took just over a week. The legs were less than a light-year each, and the time to recalibrate was about fifteen hours. In fact, if the ISA had existed back then and knew what we know now, there's no way they would have allowed such a risk in getting to Yurob."

"Well, thank the Ancestors the ISA didn't exist back then."

"Amen to that," said Sigmun. "And the computers are now able to gather local space-time data much faster now?"

"Yes," said Mika. "More accurately too, since even an error of less than one in a million could have disastrous results."

"Like finding yourself in the center of a star," observed Sigmun.

"Or any other solid or gaseous object," added Ayanna.

"Exactly. So, the fluctuations of local space-time conditions prior to taking the next jump must be fully computed using Hyper-Analysis. And as you have learned, it makes tensor analysis look like child's play."

"And Hyper-Analysis was Mat's biggest contribution," said Ayanna.

"Hardly," said Mika, almost disdainfully. "Hyper-Analysis was merely the tool he used to describe the paradigm. His biggest insight was…"

Ayanna was clearly deflated. Mika had never once spoken to her like that before.

"I'm sorry, Anna," he said, scrunching his eyes up and sucking air through his teeth. "It's just…"

"No problem, Mika. I understand." But she didn't really understand at all.

"What in the heck was all that about?" said Ayanna, as she stormed into their hotel room and slammed her purse on the table.

"Slow down, Anna," said Sigmun. "There's obviously a lot more going on here than…"

"Don't tell me that! You have no idea!"

"Ayanna!"

"I'm sorry, Sig. It's just that you can't possibly imagine what it was like to be joined soul-to-soul to Shay and Mik as we battled the Dark Ones on *Revenge*, and even more so as we battled Denab. And now – to be shut out like this." She broke down and started crying.

"Ayanna, I had no idea…"

"It's like part of me has died," she struggled through her tears. "It's as if Shay and Mik have died. Oh, I can't explain it."

Sigmun put his arm around her. "Ayanna, you have to trust Shaylae. I'm sure she's not deliberately trying to hurt you. There has to be a good reason."

Ayanna nodded and sniffed. "I guess you're right." She wiped her eyes. "Look at me. I'm balling like a kid."

The remainder of their training took on a very formal, even cold atmosphere. Mika was thorough, but other than teaching them, he hardly said a word.

Finally, their orientation and training was over, and they traveled to the ISA launch facilities in Florida, where they were joined by Harley and Anne to go over the details of their mission. Shay-Anne was almost ten, and Harley junior was seven. Of course, Harley junior and Tok were already best buddies, even though they had only seen each other a handful of times. Shay-Anne was a beautiful young woman, who loved taking care of Luci.

"Full uniform from now on," said Harley as he showed them into their quarters on the base. "You'll find them in the closets. Blues for regular wear around the base, Whites for formal farewell and take-off, and grey casuals while in flight."

Once they were settled, and dressed in their new uniforms, they headed over to launch control.

"OK, you don't need to make up your mind just yet, but here are the files on the ten star systems we have selected as possible destinations." He handed them a rom chip.

"Can we have a quick look now?"

"Sure." He motioned to a console; Ayanna sat down and inserted the rom chip.

A page came up with a display of ten star systems.

"Of course, these are all based on statistical probability, although we do know that all ten of them have luminosity, temperature, and variability well within the limits for life; all ten have planetary systems, although we cannot be sure that any of them are terrestrial.

"Which one does the ISA favor?"

"To be honest, all ten are just as likely to have a terrestrial planet with life, but my personal favorite is this one." He scrolled down to one of them. "This one is Delta Pavonis." He zoomed in on it. The computer had projected a system of fourteen planets. "It's roughly the same age as Sol, and there's a high probability that the fourth is a terrestrial world."

"Interesting. So life will have had as long as life on Earth to evolve," said Ayanna.

"I have a good feeling about Delta Pavonis. I think this is the system I want to visit," said Sigmun.

"Fine with me," said Ayanna.

"OK. But you should look at all of them before you make a final decision." He looked at his watch, "I can't stay much longer, and I'd like to introduce you to your ship and your crew..."

"Sure, we can check it out later."

"Come on then. I have a jeep outside waiting for us."

Their driver, a Marine gold-bar Lieutenant, saluted crisply as they climbed into the jeep; Harley sat in the front seat with the driver, Sigmun and Ayanna in the rear.

"I'd like you to meet Second Lieutenant Tyler Martin."

Martin saluted crisply; Ayanna saluted back. This military stuff was going to take some getting used to.

"In addition to Martin, your crew will consist of Lieutenant JG Jane Hansen, and Chief Petty Officer Mark Olsen. Immediately after graduating Annapolis, first in her class, Hansen was excused from duty to complete her PhD in Hyper-Analysis, which she received six months ago from MIT. Olsen can fix anything from welding the drive shaft of an internal combustion engine to micro-wiring the distribution center of your control panel. He'll not be much help with the Hyper-Drive, but you also have two TFC's, both Petty Officers, second class: Steve Jennings is a hyper-drive specialist, nuts and bolts, types, not a mathematician. Ryan Morris is a hyper-fusion specialist. He will take charge of the normal space flight."

Ayanna nodded. It was still sounding too good to be true. "And what's your specialty, Lieutenant?"

"In addition to being a combat platoon leader, I'm an astrophysicist, specializing in planetary system theory."

A fighter and physicist; an interesting combination, thought Ayanna.

"He's also a top notch cosmologist and practical astronomer to boot."

The jeep pulled into a huge hanger. At the far end was what looked like a regular shuttle, although at seventy-five meters in length, it was significantly larger. Ayanna had seen the specs, but the sight of her was much more impressive. Standing on its landing gear, it towered thirty-five meters above them, sixty at the tail with a wingspan of forty-eight meters, and five huge engine exhausts at the rear.

"So, this is your ship," said Harley. "She can take off and land vertically or horizontally, although, seconds into a horizontal take off, she assumes a vertical orientation."

"Will we be performing a horizontal takeoff?"

"Yes. We estimate another week to get her ready, and then two days after that..." he made an upward swooshing motion with his hand.

There was some kind of commotion going on around the ship. As they drew closer they could make out the shouting. A CPO in his forties was yelling at a Technician First Class; other Crewmen and Technicians were standing around looking quite nervous.

"Look, you malodorous mutant, I don't care how many times you've checked them, I want x-rays of every weld. Every weld! You understand."

"But, sir, as I've already told you, that's not standard procedure," replied the unyielding TFC.

"This boat is not standard procedure you anorexic asswipe. It's the first to fly hyper! You got that? X-rays, every weld, my office, first thing in the morning, or I'll bust you down to Second Class."

"Yes, sir, if that's what you want."

"Yes, *Chief Petty Officer*, you fatuous..."

"Olsen," shouted Harley, interrupting the alliterative expletive.

Olsen spun around, and clicked his heels when he saw who had interrupted him.

"Admiral," he said with a sharp salute.

The hanger was immediately silent as everyone came quickly to attention.

"At ease," said Harley. Then turning to the object of Olsen's diatribe he said. "What are you waiting for Crewman? X-rays at the double. Have them finished them by midnight tonight, and a second set on my desk."

"Yes, sir," stammered the Technician.

"And argue with a CPO once more like that and you'll be before a review board before Olsen can finish cussing you out. Dismissed!"

The technician ran off, beckoning two other technicians to follow him.

"Chief, I hope that TFC wasn't part of the mission."

"No, sir. If he was I would have requested his removal."

"Good. I'd like to introduce you to your new Commanding Officer, Lieutenant Commander Ayanna Hale, and her First Officer, Lieutenant Commander Sigmun."

He saluted. "It's an honor, ma'am, sir," he said.

Ayanna and Sigmun returned the salutes, and then Ayanna offered her hand to him. He started to extend his hand, but withdrew it quickly. "I'm afraid I've been working, ma'am. Bit dirty," he said, wiping his hands on his overalls.

She stuck her hand more resolutely toward him. "Starting today, Chief, I'll be sharing the dirt, beginning with the dirt on your hands."

Olsen took her hand, and shook it vigorously, with an enthusiastic gleam in his eye.

She turned back to Harley. "Now, can we look her over?" asked Ayanna.

"Certainly, Lieutenant Commander, it's your ship. And of course, in the tradition of ships at sea, on board you will be referred to as Captain."

She nodded, then turned toward Martin. "And to keep ranks in naval tradition, can we refer to Second Lieutenant Martin as Ensign Martin."

"Captain's call, although most do adopt ISA ranking structure within their ship."

"Ensign Martin it is then," she said.

"What will you name your ship, Captain?" asked Harley.

"*Enterprise*," she replied. She noticed out of the corner of her eye that Ensign Martin smiled.

"*Enterprise* she is. Any particular reason?"

"It's a twentieth century thing, Admiral," she said with a quirky smile.

"OK, let's begin the tour." He made as if to lead her to the elevator.

"With all due respect, Admiral, can we have the Chief show us around?"

Harley snorted and laughed. "Of course. She's all yours, Mark," he said. He motioned Martin out of the driver's seat. "Take the tour also, Tyler."

Poor Ensign Martin, he almost fell in his hurry to climb out of the jeep. His cap fell of and he scrambled to retrieve it. Harley smiled and waved as he drove off.

Olsen chuckled and whispered to Ayanna. "He'll be OK, once he gets over the weight of that brand new gold bar on his collar," said Olsen. "I hope you don't mind, ma'am, but I asked for him. I've known him since he was a pup; he's a good man, plus, I've served with his father."

"His father? Not Major Martin, Marines?" said Ayanna with surprise.

"Short Colonel now, ma'am."

"A good man. A great man," said Ayanna.

"More than that, ma'am. But I doubt he'll ever make Full-Bird, he's too down-to-earth for a political appointment like full Colonel. Once I found out you were to be the commander, I petitioned to be your Chief. Cashed in every IOU I had."

"You did? Chief, I'm honored."

"On the contrary, I'm the one who's honored. Martin told me what you and your friends did on Yurob…" Olsen shook his head, as if in awe of her.

She laughed. "A court martial offense as I recall. Top secret, no?"

He shrugged. "Deeds like that don't go unsung, ma'am. I'm sure the whole Corps knows all about you by now."

"He was probably exaggerating anyway."

Ensign Martin had joined them in the elevator. "My father doesn't exaggerate, ma'am. He's told me more than he probably should."

Olsen nodded his head in agreement. "I've seen the video of the final battle in Denab's headquarters. I've seen you fight, and if we're ever in a close combat brawl, I can't think of a better person to be at my side." He saluted again.

Ayanna wanted to hug them, but decided it would be quite improper. "Well," she said, her voice cracking. She cleared her throat, fighting back the tears. "Let's continue with the tour. Lead on Chief."

On the ship things looked busy. They began with the control rooms, the hyper-engine room first. Lieutenant Hansen was sitting over a computer display, a worried look on her face. A Technician had an access panel open, and was making adjustments to what looked like a sensor array.

"Captain on board," barked Olsen.

Hansen did not turn around. She held her hand out toward them, index finger extended, clearly asking for silence. "A moment, ma'am. A delicate adjustment."

Olsen was about to say something, but Ayanna shook her head. The last thing she wanted to do was to interrupt the calibration of the hyper-analysis machine.

"Try two more arc-seconds of spread, Jennings."

Jennings adjusted a control. "Done."

"No, too much. Go back half an arc-second."

"How's that?"

Hansen shook her head. "No, it's still out. How much granularity do we have?"

"Half an arc second is it," he said.

"Well, I'm still not happy. Keep working on it," she said as she stood up and saluted. "Welcome aboard, Captain Hale, Lieutenant Commander Sigmun."

Jennings stood and saluted also. "Yes, welcome, Captain."

Ayanna and Sigmun shook hands with both of them.

"What's the problem Lieutenant?" asked Sigmun.

"Take a look for yourself, sir" she said, indicating the display. "I can't zero adjust this one sensor."

"Which sensor array is this machine using?" he asked.

"It's the latest; sextuple tetrahedron."

Ayanna knew this configuration; it was the last one Mika had covered when explaining the mathematics and logistics of collecting local space-time fluctuations. It consisted of six tetrahedrons at right angles to each other, joined at one of their four vertices in an x-y-z pattern. A sensor on each of the three remaining vertices provided a total of eighteen, each one feeding ten million readings a second to the hyper-analysis computer.

"May I?" asked Sigmun.

"Certainly," she said, standing up, offering Sigmun her chair.

He um'd and ah'd over the screen for a few minutes. "So, it's just this one sensor you can't align?" he asked, turning to Technician Jennings.

"Yes, sir. I've replaced it a couple of times, same result."

"Then it's not the sensor. What else could it be?"

"Got to be a bug in the software," said Jane.

"I agree," said Steve. "The housings are self-correcting."

"And you think it's a problem that needs fixing?"

"Yes," replied Jane.

"But one sensor out of eighteen," said Ayanna. "Don't they cross-check each other? Eliminate conflicting results?"

"On each tetrahedron two of the three sensors must agree; if none agree the machine basically shuts down."

"But before this particular array was used, the standard was a simple tetrahedron with one sensor on each of the four vertices. Surely, even with one sensor out of eighteen faulty, we're still way more accurate than any previous array."

"This is true, ma'am. But I'm still not comfortable."

Ayanna looked at the Chief, who shrugged.

"OK, keep working on it. Let me know if you find anything else."

As they made their way through the rest of the ship, Ayanna asked Mark what he thought. He shook his head. "It's not my field, Captain. But take into account that this is her first mission since graduating."

"You think she's overly-keen?"

"Perhaps."

"You think I should take it up with Mika Hale?"

"Couldn't hurt," he said, shrugging his shoulders. "In the meantime these are the hyper-fusion engines, and this is Technician First Class Morris. A better hyper-fusion engineer you'll not find."

Morris saluted. "Welcome aboard, ma'am, sir."

"Ah, yes," said Sigmun. "Ingenious little critters these latest hyper-fusion engines."

"Yes, sir," he said. "In a pinch we can use anything that contains even trace amounts of hydrogen, but distilled water is what we use," said Ryan. "Deuterium or tritium would be even better, but why go to all the trouble."

The actual engines, five of them—one connected to each of the huge exhausts—were quite small, consisting of an intake valve for fuel, a storage tank for propellant, and a complex array of coils and wires surrounding the engine. The console housed three computer screens.

"Here's where we create and adjust the hyper-space field," said Ryan, as he sat down at one of the screens. "We create the hyper-space field around a measured amount of fuel, compress the field until we achieve the internal temperature we require…"

"What temperature is that?"

"The computer controls it based on the acceleration we call for, constantly adjusting it ten times a second, but a one-gee acceleration requires somewhere in the region of fifteen million Kelvin."

"What propellant does it use?"

"Again, we can use just about any solid or liquid that will form its gaseous state quickly, but what we are using here is a silica compound."

"Sand?" asked Ayanna.

Morris smiled. "Sort of, although it has been super refined, you wouldn't recognize it as such."

"And how much propellant do we carry?" asked Mark. "I mean, how long can those engines provide thrust?"

"Well, Chief, since we only need the fusion engines for takeoff, landing, and maneuvering in space, we actually need very little."

"How much?" asked Olsen again.

"At a constant acceleration and deceleration of half-gee, it would get us to Delta Pavonis and back with fuel to spare."

"Taking a little longer than it will with hyper-space."

He nodded his head. "About twenty years longer. But I should add, once we get to one percent of light speed, we can collect both fuel and propellant from space. So, in reality, if you had lots of time on your hands, you could travel anywhere in the galaxy."

"What is the maximum thrust these engines can produce?" asked Tyler.

"About fifteen million Newtons each, Ensign."

"Could you run all five engines at that peak?"

"We could, although the acceleration would be crippling."

"What would such a thrust do to the structure of the boat?"

"It would have no effect on the structural integrity of the vessel, but as I said, the acceleration makes it impractical."

"How much thrust to maintain a one-gee acceleration? And how many engines?"

"Two engines at sixty percent, or three at forty for a total of about twenty million Newtons."

"Does she have any other propulsion systems, other than the hyper-drive and the fusion engines?"

"Actually yes," said Morris, turning to another set of consoles. "Twenty attitude jets. Not very powerful, but they are controlled by the computer, or the pilot through motions of the joystick."

"And the fuel?"

"On earlier shuttles they used jet fuel, but our baby uses traditional rocket fuel."

"Solid or liquid," asked Ayanna. She cringed; at once she realized it was a stupid question.

"Liquid, ma'am. Solid rocket fuel cannot be turned off once…"

"Yes, of course," she said. "I'm sorry, it was a silly question."

"How much rocket fuel do we carry?"

"Two thousand tons."

"Two thousand tons! Why so much?"

"A good question, Lieutenant Commander. And the answer – I have no idea. Somewhere in their heads, the brains at ISA have decided the shuttle needs an emergency tertiary propulsion system."

"That's ridiculous," said Ayanna. "That much rocket fuel wouldn't even get us to the moon and back."

"You're right ma'am. Actually it wouldn't even get us half way there."

"Maybe we should jettison it once were in space," quipped the Chief.

Ayanna smiled and shook her head. "Bureaucrats," she said with exaggerated sarcasm.

"Okay, let's move on," said Mark. "I've saved the best 'till last."

"The bridge?" said Ayanna.

"The bridge."

The bridge was spectacular. At the front of the cockpit was a curved array of windows, although because of their attitude, all she could see was the roof of the hanger. Two impressive command chairs, each with a typical joystick configuration, sat behind an array of control panels and instrument displays, with additional controls in the armrests. They were similar to the ones Ayanna had used in the simulators and the training shuttle, but they looked significantly more classy. Behind the command chairs were two rows of three more chairs, each with their own consoles built into the armrests.

Ayanna walked over to her chair, and ran her hands over the luxurious leather. It felt good. She sat in it, unabashed excitement lighting up her eyes. She took hold of the joy-stick and pulled it back, turned it, like a child playing in the driver's seat of her dad's hover car.

"Come on," said the Chief, a glint in his eyes too. "Time to put away your toys."

Ayanna laughed.

"Thanks, Chief," said Ayanna as they took the elevator down at the end of the tour. "A tight looking ship and a good crew."

"Yes, ma'am, I think we have the best."

"But I think I'll see if Dr. Hale can't check out that sensor. It's probably nothing, but I don't think we should take any chances."

"Agreed," said Sigmun and Olsen in unison.

CHAPTER 19

Once back in their quarters, they spent a few hours looking at the other star systems the ISA had selected as possibles, but came right back to the decision they had made earlier: Delta Pavonis.

"I wonder what kind of life will have evolved on Delta Pavonis 4," said Sigmun.

"Well, I've told you what I believe."

"That all intelligent life will have evolved to look like us; because we are all children of the Holy Ones," said Sigmun. "You really believe that?"

"Yes. We're all made in their image."

"What if that image refers only to the spirit?"

"I don't think so. Shaylae says she saw them, and they looked like us."

"It's possible that they may have showed themselves to her that way so as not to startle her. I mean, aren't they just spirits?"

"I don't know. Something Shaylae said a few years ago makes me think that they do have bodies."

"I don't get that. How could they be the creators of this universe, and be a physical part of it at the same time?"

"Okay, we're never gonna figure it out tonight." She got up and walked over to the children's bedroom and peeked in. "They're asleep. Let's go to bed."

"You tired?"

"No," she said with a huge smile.

Mika called them the next morning.

"What's up, Anna?" he asked. He still didn't look himself, in fact he sounded quite distracted.

"I wanted you to look at that sensor."

"Yes, you sent me the details in your communiqué."

"What do you think? You think you should come over and check it out?"

"It'll be fine. It's only one of eighteen sensors, and it's not that far off."

"You're sure?"

"Sure enough. I wouldn't risk you and Sigmun if I thought there was any danger."

"OK, Mika."

There was an awkward silence.

"Are you sure you're OK?" she asked after a few moments.

"Yeah, I'm sure." He said, not looking sure at all. "Anyway, have a good flight."

"OK."

And he hung up.

The next week was spent in some fairly intense preparation. Ayanna had already trained on a simulator, but now she was happy to be sitting at the controls of the real thing. There was a joystick, of course, although it would probably never be used; only if there was some catastrophic system failure, and a dead-stick landing was a last resort. The ship basically flew itself, even during takeoff and landing; everything was computerized. However, the ISA still insisted she do four dead-stick landings in the simulator, and one on a real shuttle. She nailed all five. Smooth as silk, Chief Olsen said.

Their pressure suits were custom made, fully self-sustaining, in case of an unplanned EVA. They were tricky to put on, but once on, they were extremely comfortable and flexible; a significant improvement over the suits the first astronauts wore back in the twentieth century.

One whole day was devoted to going over all of the emergency equipment. The shuttle had a small self-contained escape pod. The chief dubbed it the panic room and the name stuck.

"You will almost certainly never have to use this," said Harley. "But regulations require that you be fully familiar with its operation."

It was roughly spherical, with an internal diameter of about twenty meters, and an external diameter of thirty. Ten grav-couches were arranged around its inner surface. It was basically a large gel-chamber; it could be filled with grav-gel in less than five minutes. Ayanna shuddered as she recalled the terrible experience when Shaylae had to be placed in a smaller gel-chamber.

"It can withstand a fairly intense acceleration, as much as twenty gee, and a fairly brutal crash-landing."

It was a sobering thought.

"But, of course, you're not going to need it."

The beginnings of a dark foreboding began in Ayanna's heart. It's just nerves, she reassured herself, as she buried the thought way in the back of her mind.

Finally launch day arrived. It turned out to be the most tedious day of the last seven weeks. Press conferences, media vid ops, local and federal dignitaries with sweaty hands to shake; it was never ending; like a circus; went on for more than five hours. The saddest part was saying goodbye to Tokala and Luci. Ayanna's parents were on hand for the launch, and they would be looking after the kids for the two months for which the mission was scheduled.

Once the hatches were sealed, the crew on board, Ayanna said, "OK, we've got about fifty minutes until liftoff. Let's get into our grays; back here in thirty minutes."

Once in their cabin, with the door firmly shut, Ayanna took hold of Sigmun in an enormous hug. "Sig, I love you. I love you so much."

He kissed her. "And I love you, Anna. So much so it hurts."

"How do you feel about this flight?"

"Good. No, I feel great. Why do you ask?"

"Oh, I don't know. It's probably just nerves. I'll be okay. It is the opportunity of a lifetime, yes?"

"Ayanna, everything will be fine," he said kissing her cheek.

By 14:00 hours, they were strapped into their grav couches, Ayanna at the helm, Sigmun next to her, and the others in three rows behind them.

"OK, *Enterprise*, everything checks out one hundred percent." Harley's voice sounded almost as excited, and nervous, as Ayanna felt. "You have the con, Captain Hale. Bon voyage, God's speed, and may the wind fill your sails."

"Thank you Admiral. May we have the word."

"The word is given."

Even though it could have been controlled by computer, it was tradition to allow the captain and crew to engage the engines. Ayanna stared at the five kilometer runway laid out before her, beckoning her. "Bring up engines one, three, and five, Technician Morris."

Ryan hit the buttons on his arm rest, looking at the heads-up display above his couch. "Engines coming up, Captain," he said. "Ten percent... twenty... forty... seventy-five

"Prepare to inject three micrograms of H_2O into each when we reach one hundred."

"One hundred; injecting fuel."

"Bring the hyper-field generator on line."

Morris moved three fingers along on-screen sliders. "Core temperature rising. One million degrees... five million... eight."

A rumbling began far beneath them as the fusion process began, super-heating the propellant, ejecting the gasses out of the exhausts.

"Thirteen... sixteen... holding at sixteen."

The *Enterprise* started moving along the five-kilometer runway, slowly, ever so slowly, but the force continued to build. Ayanna felt herself being pushed back into the couch.

"Prepare to increase core temperature to twenty million, on my mark."

There was a slight bump as the ship lifted off. "Twenty million," she called out.

"Increasing core temperature, Captain. Seventeen... eighteen... eighteen point five... nineteen, nineteen point three..."

She retracted the gear as the ship began to automatically orient itself vertically. She watched the altimeter climb. The shuddering increased, as did the gee-force pushing her back into her couch. The altimeter counted off their height, faster and faster as *Enterprise* picked up speed. "Hold at twenty million Kelvin."

"Holding at twenty million," said Morris.

"Prepare to reduce to fifteen million and cut engine five at my mark." The ship was now accelerating at three point five gee. It was uncomfortable, but certainly not unbearable. They would accelerate like this for approximately three minutes and five seconds, until they reached six-hundred kilometers, when they would resume one-gee acceleration. The shuttle shook violently, and even though Ayanna knew it was built to withstand a much more punishing acceleration than this, her heart still pounded with nerves and excitement.

The three minutes passed slowly, almost languidly as the ship left the atmosphere, and the once bright blue sky became black. Thousands of stars appeared, shining at her through the bridge window. Finally, the altimeter read 600 kilometers. "Mark."

There was an immediate reduction in the gravitational force, and a commensurate reduction in noise and shaking.

"One gee," announced Morris.

"Take us to thirty-five thousand kilometers and park us in geo-synchronous orbit at your pleasure, Mr. Morris; and nicely done Crewman."

"Thank you, Ma'am."

There was a collective sigh of relief from her crewmates, although none were likely to admit it. During takeoff, their grav-couches had oriented themselves vertically, matching the direction of the force of the engines, and what had been the rear wall of the cabin was now the floor. Around the cabin, were twenty large windows, currently covered in delta-titanium heat shields. She hit the control, lowering them, and again, there was a collective sigh, this one more of admiration than of relief. The universe was spread before them. Thousands of stars shone in a dramatic blacker-than-black sky.

"Thank you, Holy Ones," she breathed, as much in appreciation of the glories she beheld, as for the safety of the takeoff.

CHAPTER 20

"How come it takes two hours to calculate the jumps, Lieutenant?" asked Technician Morris.

"The calculations have to take into account thousands of variables," said Jane. "First there's our motion. The motion of this shuttle around Earth, the motion of the Earth around the Sun, the motion of the Sun around…."

"OK, I get it, we're in motion," quipped Morris.

"Well, Ryan, you did ask," said Jane, smiling.

"I guess I'm more interested in the variables the hyper-analysis computer is measuring."

"Well, compared to calculating our absolute motion, if such a thing exists, calculating the fluctuations in space-time is like comparing kindergarten arithmetic to advanced calculus."

"How so?"

"As you know, space-time is not continuous, contiguous, or linear in any of the normal spatial dimensions. Another way to look at it is in terms of the old notions of the curvature of space. Imagine a non-uniform solid. Every point on its surface has a different radius of curvature."

"What about the flat parts of its surface?"

"OK, you're getting ahead of me, but the quick answer to that is that there is no way to determine if any surface is in fact flat. Kind of like the problems with event simultaneity."

"Then," said Martin triumphantly, "there's no such thing as a uniform solid."

"Touché. Regardless, the curvature of space is significantly more complex than scientists had imagined, prior to Dr. Rodrigo's theory of hyper-space. The notion of bending space is OK for the layman, but it's not what's happening. Hyper-space itself is just another way of looking at the irregularity and granularity of space-time itself."

"OK, you've lost me," said Steve Jennings. "I know how to adjust and set those things, but the math – that's way beyond me."

"To be honest, we're still struggling ourselves with the *why*, we are only just learning to deal with the *how*. Let's just say, it's like looking at an object from an infinite number of different angles at once."

"And that's what the computers are doing now?"

"Yes, they're developing an algorithm that describes the region of space we are in."

"But if we're constantly moving…"

"That's why it's developing an algorithm. The differences, though non-linear, can be statistically predicted across limited distances, given enough sampling data."

"So, it's a constantly changing solution."

"Exactly. Again, another way to look at it is the way chess programs work. Given any position on the board, the computer will work out every possible combination of moves until it runs out of time, constantly upgrading its current solution with each better one it finds."

"But when its opponent makes a move, it starts the whole process again."

"Not entirely true. That may be true of earlier chess programs which were stateless, but modern ones are constantly learning from their own moves as well as their opponent's moves."

"So when a computer finds a solution which leads to checkmate, regardless of any defense, it stops, and plays out that scenario."

"Yes, but again the level of complexity is orders of magnitude greater. Unlike a chess program, our computers will never reach a probability-one state. Instead we are looking to get within a margin of error of one in a trillion."

"And that's why it takes two hours?"

"We hope. If we are in a particularly unstable region of space, it may take much longer, but on average, we expect it to complete within two hours."

Ayanna walked into the control room, signaling to the two crewmen at ease.

"And how's it doing so far?" she asked, looking at her watch. "It's been going for half-an-hour."

"Let's look." Jane picked up her PID to check the results. "It's just about at one in nine hundred billion."

"Then it's almost done?"

"No, the progression is logarithmic. Just like a chess program, the further out it goes, the longer it takes to get to the next move."

"Does it give you any estimate as to how much longer it may take?"

"Not really, but a rule of thumb is that once it gets to one in nine-hundred billion it's approximately half way there."

"Is there anything else you need to do while it crunches?" asked Ayanna.

"No. It will let me know when it is getting really close," she said, tapping her PID.

"Then I suggest we grab some food while we have the chance."

Everyone nodded their agreement.

Five minutes later they were seated round a table in the observation deck eating their first meal on board the *Enterprise*. The conversation was lighthearted, amusing, and genial. Ayanna was happy. The members of her crew were comfortable with each other and with themselves. They all seemed to be well balanced, well rounded, and well educated. During one particularly loud outburst of laughter, she turned to her chief and quietly said, "We've got a good crew."

"I think so," he agreed.

"You chose well."

"Captain, can you tell us more about what happened on board *Revenge*, and also on Yurob when you defeated the Dark Ones?" asked Lieutenant Hansen.

Ayanna looked at Olsen, who pursed his lips and shook his head.

"I'm afraid you don't have the security clearance, Jane."

"But the rumors are everywhere. I mean, what sort of person is your friend Shaylae Lucero? According to the scuttlebutt, she's some sort of goddess."

Ayanna laughed. "She's not a goddess, although she is a very unusual person."

"She saved my father's life," said Tyler. "And she almost died retrieving the bodies of two of his platoon."

"That will do, Ensign. I would tell you if I could, in fact, nothing would please me more to tell you all about Shaylae, but…"

Lieutenant Hansen reached for her beeping PID. After looking at the read-out for a moment, she said, "Well, shipmates, it looks as if we're just about ready for our first jump."

CHAPTER 21

"I want everyone strapped in for this first jump," said Ayanna.

"It's not necessary..." began Steve.

"Strapped in." interrupted Ayanna. "How close are we, Jane?"

"We're already past our target of one in a billion, but the accuracy continues to get better."

"Recommendation?"

"I say we wait until it asymptotes," replied Jane.

"But if it's already past..." began Steve.

Ayanna interrupted him. "Then we wait. It's your call Lieutenant." She sat in her command chair and began to strap herself in. "But we might as well be ready." The others followed suit. "How many of us have jumped before?"

"This will be my first time," said Tyler.

"Mine too," said Jane.

"Really?" said Ayanna. "And yet you are a leading mathematician in hyper-analysis."

"There has to be a first time for everyone," she said with a chuckle.

"What can we expect?" asked Ensign Martin.

"Vomit," responded Ryan.

"Ignore him, he's exaggerating," said Sigmun. "There is a moment of disorientation, but it passes quickly."

"What causes it?" asked Tyler.

"We're not exactly sure," said Jane. "There's no sensation of movement; none at all, but for some reason, something inside your body contradicts that."

"Like when you're on board a ship on a rough sea," said the Chief. "If you look at the deck your eyes are telling your brain that you're stationary, but your middle ear is telling your brain a totally different story."

"And the conflict causes nausea," said Jane. "So, we're not sure what it is. All we do know is that each atom of your body travels its own route through hyper-space."

"Whoa! I've never heard it explained that way before," said Ayanna. "Does that mean we're somehow disintegrated and reassembled, like in the old Star Trek show?"

"You like Star Trek?" said Tyler, perking up. "I love that show!"

"What's Star Trek?" asked Sigmun.

"I'm gonna have to play some episodes for you when we get back," said Ayanna. "I can't believe I missed that important part of your orientation to Earth Life."

"Yeah, it's as corny and cheesy as any TV show ever made, but I can't resist it either," said Mark.

"Now I get it," said Tyler. "Then that's why you named the ship *Enterprise*."

Ayanna smiled and nodded. "So, back to the question; is hyper-travel like being *beamed* then?"

Jane laughed. "Not at all. If you think about it, your atoms are already traveling through space-time on their own due to the problems with simultaneity and uncertainty, but the difference is negligible; less than that, it's infinitesimal. No, your body is intact at all times."

"That's a relief," said Sigmun. "I don't want to be falling apart."

Jane's PID beeped again. "Aha! Looks like we've reached a stability point." She laughed out loud. "At one in a billion, three hundred thousand."

"Was it worth waiting for?" asked Ayanna.

"Probably not," replied Jane with a shrug.

"Okay, let's do it."

"Prepare to engage hyper-field, Steve."

"Ready when you are, ma'am."

"The course is plotted and entered. Permission to engage, Captain?" asked Jane.

"Engage," said Ayanna.

There was that sudden feeling of disorientation she was familiar with when she shifted with Shaylae, but it was over very quickly. She thought it odd that it was not something that diminished with each jump; that your body never acclimatized itself to it.

"OK, let me check how accurately we made the jump," said Jane.

"That's it?" asked Martin. "We already jumped?"

"Yes, we're already two-point-five light years from home."

"I didn't feel a thing," he said.

"Some don't. I understand that your father and his platoon that came to rescue me on Yurob felt nothing either."

"Must be a marine thing," said Steve, with a little sarcasm.

"Must be," said Tyler smugly.

Jane gasped. "I don't believe it," she said.

"Something wrong?" asked Mark.

"On the contrary, Chief, according to these initial calculations we're within ten kilometers of our projected destination."

She sounded surprised, no, more like shocked thought Ayanna. "How does that compare to the current Yurob-Earth hyper-transport," she asked.

"Three orders of magnitude more accurate."

"No way!" said Sigmun. "You mean they base their jumps on an accuracy of ten thousand kilometers."

"Or more when they allow a margin of error. And that's over a distance of less than a light year."

"Wait, said Tyler, "That means our margin of error is less than one in two-point-three trillion."

Mark whistled.

"How do you explain this accuracy?" asked Sigmun.

"Well, we've just completed the first jump calculated by the sextuple tetrahedron array."

"Why don't we try jumping in longer legs then?" asked Sigmun. "Perhaps as much as ten light years."

"Well, initial indications would suggest that it's a possibility," said Jane. "Although I don't think we should base such a decision on just one jump."

"I agree with Jane; let's stick to the current flight plan," said Ayanna.

"Anyway," continued Jane, "The accuracy is exponentially proportional to the distance of the jump. So, yes, let's stick to our original plan."

"How long to calculate the next jump?" asked Mark.

"Hard to say, Chief, until we know more about the conditions of space-time in this location."

"In the meantime, how about some Star Trek?" said Ayanna.

"Sounds good to me," said Sigmun.

The computers calculated the next jump in less than an hour.

"Space-time is much more stable here than it is around Earth," said Jane "Of course that's to be expected."

The next jump took place with the same ease as the first, and with similar accuracy. It was the same for the next seven jumps, until at last they were within two light years of the star Delta Pavonis.

"How much detail can we see from here?" asked Tyler.

"Not much," answered Sigmun. "In fact we won't even be able to resolve the disk of the star."

"What about the planets?"

"We won't be able to see any at this distance. We would if it wasn't for the brightness of the star. A planet at the distance of Pluto would be separated by an arc-minute, but then again, if the star was any dimmer, there wouldn't be any reflected light to see it."

"Then how will we determine the plane of its elliptic, to figure out its z-axis?" asked Mark.

"The hyper-analysis sensors will be able to detect gravity fluctuations; enough to give us an approximation of any planetary objects, including their plane," said Jane.

"Even at this distance?"

"In theory, they could do it over any distance. In practice, it's only accurate for what we need within about three light years."

"Will that take long?" asked Ayanna.

"It might, but they're already crunching the numbers."

"Any one feel like eating again?" asked Steve.

Steve's comment reminded Ayanna that she was indeed hungry. They hadn't eaten since their first meal in space. "Okay, let's eat."

Hardly had they sat down when Jane's PID rudely interrupted. She looked at it and smiled. "Well, we have an elliptic."

"Excellent," said Sigmun. "Which also means we have a planetary system."

"Hmm," said Ayanna. "I hadn't thought of that. I guess I'd always assumed that all stars would have planetary systems."

"Let me just set the computers crunching on the local space-time fluctuations so we can make our next jump, now that we know where we're going."

She soon returned. "Well, they're on it, although the local fluctuations are much higher than I expected."

"How is that rogue sensor holding up?" asked Ayanna.

"No change. Still less than half an arc second out."

"Any problems with any of the remaining seventeen?"

"None whatsoever. I think they've all performed admirably."

"Agreed. I think I'll give them a field promotion," said Ayanna.

Everyone laughed.

The calculations took three hours, but finally they were ready to make their penultimate jump, which brought them to within one-point-five billion kilometers of the star. At this distance, the disk was clearly visible, at almost three arc-minutes.

"OK, Tyler, start scanning for planets."

He set the sensors to scan space for an angular radius of fifty degrees around the sun. Almost immediately, they detected a few gas giants. The excitement level in the observation deck was electric.

"OK, we've got a Jovian at 6.6 AU, and another at 12.4 AU."

Ayanna realized her heart was beating faster. Another beep.

"Two sub-Jovians at 2.67 and 15.85 AU."

The sensors were silent for about ten minutes. Ayanna could hardly contain herself. Why were they taking so long? Were these four planets the only ones circling Delta Pavonis? No, she reassured herself, the smaller planets would take longer to detect. More beeps.

"Ice planet at 44.25, and a water planet at 1.6."

"Water planet?" said Steve. "That sounds promising."

"Hmm, not really," said Tyler. "It has approximately the same density as Earth, but it's almost three times as massive. And its exospheric temperature is 200 degrees K cooler than Earth."

Ayanna was suddenly despondent. Maybe there would not be a terrestrial planet around Delta Pavonis.

"Hold on...," said Tyler, excitement building in his voice.

"What have you got?"

"Let me make sure of the details before I get anyone's hopes up."

"Spill it Ensign!" said Ayanna.

"OK, here comes the analysis." He paused. "Oh no, this can't be; it's almost too good to be true."

"Martin!" yelled Mark, Sigmun and Ayanna in unison.

"Terrestrial planet at 0.98 AU, 1.13 Earth mass, 1.08 gee surface gravity..." He paused. "I told you; it's... well, it's just plain uncanny."

Ayanna whistled. "I'll say," she said.

"Incredible," said Mark.

"Any sign of pollutants?" asked Sigmun.

"Hard to tell at this distance, but I'm not detecting any ozone."

"Look, Ayanna – I'm sorry, Captain," said Tyler.

She waved him off with a smile.

"We've got a visual on the terrestrial."

She looked at the screen. In front of her was an image of a planet every bit as lovely as Earth. She whistled through her teeth. "Oh my," was all she said.

"Axial tilt is nineteen degrees, which means she won't have quite the range of seasons we have on Earth."

She turned to see Jane and Steve conferring, worried looks on their faces.

"What's up with them?" asked Mark.

Ayanna's smile disappeared. "Problems with the sensor array."

The mood of the four others immediately changed from one of utter excitement, to one of worry and concern. Steve and Jane left the observation deck in a hurry.

"Well, there's nothing we can do about it until our experts have done some more investigation. So, let's get a closer look at Vulcan."

"You can't be serious?" said Mark. "Spock's home planet?"

"Yes, I'm joking. But we, all of us, get to have a say in naming her."

"Unless her inhabitants have already got a name for her," said Sigmun.

Now that was an interesting idea.

CHAPTER 22

"Okay, let me check how the calibration's doing," said Jane, pulling up another display. "Now there's a surprise!"

"What?"

"It's already to one in a billion – and climbing."

"That is a surprise."

Something about this was all wrong. Jane couldn't put her finger on it. The sensors were as good as they were when they left Earth orbit; the calibration algorithm was performing perfectly. What could possibly be wrong? She shook her head a couple of times, trying to figure out what to do, what to tell the Captain.

"How's it going?"

Jane whirled around. The captain was at the door to the equipment room.

"It's normal – well it's better than normal. All sensors except the one that was off when we left Earth are still dead center."

"That's good isn't it?"

"And according to the analysis computer, we're already ready for our final jump."

Jane watched as the captain digested all of this. Was she going to tell her to get ready for the jump?

"You're not happy though?"

"No, Captain. And I don't have any logical reason to feel that way."

"What about you, Technician?"

"Don't know, Captain. But I do know this; there isn't a better hyper-analyst than Lieutenant Hansen."

"What if you powered everything down, reset every sensor, and started the calibration over from scratch."

"I think I'd feel a lot better. No logical reason, just a hunch, I guess."

"Then do it." She turned and left the equipment room.

Jane's respect for Captain Hale took a few steps forward. She was half expecting to be told, 'you're being overly cautious,' or 'it's probably just nerves.' Instead, her captain had trusted her judgment.

"Everything? Start from scratch?" asked Steve with disbelief.

"Everything, Technician Jennings. Now, let's get started."

"Yes, ma'am."

"Well?" asked Sigmun as she walked back into the observation deck.

"Jane's recommendation is that we shut everything off, realign every sensor, and then restart the calibration program."

"Was it that bad?" asked Mark.

"Actually, Chief, it looked better than it did when we were in Earth orbit."

"Huh?"

"All sensors, except the one which was off originally, are dead center, and the calibration program had finished."

"Then why restart everything?"

"Jane had a hunch."

"Female intuition?" said Sigmun, half-jokingly.

"Watch it, Lieutenant Commander," said Ayanna with a short laugh. "No, I actually had the same feeling of uneasiness."

"Any reason?"

"Not really. But it did seem odd to me that the calibration had finished. It had been running less than an hour."

"And it was Lieutenant Hansen's call?"

"Exactly. Her recommendation; I agreed."

"How long does she expect it will take?"

"Two hours to realign the sensors, then two hours, maybe three, to re-run the calibration program." She turned to Sigmun. "In the meantime, let's get a transmission back to Earth. Let them know everything about the Delta Pavonis planetary system, as well as the problems we've been having with the sensors."

"Will do," said Sigmun.

"Captain, would you like to see the full details of the planetary system?" asked Ensign Martin.

"Sure," said Ayanna.

He pulled up a display, and routed it to the wall screen. "Okay, here's what it looks like."

"And here are the details of all thirteen planets..."

"Tell me quickly about the two Jovians. Either of them have rings?"

"Both, just as in our own system, although neither of them match the magnificence of Saturn.

"What about satellites; moons?"

"The usual. Very small compared to the primary"

"How about the terrestrial?"

"Here's the odd thing, it has a moon similar to Earth's moon."

"It has its own Sister Moon."

"What?"

"Oh, nothing," she said with a smile. "But why do you say it's odd?"

"This is the third terrestrial planet we are aware of, and all of them have moons approximately one-fourth their own radius."

"Yes, but I still don't see why that is odd."

"It's too much of a coincidence."

"Ah, but it's not a coincidence," said Ayanna. "What would happen to a planet with no large moon?" Before anyone had a chance to answer she answered her own question. "It would wobble, like Mars does at home, making civilization extremely unlikely. No, Ensign, it's no coincidence; it's by design."

Ensign Martin looked embarrassed. "Well, yes, it's designed. It has to be. The probability of it happening by chance is inconceivable, given the unusual way Earth gained its moon. And I'm guessing each one of the other planets gained their moon in a similar way. So, yes, Captain, the only explanation is that was designed. I just meant that scientifically, statistically it was odd..."

Ayanna smiled. "Of course, Ensign, I was just giving you a hard time. Okay, let me see the details of the terrestrial."

He hit another button, and a table of the planet's statistics filled the wall screen. Everyone was silent as they absorbed the contents of the table. Many long in-drawn breaths as the significance of the comparison between Delta Pavonis 4 and Earth sank in.

"Blessed Ancestors," said Ayanna. "It's uncanny, too good to be true. It's almost identical to Earth, even the length of the day and year, are close."

"Yes, Captain. I think it's… miraculous."

"And look at the atmosphere. Very close to Earth; maybe slightly higher carbon dioxide."

"Which means it probably has an abundance of photosynthesizing plant life, as well as oxygen breathing animal life."

"Indeed," said Ayanna feeling a surge in excitement. Her team would be the first human eyes to view this life. What would it be like?

"Any sign of pollutants in the atmosphere?"

"None."

"Any electromagnetic radiation?"

"Background only. Nothing that could be any kind of radio signal?"

"Any other signs of intelligent life? Cities, roads?"

"Hold on a minute. We don't have those kinds of sensors yet. I'm not Spock aboard the USS Enterprise, NC-1701."

She laughed.

CHAPTER 23

"I just don't get it, Steve. Everything checks out."

Jane and Steve had just finished rebooting the hyper-analysis machine. They recalibrated every sensor and every one was dead center, except the one which had been off when they left Earth, and it was still off by the same amount.

"What's the problem?"

"I don't know. The computers have now told me the same thing twice, so it would be foolish to ignore them. But I still have the feeling that something's not right."

Steve looked at her, as if not knowing how to respond. "Why don't we run the fluctuation analysis again, and see how that checks out."

She shrugged, shaking her head. "Sure. I can't think of anything else we can do."

"You want me to focus on the same point, one million kilometers above the surface?"

She didn't answer; her thoughts were many kilometers away.

"Lieutenant, do you want me to focus on the same…"

"Oh, yes. Repeat the last analysis. Kick that program off, and then let's go relax for a few hours; get something to eat; maybe grab a quick power-nap."

"Sounds good to me."

When they got back to the bridge, Captain Hale and Ensign Martin were ogling the screen displays of the planetary system they were about to explore. They turned as she and Technician Jennings came in.

"Jane, come and look at this, you too Steve. This planet is… well, it's almost miraculous."

Jane joined them at the computer console. Her eyebrows rose as she surveyed the data. "Wow!"

"Isn't it though? And based on the atmosphere, there's plenty of life down there. I can't wait… How's the analysis coming?"

"We've recalibrated every sensor, everything checks out perfectly, except for our black-sheep sensor, and he's no worse."

"What about the fluctuation analysis?"

"We just started it. We were hoping to grab some food while it chunks away."

"And maybe a nap," added Steve.

"That sounds like a good idea to me," said the Captain. "Why don't you two do just that?"

"Okay, thanks, Captain," said Jane.

She turned and started to head toward the mess room.

"Hold on, Jane," said Captain Hale. "Give me your PID. I'll wake you when it reaches a solution."

"But, Captain…"

"That's an order. We're in no hurry are we?"

"Well, no…"

"And it won't matter if we leave the program running?"

"No, Ma'am. It can run indefinitely, continuing to make incremental improvements to its calculation."

"Even better; maybe you'll feel better after some food and some sleep, as well as getting the most accurate result we can."

"If you say so, Captain."

"I say so. Now git! You too, Steve. Food then sleep, you got that?"

"Yes, Ma'am."

Once in the mess room they grabbed some food. Steve must have been quite hungry, because he devoured his as if he hadn't eaten in days. He's a good man, though Jane, I'm lucky to have him. But her mind was not on food.

"I'm not hungry," she said, pushing aside her food. "I think I'll just sleep."

"See you when you wake up," he said, through an overly-stuffed mouth.

When she got to her cabin, she slipped off her shoes and flopped onto the bed, and was asleep in a matter of seconds.

When she awoke, she looked at the clock; she had been asleep for three hours. The Captain wasn't kidding when she said she wasn't in a hurry, but Jane knew better. If ever she had seen someone about to burst at the seams, it was Ayanna Hale, waiting to see the surface of a new planet.

She climbed off the bed, threw off her clothes and jumped in the shower. As she stood there, under the warm, soothing water, she began to feel better. There had been no reason for her concern; the equipment was performing perfectly, had performed perfectly on every jump. Like the first jump, all subsequent jumps had been within ten to fifty kilometers of their plotted position. She looked directly into the flow of water, letting it run over her face, indulging herself in the sensation of those warm fingers of water revitalizing her body.

She climbed out of the shower, dried herself off, and dressed in fresh clothes; yes, definitely, she felt orders of magnitude better than she had three hours earlier. She hurried to the bridge, where she found everyone in a heightened state of excitement.

"How's the analysis doing?" she asked.

"Ah, Jane. You look a lot better. You sleep well?" asked the captain.

"Actually, I did. Kinda surprised me. I was asleep even before my head hit the pillow."

"Good." The captain held out her PID. "See for yourself; looks like we're ready to go."

Jane took the PID and nodded. "It certainly does," she agreed. The display was showing an accuracy estimate of better than one in 1.5 billion.

"Your call, Jane. Are you recommending the final jump?"

"I am, Captain," she replied with heartfelt confidence.

Ayanna strapped herself into her grav-couch, her anticipation almost overpowering her. She looked at Sigmun as he strapped himself in. He gave her an enthusiastic thumbs-up; he was excited as she was.

"Everyone ready?"

"Ready, Captain," came the unanimous response.

"Lay in our course, Lieutenant."

Jane tapped her sleeve PID. "Course laid in, Captain."

"Fire up the hyper-drive and engage at will, Lieutenant."

"Aye-aye, Cap'n," replied Jane, in a very poor imitation of a Scottish accent. Everyone laughed; well, everyone who was familiar with Star Trek. "Prepare to engage hyper-field, Steve."

"Ready when you are, ma'am."

"The course is plotted and entered. Permission to engage, Captain?" asked Jane.

"You may call it, Lieutenant," said Ayanna.

"Engage," said Jane.

There was a tremendous, horrific jolt! The shuttle pitched upward, at the same time yawing slowly to starboard, and rolling lazily in an anti-clockwise direction. There was a definite feel of gravity as Ayanna's inner ear confirmed the unexpected movement of her ship.

"What happened?" she shouted.

"Captain," said Tyler, "we're in the planet's atmosphere."

"What?"

"We're in its thermosphere, about 400 kilometers… and falling."

"How did that happen?" asked Ryan.

"No time for that now, Ryan. Just tell me how long will it take you to fire up the fusion engines?"

He sighed and shook his head. "Fifteen minutes. Twelve if we're lucky."

"We don't have that long, Captain," announced Tyler. "We're already traveling at about 3,000 klicks, and accelerating. We'll be coming into the mesosphere in twelve minutes, or less."

"Damn!" she said. Damn, she repeated to herself. Why didn't I have the fusion engines on line? She had to think… quickly. "What speed can this bucket hit the stratosphere?"

"It's never been tested," replied the Chief. He sounded calm. Damn! We're about to die, and he sounds calm.

"Best guess."

"Probably ten-thousand klicks, if we hit it belly first," he replied.

"Tyler, best guess, what speed will we hit the stratosphere."

"Give me a second…" he entered data into his PID. "At this speed and acceleration, between ten and fifteen-thousand."

Not good, she thought. "Do I at least have attitude engines?" The attitude engines were not intended for drastic changes in direction, only minor adjustments during flight. There were twenty positioned around the fuselage, each one fueled with traditional rocket fuel.

"Yes, Captain. They should respond immediately," said Ryan.

Well, that was something. Ayanna's mind turned over frantically. First, she would have to stop the yaw, pitch and roll, and turn the boat belly-down; the attitudes should help her there. Then she would have to pray that the atmosphere would slow her down. Then what? Adrenaline flooded into her body, heightening her awareness. She would have to dead-stick land it, but where? She knew nothing about his planet; no one did.

Quickly she reached her decision. Everyone was silent, waiting for her orders.

"Okay," she said quietly. "Okay, you six head for the panic room, suits and helmets on, and fill with gel."

There was a cacophony of disagreement.

"Silence," she shouted. "That's my order. I'm the only one with a chance of landing this boat; the rest of you will have more of a chance in…"

"Captain, no, let's go out together," said Ensign Martin, panic, yet bravery in his voice.

"Brave, Tyler, but very foolish." She raised her voice. "My answer is no, and you're wasting time. Now go! That's a direct order."

The noise level rose again.

"Damn it, she's right," shouted the Chief, above them all. "Now, do as the Captain has ordered, or do I have to manhandle you?"

Everyone was silent, and motionless.

"Do it," he shouted, his commanding voice filling the cabin. "Now!"

They were suddenly galvanized into action, and headed toward the escape pod; everyone except Sigmun.

"Ayanna, I would rather be with you, come what may…"

"Sigmun," she said, fighting back the tears. "We have kids! One of us has to survive. Do you understand? Now go, before I have the Chief carry you."

"Come along, sir. She is right, and you know it."

Sigmun's head dropped, and then he too followed the others, fighting the motion of the shuttle, and his own tears.

"Keep me posted on how you're doing, Chief."

"Will do, Captain. It's more than an honor…"

"You already said that; now git."

Once she was alone she took stock of her situation. She was feeling oddly calm, and thinking very clearly. She grabbed the joy stick. It controlled not only the control surfaces of the wings and tail, but also fired the attitudes in accordance with her movements. She decided to control the pitch first. She nosed the joystick down, slowly, slowly. To her amazement, the ship responded perfectly, righting itself. Next the roll. She had to fight with the ship to get her to stop rolling. She would overcorrect, and then over compensate the other way. It took her a few minutes, but finally, she had it; the ship was flying horizontally. The yaw wasn't as serious. As long as she hit the stratosphere belly first, the ship's heat shields should protect them. Once she was flying in the troposphere that was a different matter. She would need the yaw under control by then.

"Chief, how are you doing?" she asked, while slowly moving the joystick to the left. Once again, she had overcompensated. "Damn."

"Ayanna, are you…" she cut Sigmun off. She could not bear to hear his voice. It might be the last time she would ever hear it. She cut all comm links, except to her Chief.

"Almost ready. We should be suited up and helmeted within another minute."

"Start filling, using the floor nozzles."

"Good idea, Ma'am."

She heard the admiration, and the sadness, in his voice. "Let me know when everyone is strapped in and the pod is filled."

"Aye-aye."

She finally had the ship stabilized. She checked the altimeter. Sixty kilometers. The hull temperature was climbing, it had almost reached six hundred degrees Kelvin, almost the melting point of lead. "You need to be strapped in. We're entering the stratosphere."

"All strapped down, fifty percent full."

"Good. Get ready for a roller coaster ride, Chief."

She checked her speed. Seven-thousand klicks. Damn it! Faster than expected. The ship began to shake as the atmosphere buffeted it mercilessly. The joy stick threatened to yank itself from her hands, but she fought with it; she would not let go, she refused to let go. Altitude fifty klicks, speed almost eight-thousand, temperature fourteen-hundred degrees; iron would be turning white, she thought.

It was getting harder to control the ship now. She was using every ounce of strength just to hold on to the joystick, but somehow, she was keeping her ship level. Thirty-five klicks, temperature nineteen hundred and fifty, speed nine-thousand. Titanium is now a liquid, but for a while at least, she was safe; the delta-alloy should be able to withstand three-thousand. The shaking was getting worse. How much punishment would the hull withstand before it came apart? It was academic; if it happened, she wouldn't even have time to mutter 'shit', before she disintegrated in a fiery blast. She chuckled. Quite an exit.

"Everything okay, Captain?"

"Just ducky, Chief. How about you?" Her voice was quivering, not in fear, but in response to the violent shaking of the ship.

"We're as ready as we'll ever be. The pod is full."

"Good. We'll be hitting the troposphere in about fifteen seconds."

"God's speed, Captain."

"And may the Holy Ones bless you, Chief."

The buffeting increased dramatically as the ship passed fifteen kilometers. The joy-stick was yanked from her hands. She grabbed for it, but it had a mind of its own, thrashing around like a reed tossing in a hurricane. Her whole body was shaking so much she couldn't see any of the read-outs; they were a meaningless blur. This is it, she thought.

And then, without warning, the buffeting stopped. Of course, she thought, as she realized they were safely into the troposphere. For a moment, she felt euphoric, but the ship, though no longer shaking, was not behaving well. It nosed down, and increased speed. She quickly regained her composure, and grabbed the joystick, easing it backward. Nose up, she thought, keep the nose up. Let the wings and the belly slow me down.

"Okay, Chief, we're gliding."

"Air speed," he asked.

She checked the readout. "Damn! Three thousand."

"Way too much, you have to reduce speed. Keep her nose up. Keep her at her current altitude as long as you can."

"Okay."

"What is your altitude by the way?"

"Twelve klicks."

"Good, then the first hurdle is safely passed. Let her glide as long as you can."

"You know, I almost feel safe and secure up here."

"I know, but it won't last. What do you see out there?"

"You have any view screens in there?"

"No, I guess they didn't think anyone would want to watch themselves crashing."

She laughed. "I guess not."

"What do you see?"

"We're on the night-side."

"Good."

"Good? I won't be able to pick out a landing site."

"You should be able to glide for at least another thirty minutes, and at the speed you're traveling, you should easily make it to dawn. But I wouldn't want you to head into another night."

"Gotcha."

"What is your current speed?"

"It's fallen to five-thousand."

"Better, but hardly landing speed."

"You've got that right. If we hit the ground at this speed, we'll become an instant twenty kiloton explosion."

"It'll be quick."

"That it will."

There was silence for the next ten minutes, as she continued to hold the nose up. The ship fell; its speed dropped. By the time she was at two klicks they had dropped to two-thousand, leaving quite a sonic boom in their wake but still too fast. It was still dark, but she could see the dawn ahead of her. One-point-five klicks, she was doing fifteen hundred, but dropping. Fourteen hundred, twelve hundred. This was a good sign, but still too fast to attempt a landing. The ship felt good underneath her hands. It was gliding smoothly, and so far, there had been no unkind weather to jostle them. The sun burst into view before her, almost blinding her, but the automatic shields in the cockpit window quickly compensated. She was flying over an ocean, but ahead of her, maybe a hundred klicks, she saw land. At this speed, she'd reach it in six minutes.

She was losing altitude too quickly. Less than a kilometer, and her air speed had dropped below mach-1, but it was still over a thousand. No, she couldn't have come this far, only to burst into a spectacular fire ball. She eased the nose up a little. She had to be careful; too much and the ship would stall, then they'd fall like a stone with no hope of any kind of landing. But luck was with her. LUCK! No, she didn't need luck; she needed the Holy Ones.

"Holy Ones, be with my crew as we face these next few perilous minutes. Let my last act in this life save the people whose lives are in my hands. Bless my husband, bless my children, and bless my crew. I die willingly to save my friends."

"Amen," said the Chief. "Except, dear Lord, please also spare Ayanna Hale. In Jesus name."

It was a touching moment. It was the first time she had heard him use her name. She cried. "I thank you, Mark."

Nine hundred kph, altitude five hundred meters. The ship passed over the coastline. The land in front of her looked flat, a huge coastal plain that seemed to stretch for perhaps thirty kilometers in front of her. She reported that information to her Chief.

"Gear up or down?" she asked.

"I can't advise you, Ayanna…"

"Up," she said, resolutely. If the ground was soft, the gear would bite into it and roll the ship before it had any chance to slow.

Seven hundred, altitude fifty meters. She was still losing speed, but it was still too fast.

She switched on the comm link to the rest of her crew. "Brace for impact. Five seconds."

The ship hit the ground with a violent crash, which almost threw her from her seat, even though she was strapped in. May the bolts hold, she prayed, may the seat not come loose. She eased the nose up again, hoping it would reduce her speed. The scenery flashed by her ridiculously fast. But so far she was holding together. Five hundred, four hundred; she was losing speed quickly, but she was still hurtling ahead dangerously fast. If they hit a large rock, or a hill at this speed…

Suddenly, they were in the middle of a forest. The ship plowed through it as if it was a field of corn. The tail began to swing inward. "No," she cried.

If the ship turned sideways into its direction of motion, it would surely roll. Damn. The tail continued turning as the ship skidded to the right. She closed her eyes. This is it. Finally, the momentum was too much and the ship bounced violently once, and rolled. Endlessly she rolled, over and over she rolled. Then her worst fear was realized; as she rolled she caught the horrific sight of a cliff, towering above them, only a hundred kilometers ahead of them.

"Impact in three seconds," she shouted, and everything went red, then black. A bright light filled her eyes. It was the last thing she saw.

CHAPTER 24

"Mika, don't worry," said Reycita as she handed him a cup of coffee. "Our Navajo Princess can take care of herself." She placed a comforting hand on his shoulder.

"What?" said Mika looking up. "Oh, I'm sorry, Reycita. I was light-years away."

"Drink your coffee. And I've got some soup on the stove."

"Reycita, you really shouldn't..."

"Oh, stop with your foolishness. Anyway, you think I come over for you?"

Asdza and Halona were hanging on to Reycita, as they always did. They loved their grandmother, and the fuss she always made of them.

Mika laughed. "I guess not."

"She'll be back soon. She's never gone for long."

"But it's been three days. She's never been gone for three days."

For the last three months, Shaylae had returned to Dzil Na'oodilii, 500 hundred years in the past, at least a dozen times. Each time she had returned she looked wearier than the last, her eyes looked sadder, and her face grew more lines. He understood none of this, and she wouldn't give him any details. Who was this woman who had appeared to Shaylae, and why was she trying to destroy the Dine'h, at least the branch of the People descended from Nashota and her followers? With some soberness, he realized that that line included his wife, and of course White Cloud. If this woman did succeed in destroying Nashota, then his wife would never have existed and White Cloud would never have been here to discover fusion power. He looked longingly at his children. They would never have been born either. Theorists had long argued about the paradoxes of time

130

travel, but it had never really bothered Mika thus far; he was one of those who didn't believe time travel was a possibility. But then along came Shaylae Lucero and shattered that conviction.

"One thing I don't understand, Mika – not that I understand anything at all about time travel – but when she returns to us from the past, why doesn't she just return to us a few seconds after she leaves?"

Mika laughed again. "I'm still not sure I fully understand it. She's tried to explain it to me a couple of times. I think I almost have it, but not completely."

Asdza and Halona were still hanging on to Reycita. "OK, you kids. Time to go play. Off with you now."

They giggled and ran into the yard to play.

Reycita put her hands on her hips. "Try me," she said.

Mika wasn't sure if she was just trying to distract him from worrying about Shaylae or if she was genuinely interested, but either way, it was something he liked to talk about. "You're of course familiar with problems of simultaneity in a speed-of-light, or close to the speed-of-light experience."

"Yes, it was something pointed out by Einstein almost two hundred years ago. No two events in the universe can ever be proven to be simultaneous, because there is no way to measure both the time and the place accurately."

"Well hyperspace introduces a whole new slant on the problem."

"Yes, so now it is possible for us to talk to Ayanna and Sigmun on Yurob, eleven light years away, and enjoy a simultaneous conversation."

"Well, as close to simultaneous as our conversation right now."

Reycita gave an *of-course* nod of her head.

"So when an hour passes on Yurob, an hour passes here also. Or when we travel through hyperspace to Yurob, spend an hour there, and return to Earth, the same hour has passed here. Kinda puts twentieth century science on its head."

"Yes, hyperspace has certainly given us a lot to re-think."

"So, here's the part I don't understand. She tells me that there is a continuity, a continuum if you like, between time and space-time. Not that they're the same thing, but that there is a relationship. Time continues to move forward, even as you travel through space-time."

Reycita shook her head. "Sounds like a contradiction to me."

Mika nodded. He took at a piece of paper and drew a line across it, and then a line perpendicular to it. "OK," he said. "In two dimensional space, if I were to move up the Y axis at a constant speed, like this," he drew another smaller perpendicular line in the middle of the horizontal line, and then switch my X coordinate over here, and continue moving up the Y axis at the same speed, no matter where you were on the X axis, your position on the Y axis would increase by the same amount over time."

"Okay."

"Now, instead of X and Y, we called the X axis space-time, imagine space-time condensed into one dimension, and the Y axis time," he made the changes to his drawing. "That, she tells me, is how time and space/time interact."

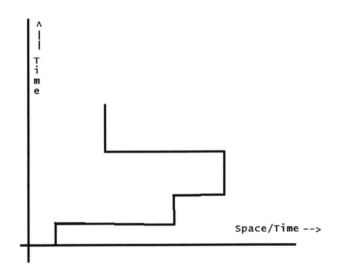

"So no matter where you are in space/time, time continues to move forward, independent of it? Space-time independent of time? No, that's just too much to absorb."

"I know. Somehow she seems to think it's easy..."

Reycita's jaw dropped. "Shaylae!"

Mika whirled around. There she was, standing at the doorway to their kitchen, her face and arms covered in ugly cuts and bruises.

"I had to wait until the kids weren't around," she said. Her eyes rolled, and she fell to the floor in a faint.

Mika was the first to reach her. Her eyes fluttered and then opened. "Shay! What is it, are you OK?"

"Yes, I'm OK, and I think it's over – for now at least."

That should have reassured him but it didn't. Here she lay before him, bruised and broken, tears in her eyes.

"Carry her to her bed, Mika. I'll get a cool glass of water, and maybe try her with some soup."

Mika didn't move, he just held on to his beloved, looking into her sad eyes.

"Mika!" said Reycita. "Take her to her bed."

He nodded, easily gathered Shaylae in his arms, and carried her to their bedroom. As he laid her head on her pillow she smiled and looked into his eyes. She stroked his cheek. "Don't worry my lover. I'm home." She pinched his cheek. These little intimate moments with his wife told him volumes that could never be expressed in words. "And you're here with me. I'm fine, really, but I'm so tired. I have to sleep."

"Okay. I'll just stay here though, he said, as he sat on the recliner next to their bed.

She closed her eyes, a beautiful smile gracing her face.

Reycita walked into the bedroom with a tray, holding soup and bread. "She's asleep, but she'll be fine."

"Then you eat the soup and bread."

She was insistent, so Mika could not resist her. He swung the table over his chair and nodded. Reycita placed the tray before him and he picked up the spoon and began to eat.

"Mmm, you've outdone yourself this time. Delicious."

He was beginning to feel himself again; after all, Shaylae had said it was over, even if only for a while.

"I'll stay a little longer," said Reycita. "I'll get the kids something to eat. I'll stay at least until she wakes up."

Mika knew it would be impossible to dissuade her, so he didn't even try. "Thanks, Reycita." More to the point, he wanted to stay by Shaylae's bed-side and someone had to be with the kids.

"Call me, if you need me," she said, as she left the bedroom.

It wasn't long before Mika settled into a peaceful sleep, the first he had had in three days.

When he awoke, it was already dark outside. He could hear Reycita getting Asdza and Halona ready for bed. God bless Shaylae's mom.

He turned toward the bed, and jumped. Shaylae was sitting up in bed staring at him, a huge smile on her face. All of her bruises, cuts and swellings were gone, and her skin had returned to its beautiful, unblemished perfection. There was a time when Shaylae could not heal herself, only other people, just as she had healed Ayanna and him at Dzil Na'oodilii at her Kinaalda, but now, it seemed, her powers had no constraints or limits.

"So, what happened?"

"Tomorrow we can talk about it. Tonight, I just want to relax, forget about it for a while." She patted the bed next to her. Come, lie next to me, my husband,"

Mika climbed on the bed next to her. She laid her head upon his chest and wrapped her arm around his body, as he put his arm around her shoulder. It was what they called their sweetheart's embrace. They often fell asleep like this, nestled together; there was something so intimate and right about it, as if the Holy Ones had created this embrace just for them.

"*Mika.*" Shaylae's tentative thought came into his mind.

He willingly accepted her into his soul, as they fell asleep, joined in an even more intimate embrace – a sweetheart's embrace of the spirit.

"*My little Luyu,*" he said. "*My Wild dove.*"

It was still dark when she awoke. She let out a huge contented sigh. She felt good; better than she had in months. Though she knew that her struggle with the woman was not over, she hoped that there would at least be a lull. The steady rise and fall of Mika's chest, the smell of his skin, and the warmth of his body were intoxicating.

He stirred and yawned. Reaching across his body, she pulled him toward her until they were face to face on her pillow.

"What time is it?" he said sleepily.

She kissed him tenderly, ignoring his question. "I'm carrying your daughter."

"You are?" He sounded excited, pleased, and suddenly wide awake.

She nodded her head vigorously.

"When? I couldn't tell."

"Thanks for the complement."

"How long?" he asked, repeating his question.

"I'm three months along. It must have been just before my first encounter with the woman."

"She hasn't been harmed…" worry began to creep into his voice.

"No, she's perfectly fine."

"How long have you known?"

"Six weeks… or so."

"Why didn't you tell me?"

"It wanted to wait until the right moment."

He turned around and switched on the bedside lamp. The lines in his face deepened. "You said the struggle was not yet over."

Uneasiness crept into Shaylae's mind too. "Yes, and I'm not sure when it will resume." She was silent for a moment. "But I think it will be before I deliver."

"Shaylae!" Mika was clearly disturbed by this. "But what will this mean to our baby? To you?"

She shook her head. "Mika, I really don't know, but there's nothing we can do about it now." She took his hands in hers. "All we can do is trust the Holy Ones, and take each day as it is given to us."

"Carpe Diem," he said, resignation in his voice.

"Exactly!" She leaned up and kissed him. "Oh, Mika Hale, I love you so much."

"And I you, Shaylae Lucero."

Even though she only lived a few blocks away, Reycita had stayed overnight. When Shaylae went into the kitchen the kids had already been dressed and fed. As soon as they saw her they ran to her and jumped up on her, almost knocking her over.

"Hey, you two, slow down," she said, picking one child up in each arm, and sitting down on the couch with them. She snuggled their faces, kissing them and cooing in their ears. "Oh, I love you guys so much."

"Oh, mommy, stay with us today. Don't go away again," said Asdza.

"Yes, stay," echoed Halona.

"Take us into the mountains," demanded Asdza.

Shaylae laughed at her precociousness. "OK, sounds like a great idea to me."

"Daddy too," pleaded Halona.

"I don't know," said Mika, who joined them in the breakfast room.

"Oh, don't be such a spoilsport! I'm sure your boss will understand," said Shaylae.

Mika shrugged. "My boss is your dad!" But the pull of spending a day with his wife and kids overpowered his obligation to go into the lab. "OK, I'll give Mateo a call."

"Sounds like you don't need me anymore," said Reycita, grabbing her purse. "And since we'll be short-handed in the lab, I guess I'd better get going."

Shaylae shook herself free of her kids and stood up and gave her mom a hug. "Thanks, mom." It was all she had to say; Reycita knew exactly how much Shaylae appreciated her willingness to look after the munchkins.

"Well, have fun," she said, and she waved as she left.

"OK, let's pack up a picnic," said Shaylae, clapping her hands together. She stopped suddenly and held her hands up. "Wait, even better! Let's go visit Ayanna!"

"You serious?" said Mika.

"Yes, Ayanna and Sigmun. Let's go to Yurob," said Asdza.

"They're not on Yurob anymore," said Mika. "They took off on their mission to Delta Pavonis two days ago."

"Even better!" said Shaylae. "I can find them. I could find Ayanna anywhere."

"You're not worried about the ISA?"

"Me?" she said with a mock sneer. "Me worried about the ISA?"

Mika shrugged. "OK, let's go," he said. "In fact, we should head over to the office; find out exactly where they are."

"Come on kids, let's go."

CHAPTER 25

Nashota sat cross-legged on a gentle hill overlooking the ocean, drinking in the beautiful sunset. This was her favorite place; had been since the first day they had arrived at their new home five-hundred years earlier...

For a long time after they arrived nobody had said anything. One moment they were surrounded by their loved ones, and less than a hair of time later they were standing on a beautiful hillside, looking west over an endless ocean to a glorious Father Sun, about to set. The ground beneath their feet was soft, covered in a carpet of thick green grass. Trees grew tall with huge leaf-laden branches wafting gently in the breeze providing cooling shade. Thousands of wild flowers dotted the hillside in a blaze of glorious colors. None of them had ever seen such lush vegetation, such brilliant colors. None of them had seen an ocean or the beauty of Father Sun as he sank behind it.

"It's wonderful," said one.

"Is this the land of the dead?" asked another.

"No," said Nashota. "It is the home of our blessed ancestor, Asdzáán Nádleehé. And now, it is our new home."

They arrived at the beginning of springtime in their new home. It did not take them long to build their Hogans, till the ground, and plant their crops. The first harvest was abundant, providing wondrous varieties of fruits, vegetables, herbs, and roots. In fact, the food found growing naturally was more than enough to sustain them until that first harvest. It was not until they had been there twenty days that they realized that they had not eaten any meat, nor had they had a desire to do so.

"Have you also noticed that the animals do not prey on each other either," said Niyol.

"I have," said Nashota. "The rabbits and squirrels play in the open with no fear. And they have no fear of us." Nashota smiled as she remembered the first meal she and Niyol had eaten together; a rabbit that she herself had caught.

"Then what do the coyotes and wolves eat?"

"I don't know," she said, laughing. "Maybe we should follow one and find out."

"Maybe we should."

Nashota took Niyol in her arms and kissed him. "Oh, my husband, I do love you."

"And I love you."

"I want to bear your children, Niyol Swift Wind."

As their first winter on Tal'el'Dine'h approached, Nashota was surprised that even as the days became shorter, it did not become as cold as it had in Dinetah. Even the storms were gentle. When it rained, it did so without the harsh thunder and lightning she remembered back home; the winds not as fierce, and the sky not as black. Niyol carefully tracked the position of Father Sun in the sky, marking his rising and setting, and his high point.

"Tonight will be long night," said Niyol. "Beginning tomorrow, the days will get longer once more."

"And by tomorrow you will be a father," said Nashota, rubbing her belly.

"It is time?"

"It is time."

Little Halona was the first child born on Tal'el'Dine'h since Asdzáán Nádleehé had left, twenty-five hundred years earlier. Nashota marveled at the ease with which she had come into the world, but not as much as she marveled at the beauty and perfection of her first child.

Over the next few months there were many babies born, each with the ease of Nashota's delivery, and each as beautiful and perfect as little Halona.

"I have never heard of such a thing," said Nashota.

"Such a thing as what, my love?" said Niyol.

"Forty babies have been born since we arrived, and we have not lost one child or mother."

"It does seem unusual," agreed Niyol.

"Yanaba did say that Tal'el'Dine'h was special, that it was protected."

"Yes, the protection of the Holy Ones."

The next thirty years brought great changes among the People. More than two hundred babies were born, and still, not one had been lost. Not one person had had a day of sickness, not one had fallen and broken a bone, not one had even received a cut. Even greater changes had taken place in the knowledge and understanding of the people. As they grew, they grew in kindness and wisdom, and born of that kindness and wisdom came great power. Everyone learned how to mind talk, everyone learned how to shift, and everyone began to understand the nature of the Universe. Even children, by the time they were five years old, had already begun to acquire the knowledge and power.

Nashota and Niyol had two more children; most families had two or three children, but none had ever had more. By now it was also beyond doubt that they were not aging. Nashota was forty-five summers, but did not look a day over twenty-nine; none of them did.

"What can this mean?" asked Niyol one day.

"The Holy Ones visited me in a dream last night," said Nashota. "They told me that this world was in its paradisiacal state. That there was no death, no disease, no pain, and that there was no growing old."

"How can this be?" asked Niyol. "And why?"

"I'm not sure I fully understand, but they told me that when everyone is completely in harmony with the Holy Wind, when a people live as one, it is a natural consequence of the Universe that they and the world in which they live enter this paradisiacal state."

"Yes, since the first day we arrived," said Niyol. "There has been no fighting, not even any arguments. Everyone is as concerned with the happiness and welfare of everyone else, as if they loved everyone as much as they love themselves."

"We have a great future, Niyol. We must prepare for the coming struggle with the Dark Ones."

CHAPTER 26

The escape pod finally stopped rolling. The impact had not been bad for those inside, although the last communication the Chief heard from his captain had not been so good.

"Impact in three seconds," she screamed, then, an almighty crash, and nothing but static, as they rolled.

"Emergency evac," he shouted. The gel immediately began to drain from the pod, but it was too slow. Mark was too impatient to wait so he removed his harness, waded toward the hatch and flung it open. The rest of the gel cascaded out, almost dragging him with it.

"You think she's alright?" asked Sigmun.

No one answered.

Mark was first outside, followed by Sigmun. Their eyes were met by a scene of warlike destruction. Behind them was a swath of flattened trees, a two kilometer path, a hundred meters wide, cut as a knife cuts through butter. Further away, past the edge of the forest, they could see the track made by the shuttle in the desert floor stretching for five kilometers. Mark whistled when he saw how perfectly straight that track was.

The escape pod had been thrown loose, and had come to rest against a small hill next to a large lake. Mark was glad they had not landed in that, would have been a problem. They turned around. Ahead of them, a kilometer away, lying up against a cliff, was the tangled wreckage of the *Enterprise*, dust still swirling around it. It bore no resemblance to the elegant space ship she had once been.

"Come on," said Mark. "She may still be alive." He started to run, but the flash almost blinded him. In one motion he dived for Sigmun, and threw them both back inside the pod as the blast hit them. Molten metal bounced off the sides of the pod. Mark's heart sank in despair. No, he thought. No! It can't be. It took a few seconds for the blast to dissipate, and once again he and Sigmun were the first outside. He almost vomited at the sight he beheld. Where the wreckage had been was a huge fireball. They could feel the heat, even at this distance.

Sigmun started to run toward it.

"No, sir, it's too late," said Mark, running after him and holding him fast.

"But she may still be alive," he screamed hysterically, trying to break free. "You said so yourself."

"She's gone, Sigmun. She's dead." Mark had faced death many times, but this was the worst thing he had ever experienced. He too wanted to cry. His eyes were already wet, and a scream was bursting to escape his constricted lungs, but he would not let it out.

The others had left the pod and were standing, dazed looks on their faces.

"What exploded?" asked Steve.

"The rocket fuel," said Ryan. "There was enough of it to …" He left the sentence unfinished.

Sigmun had fallen to his knees, sobbing. Mark knelt down and put his arm on his shoulder. "Sir, she's gone, but her death will not be in vain; she died saving us. No greater act of love can one person show to another, no greater show of bravery. But you will live, you must live. You will return to your children, and they will grow up calling her blessed." His voice softened. "Her death will not have been in vain, Sigmun. Don't let that happen." Sigmun turned his face and looking up from the ground he nodded. Mark helped him up and dusted him off. "A finer women I have not met, Sigmun. God blessed me that I should have known her but for a short while, and now, because of what she did, her place with him is assured."

Sigmun nodded, tears streaming down his cheek. "I believe that too."

Tyler joined them. "Sigmun, her Holy Ones, and our God are the same. I know she is with them now."

CHAPTER 27

"Good morning, Dr. Hale." The receptionist's breezy smile greeted them in the lobby of ISA research facility in Fort Douglas. The security guards saluted. "And welcome back, Dr. Lucero. It's been a long time."

"Morning Emma. What's going on?"

"Oh, the usual. And Asdza and Halona; I haven't seen you two in ages."

The comm-link sounded; Emma answered it. "Admiral, good morning…"

"I need to speak to Dr. Hale immediately."

"He's right here, Admiral."

"Put him on."

"I can hear you, Harley. What's up?" said Mika, a little concern finding its way into his mind.

"We've found a bug in the hyper-analysis program."

"What?"

"When? Who found it?"

"Last night…"

"What about the *Enterprise*?"

"We got a transmission from them about two hours ago, when they were preparing their final jump. We haven't heard from then since."

"But you'd already sent an abort code, right?"

"No. We tried half an hour ago, but we can't get through to them. Even their transponder is out."

"Half an hour? Why not last night when the bug was found."

Shaylae gasped. "Ayanna's in trouble."

There was a rustling behind him. He turned. Shaylae had disappeared.

"Shaylae," he said uselessly to the empty air. "Harley, let me get to my office; I'll pick up there." He motioned to the kids. "Emma, could you…"

"Of course." She shepherded the kids behind her desk. "Want me to call Shaylae's mom?" But Mika was already hurrying across the lobby.

"Okay, fill me in," said Mika as he threw his coat over a chair.

"I'll let the software manager explain…"

A worried face filled the screen.

"Go ahead," said Mika when he paused.

"The bug is in the routine…"

"You can tell me about the bug later. Why was the abort code not sent?"

"We were not sure about the bug…"

"What's that got to do with it?" Mika's voice was steadily rising.

"We didn't want to start a panic?"

"Like the one that's going on right now?" Mika asked, his voice full of both panic and anger. There was an awkward silence at the other end. "I'd beat you senseless if I was there, you…"

"Hold on now, Mika," said Harley. "Recriminations can come later. Right now, you're right; we have a situation on our hands."

"Okay," he said, trying to calm himself, worry filling every fiber of his being. "Tell me what we know. What is the nature of the bug?"

The software manager cleared his throat. "The most complex routines are the fluctuation calculations near a gravity well, such as a star."

"Yes, I know that."

"We were sure we had it all worked out. Our tests were conclusive, or so we thought."

"Get on with it."

"Leaving a gravity-well is no problem…" Again he paused.

"But getting closer to one?"

"The program gives false readings."

"How bad?"

"All jumps made so far by the mission were accurate to within ten kilometers."

If he hadn't been so angry, he would have been impressed.

"But when calculating the jump into a gravity well, the results could be out by…" he swallowed nervously, "could be out by four or five orders of magnitude."

"What? A million kilometers? Are you certain?"

"The algorithm uses an asymptotically reducing tensor of..."

"I know the math. I helped develop it."

"Of course, I'm sorry. The program was giving more weight to the readings close to the point of origin than it was to the readings at the destination."

"That's impossible..."

"It was a transcription error..."

"You mean a typo?" Mika was incredulous.

"I guess you could characterize it that..."

"So, the *Enterprise* could have materialized inside the planet?"

The silence pounded in Mika's ears.

"When we analyzed their last transmission we realized we were sure about the bug."

"How so?"

"Their last calculation took less than an hour?"

"Less than an hour. That close to a gravity well. It's not possible."

"They re-calibrated every sensor and ran the calculation again. Same thing; less than an hour."

"Harley, is there another ship ready."

"Three weeks, maybe more."

Mika banged his fist against his desk. "Admiral, I want heads. Start an internal inquiry immediately. And I'm more concerned about the delay in notifying the *Enterprise* than I am about a stupid bug!" The disgust was evident in his voice. "I want heads!"

"I'll start the build up to the launch immediately."

Mika terminated the call, sat in his chair, and buried his head in his hands. He was even angrier with himself than he was with the software department. He had plainly heard the concern in Ayanna's voice before they left, but he had brushed her aside. The fact that he was so distracted and worried about Shaylae at the time was no excuse. And now, because of him, his wife might be in as much danger as the *Enterprise*.

He raised his eyes to the heavens. "Shaylae, won't you at least let me know where you are?"

CHAPTER 28

Ayanna's sudden panic and fear filled Shaylae's soul. She gasped. "Ayanna's in trouble." There was no time to explain to Mika, as she shifted instantly to her side.

"Blessed Ancestors," she said, as she saw Ayanna's unconscious body tangled in a chaos of twisted wreckage. "Oh, may she still be alive," she breathed as she placed her hand on her chest. There was the barest of pulses. "Thank you, Holy Ones," she whispered. She let her hands roam across her friend's body. The grav-couch she had been strapped into was broken in two, and her body was bent over backward at an impossible angle, her backbone shattered. Every organ had burst and had ripped away from its proper position in her body. Miraculously, her heart was still beating but Shaylae knew it was beating its last few times. Her brain was also miraculously undamaged and, even though she was unconscious, Shaylae could feel her strong spirit somehow holding on to her devastated body. Should she shift her out of this wreckage first, or heal her where she lay. She decided on the latter; perhaps even shifting her to another location would have disastrous results…

"*Move her at once,*" came the powerful thought into her mind.

She had learned long ago not to ignore such promptings. She cradled Ayanna's head against her shoulder and shifted a hundred meters from the ship, micro-seconds before the rocket fuel ignited. She felt the heat of the blast, and instinctively shifted them again, this time in a fractional space-time displacement, as molten wreckage exploded all around them. Even though she was in no danger, Shaylae covered her face with her hands and cringed defensively. As soon as the blast had passed, she shifted them another ten kilometers away, into the middle of a beautiful lush forest by a gently running river. She began healing Ayanna's wounds. It took her a long time as she repaired every vital organ in her body, every blood vessel, her spinal column and nervous system. When Ayanna was out of immediate danger, no longer near to death, she repaired her broken bones and the ugly tears in her flesh.

She sat back and relaxed, surprised at how exhausted she was. She had been working on her for at least three hours. Strange, she thought, as she lay down, I've never felt this drained after I healed someone; but then again, she had never seen a body as devastated as Ayanna's had been. She lay down and fell immediately into a deep sleep.

***

Mark turned back toward the pod. "Let's get an inventory of what we have. As far as I remember, the pod comes with some pretty impressive supplies."

"You think there's a hyper-transmitter."

"I'm sure there is," said Jane.

"But there won't even be a shuttle available for at least another three weeks."

"Then let's hope they included some board games to pass the time," said Mark.

Everyone laughed, even Sigmun. That made Mark feel better. "Okay, let's send a message first, and then we can break out and catalog the supplies."

Nobody seemed to be objecting to Mark taking the lead, and he wasn't about to surrender it to any of these younger officers. As bright as they were, they did not have his experience. They started back inside the pod.

"Don't suppose our supplies include a bathroom?" said Jane.

Mark laughed. "I doubt it."

"Then I need to make a little call," she said, turning around.

"Go ahead. We'll start on getting the transmitter up."

The interior of the pod was designed as tightly as any cramped quarters Mark had seen. Every last space was used, and used well.

"Here's the transmitter," said Ryan, pulling a large box out of one of the closets.

"Here, I'll take that," said Steve. "I can set it up and start getting it booted up."

"Don't you need to set it up outside?" said Mark.

Steve laughed. "Chief, it's a hyper-transmitter. We could bury it twenty thousand leagues under ground and it would still work."

"Don't laugh at me, else you'll be finding yourself on the losing end of an arm wrestle."

They all laughed again. Mark was pleased that spirits remained high, in spite of their tragic loss. Once they had sent their transmission to Earth it would simply be a matter of waiting it out. Hopefully, whatever had caused the failure of the last jump would be solved in the next shuttle. "Make sure we send every detail from our technical logs. And if no one objects I think we should send our personal logs also. There may be some clues there."

"No problem here, Chief," said Ryan. Everyone nodded except Tyler.

"Hmm… with your permission, Chief, can I, umm…. edit out my reflections about Lieutenant Hansen?" he asked.

Mark smiled. He should have been surprised, but he wasn't. "Just so long as you give me your word that's all you'll edit out."

Ensign Martin held his hand up. "I swear it, Chief."

"Damn," said Steve. They all turned around to see him banging the side of the transmitter.

"What's the matter?" asked Mark.

"Damn thing won't boot up."

"Can you fix it?"

"Don't know." He flipped open the plate. "Ouch," he said, sucking air between his teeth. "This isn't good."

"What?"

"It's missing the main board."

"What? You mean we have a defective transmitter?"

"Not defective. I'm sure it would work fine if it had completed its assembly process," he said, slamming shut the plate.

"Well, I guess we'll have to wait a little longer for a rescue. In the meantime, we have lots of food and…"

"Where's Jane? Shouldn't she be back by now?" said Tyler, a little uneasiness evident in his wavering voice.

Steve snorted. "Well, if she's anything like any girlfriends I've had, she'll take forever in the bathroom."

No one else laughed. Mark felt a shiver down his spine. "I'm going out to look for her," he said. He opened the hatch and stepped out, and came to a dead stop, his heart frozen. At least a hundred men surrounded the pod. They carried wooden spears, clubs and rough stone axes. Around their waists they wore loin cloths made of uncured animal skins. Their hair was messy and long, and most had bad teeth. Their dark skin was hairless, and while they may have been stone-age, they were unmistakably human. But what caused his breath to stop was that two of them held Jane fast, while another held a spear to her throat. Her face was white with terror. The man with the spear uttered a guttural imperative. Mark had no idea what he had said, but he was certain it meant that they were to all come out peacefully, else Jane would be harmed.

"Okay, everyone, come out of the pod quietly, and no sudden moves."

"What is it, Chief," said Steve, as he came outside, immediately dropping his jaw.

"Quiet every one, and do nothing to alarm our reception committee. They're probably more afraid than we are."

The one holding the spear issued another guttural command, and beckoned to them.

"I guess he wants us to join them." He turned to the others, and motioned them to follow him. As they walked, the men closed ranks behind them, surrounding them. "We just bide our time, and try not to alarm them. If my recollection of history serves me, most encounters with native peoples start out this way, but if we keep our heads, like those that went before us, we should be friends with them within a few days."

"Maybe they'll sell us a large island for a few beads," said Steve.

Mark didn't feel like laughing. Something told him that these men would be more difficult to bargain with, than those who sold Manhattan to the Dutch.

Steve held up his hand in the universal gesture of peace. "Take me to your leader," he said with mock sincerity.

One of the natives behind Steve raised his club, but before Mark had time to shout out a warning, he felt a crack on the back of his head… and then nothing.

***

It was already dark when a grunt from Ayanna woke her. She looked up at Shaylae and smiled weakly. "Shay, you came." She hugged her, sobbing gently. "Shay, it was awful." Her eyes were suddenly wide open. "My crew, where is my crew? And where is Sigmun?"

The change from peaceful and relaxed was dramatic as she shot up with the same panther-like awareness and readiness that Shaylae had seen in her many times. She had been so exhausted after healing Ayanna that the fate of the rest of the crew had never occurred to her.

***

It took Sigmun a few moments to get his bearings as he regained consciousness. He tried to move, but he could not. He was bound hand and foot with coarse, fibrous rope. He looked up, his eyes still blurry. In addition to the ropes at his hands and feet, he was also roped together with the other men. They were in a clearing, surrounded by crude huts. His eyes hurt; he couldn't see very clearly, but torches burned on stakes, giving an eerie light as the wafting flames made the shadows dance. With a surge of horror, he saw Lieutenant Hansen tied to a crude stone altar in the center of the circle surrounded by wood. Her eyes were wide with terror.

"Let her go, you swine. Let her go."

His outburst woke Chief Olsen. "What is it, Sigmun?" he said groggily. Then he too saw Jane. "Oh, dear God," he said.

By this time the others were aroused.

"What are they doing to her?" shouted Ryan.

Steve shook the pain from his eyes. "I would say their intentions were rather obvious."

"Chief, we've got to do something," said Tyler. "Jane…"

"If I could get loose from these ropes I would fight every man of them. I'm not losing another of our crew."

Sigmun felt a presence. Was it Shaylae? A glimmer of hope sparked in his heart. Yes, he was certain. And was that Ayanna's spirit he felt? He cleared his throat and spat blood on the ground. "Shaylae's here. And I think…" His heart soared. Yes, his wife was alive, he could feel her.

"Shaylae Lucero! I don't believe it," said Mark.

"You're awake I see." The voice spoke quietly in perfect English. They all turned to the edge of the clearing to see a woman with curly blonde hair, smiling at them. It was more of a smirk than a smile, and although she only appeared to be about twenty-five-years old, her expression made her appear a lot older. "Yes, Shaylae's here. And soon she will walk into my trap. What do you think? Are you impressed by the way I lured you here?"

The men looked at each other incredulously. "Lured us here?" said Steve.

"Yes, lured you here. Mind you, even I couldn't have foreseen that spectacular crash. Wasn't that wonderful? Though it's a pity Ayanna died. She would be even better bait than you, but I guess I'll make do."

"Who are you? And what do you want?" asked Sigmun.

"I want Shaylae. She is quite intelligent, for a mere human, but with my tutelage, together we can become the most powerful force in the universe, once I've won her over that is."

"Oh, dear God, no," said Sigmun. "Shaylae!" he screamed. "Do not come here. You are in terrible danger."

"Oh, she'll come." She motioned over to the altar where Jane was tied. "In the meantime, my people need to make a sacrifice."

"You fiend from hell," shouted Tyler. "Let her go. Take me. I'll be your sacrifice, but you'll not harm her."

The woman laughed cruelly. "Silly man, they only sacrifice females."

"It's alright," said Jane. "I'm not afraid to die."

"Oh, you will be," said the woman. "I understand it's very slow, and very painful."

"I don't care. I don't know who you are, but you won't have the satisfaction of seeing me beg for my life!"

Sigmun was impressed by her courage, but he was afraid it would fail her when the flames began licking around her body.

The woman laughed again. "You think I care whether or not you beg for your worthless life? Go ahead. Die bravely, or scream like a baby; I don't care."

She motioned to the men. One of them pulled a torch from its stake, and walked, rather danced grotesquely, toward the altar.

"No," screamed Tyler.

The wood quickly burst into flame. A look of horror and disbelief filled Jane's eyes.

***

Shaylae searched, and her mind found them. "Ayanna," she said, her face drawn with worry, placing her hand on Ayanna's arm. "They're OK. They're alive, all of them."

"They are." Ayanna's eyes lit up. "Are they injured?"

"No, but they're in grave danger; they've been captured by natives, stone-aged natives. And we need to hurry." She looked once more across the distance and saw the woman. "No," she said out loud.

"What is it?" asked Ayanna.

"It's the woman."

"What woman? What are you talking about?"

"We need Mika," she said. Seconds later he materialized next to them; they immediately joined hands and in a split second she told them everything that had happened since the first night she had seen the woman. In the same nanosecond Ayanna told Mika what had happened with the mission.

Shaylae showed them the scene in the village. Mika gasped, Ayanna screamed, and then, with their souls joined, they shifted. They sprang into action even as they materialized. A globe of white light surrounded them; a fiercely blowing wind billowed out their clothes and their hair; they were magnificent. Mika pointed to the fire, which was immediately doused. Ayanna pointed to the tied up crew; their bonds were not loosed, they simply disappeared. Shaylae raised her hands toward the woman, who fell back, skidding across the clearing as if a truck had plowed into her. Shaylae was not expecting this; for a moment, she wondered if the three of them together could defeat this evil personification, but then she screamed, curdling Shaylae's blood. She stood up, and held her arms out, as flames and lightening burst upon them. Shaylae felt an unbearable pain in her chest as she stumbled, but the souls of Mika and Ayanna lifted her up. The light which surrounded them flickered, but it did not extinguish.

Shaylae threw her hands toward the woman once more, but this time it had no effect. Instead, she rose off the ground and floated toward them.

"I have to admit, you caught me by surprise. I wasn't expecting the three of you." She sighed and shook her head. "Ayanna, do I have to kill you again? An unexpected pleasure, I'm sure." She was now level with Shaylae's eyes. Somehow she had penetrated the globe of light which encircled them. Their noses were almost touching. Shaylae was sure she smelled hell fire on her breath "What does it feel like, knowing that your friend and your husband are about to die, and that you are about to become my slave?"

"No one is going to die," screamed Shaylae. "Holy Ones, Blessed Ancestors, come to my aid." Once more Shaylae thrust her hands toward the woman. Once again she was pushed backward and fell onto the ground, but quickly stood and dusted herself off.

She threw her head back and laughed. "Oh, I'm impressed; you're good, very good. You want a fight do you? This is more fun than I could have had hoped for. I was expecting to defeat you quickly, but this will be amusing." She turned and walked around the clearing, circling them. "But, you know you will lose. Even the three of you together are no match for me." She shouted the last word and once again lightening burst from her hands and knocked Shaylae to her knees. Blood and saliva dripped from her mouth, immediately soaking into the dusty ground. She tried to stand up but could hardly support her own weight on her hands and knees.

"Should I let you suffer a little longer," she said mockingly. "And how should I kill your friends? Slowly of course, with you watching every dying, agonizing breath. Fool, you are no match for me!"

Why do evil people have to gloat even after they've won, thought Shaylae? Why don't they just get on with it? She knew she was beaten, and she knew she was about to lose her best friend and her husband, and become subject to this woman's power, for what she had no idea. Her hands and knees gave way beneath her as she rolled in agony on to her side, defeated. Ayanna and Mika were already unconscious. This is it, she thought, the end. But then the words which White Cloud had uttered to her five hundred years in the past, only a few weeks ago, came back into her mind. She barely raised her head and turned to Mark Olsen. "Chief," she croaked. "She's right. Spiritually we are no match for her, but physically she is still only a woman."

The Chief did not need a second call to battle, and as he launched himself at the woman Shaylae summoned one last burst of spiritual strength and launched it at her. The woman could not fight on two fronts at once, and she knew it. Defeat was in her eyes, but the hatred did not diminish.

The Chief knocked her to the ground, but unlike the time when she had scratched, bitten, and kicked Shaylae, this time she didn't even bother. Suddenly the Chief was wrestling empty space.

For a moment, everyone stood in stunned silence, even the native warriors who still surrounded them. And then she was back, standing above them, five meters high. The warriors scattered like sheep before wolves. Shaylae's first thought was that their victory had been short lived, and they were now surely about to die. But then she noticed something... "Do not be afraid my friends; she is here only in spirit," she shouted, eager to dispel everyone's fears and doubts. "And as a spirit she has no power over us."

The girl's voice thundered over them. "Twice you have beaten me, witch. You have won two battles, but know this, the war will be mine." Her face was the personification of the most awful evil, making Denab look like a saint. How could this be? Who is she, wondered Shaylae?

"Who am I? Write this on your soul, witch. I am Istas, the White Stone, cut out without hands, who will roll forth until I fill the whole Universe. I am she who will destroy everything you cherish, everything you love. Your family, your friends, your puny worlds; everything will I destroy." Her voice reached a new pitch of power and hate. "Everyone you know and love will die as you watch them. I will slowly rip the flesh from the bones of your children and feed it to dogs." Her eyes widened and her mouth fell open. She raised her eyebrows and smiled. "Ah, I see. There is another. Her I will not kill immediately. Her you will carry to full term; I may even let her live a few years but then you will watch as she dies in indescribable agony."

Shaylae howled, like the roar of a tiger and launched herself at the hideous apparition, but she found nothing but empty space. The horrifying laughter reached a new crescendo.

"Of course, if you learn to serve me, then perhaps they can be saved. But it doesn't matter, one way or another you will serve me. Even your Holy Ones will fall to my power!"

Still laughing, the disembodied spirit faded until she was gone.

Sigmun immediately ran to Ayanna, threw his arms around her, and laid his head on her shoulder weeping. They didn't say anything to each other, they didn't have to.

Finally Steve spoke up. "What just happened? What did we just see?"

Jane stepped forward and stood in front of Shaylae, head bowed. "Thank you. Thank you for saving me." She shuddered.

Shaylae reached up and hugged her.

Tyler stared at the three friends, disbelief in his eyes. "I always thought my dad was exaggerating."

"How in the heck could you tell anyone what we just saw without them thinking you were exaggerating?" said Steve. "Dang! I was here, and I still think I'm exaggerating."

"Tyler, your father spoke of her as if she were an angel. I think he is right," said Mark.

Ayanna turned when she heard this. "No, she is not an angel, although Mika might not agree. What she has is a gift from the Holy Ones; power to call upon the spirit which is in all things, and a faith in the Holy Ones that cannot be shaken." She walked over to Chief Olsen and embraced him. "And you, Mark, what can I say? You're the best Chief Petty Officer I ever had," she said, "even when fighting helpless women."

He laughed. "As I recall, I'm the only Chief Petty Officer you ever had."

"All of you," she said to her crew. "You all were the perfect crew. I mean it. I'm, sorry I lost our ship. I'm so sorry."

"Sorry!" said Mark. "You have nothing to be sorry about! I still don't know how you were able to land the boat. What speed were you doing when we hit?"

"I didn't dare look. At fifty meters we were still doing seven hundred."

"You landed a shuttle at seven hundred klicks?" said Mika in astonishment. He shook his head. "It's not possible."

She shrugged.

"Ayanna, for five kilometers you held your ship steady," said Mark. "I saw the tracks! And without gear! If it hadn't been for the forest, she'd have been undamaged; we could have taken off in her."

Mika whistled, nodding in agreement. "If you'd lost control when you first hit, the shuttle would have rolled and everyone would have died. Even the pod was not made to withstand an impact like that, any more than a shuttle was built for a gear-up landing at seven hundred." He shook his head again.

Jane coughed and spoke up. "Actually, I'm the one to blame. Somehow I must have misread the results."

"No, Lieutenant," said Mika. "The program was screwed up even before you left."

"How?"

"The programmers had a bug in their software. It was giving more weight to the readings close to the point of origin than it was to the readings at the destination."

"Then that's why it completed its analysis faster than I expected."

"It wasn't the programmers," said Shaylae. Every one turned toward her. It was the first time she had spoken since Istas had left. "The program was sabotaged by the woman."

"How could she have sabotaged it?" asked Jane.

"And who is she anyway," asked Steve.

"I don't know. There's a lot about her I don't know."

The villagers came back into the clearing, this time they had with them women and children. They seemed to be in a daze, as if they had woken from a nightmare.

"They need help recovering from the influence of the woman. They are in tune with the Holy Wind, or they were before the woman arrived."

"Arrived from where though?" asked Ayanna.

"I have no idea."

The villagers came closer to Shaylae, Ayanna and Mika, tentatively, but worshipfully.

"I guess the first-contact protocol is out the window," said Steve.

The mood immediately lightened, as everyone chuckled.

CHAPTER 29

Shaylae and Mika enjoyed a relaxing week at home with the kids. They had gone riding everyday up Millcreek Canyon, something Asdza loved as much as Shaylae did. But all too soon, the lull was over.

"Mika, I have to go away again," she said after the kids were in bed.

"Shaylae..."

"I know, and I'm sorry."

"And I can't come with you, can I?"

She shook her head. "Not this time, at least. It's time to visit Nashota on Tal'el'Dine'h, and I think I need to go alone."

"You know I was a complete wreck last time you were gone. I'm not sure I can take another three months like that."

She took hold of his hand and squeezed. "I'm sure I'll be safe on Tal'el'Dine'h, and anyway, after my first visit, I'm coming to get you and the kids."

"What if there's trouble?"

"I swear, if there's any trouble I'll come a get you."

"And Ayanna?"

"Yes, Ayanna too."

"When will you leave?"

"Tomorrow morning."

"Then you should get a good night's sleep."

"In a half-hour or so," she said, snuggling up to him.

Afterwards Mika fell asleep quickly. How fickle men can be, she thought with amusement. Usually they fell asleep wrapped in each other's arms, but tonight she could not stop her mind from racing!

Her mind went back to that awful experience onboard *Revenge* twelve years ago, when they had almost been defeated. She had only just discovered her powers, in fact had only truly solidified them a few days earlier when she had been in Madrid. Four years later, they had easily defeated the full assembly on Yurob as well as Rolling Darkness himself. Now she was faced with an adversary who was more powerful that even Rolling Darkness. How much more powerful, she wondered.

She smiled as Mika woke briefly, said "G'night lover," changed positions and fell right back to sleep.

She looked at the clock on her bedside table. It read 4:05 and she was even more awake than when she had first gone to bed. She really needed to get to sleep! "Blessed Ancestors," she breathed in desperation. "Let me sleep."

"*Dearest Shaylae.*" It was the quiet voice of her beloved great-grandfather. "*Sleep, my precious one. Tomorrow will take care of itself.*"

She was immediately calm, relaxed, and filled with peace. She fell asleep almost immediately.

"You were sound asleep so I didn't wake you," said Mika, holding her breakfast on a tray.

"What time is it?" she asked, rubbing her eyes awake.

"Almost eight."

She was about to jump out of bed, but Mika gently put his hand on her shoulder. "Just enjoy your breakfast, my little Luyu."

She was about to argue, but felt a reassuring glow filling her. For now, everything felt fine, and she had time to relax. "Okay." She buttered a slice of toast and spread a thin film of raspberry jam on it. "Delicious," she said, with her mouth full.

"It's only toast," said Mika, laughing.

"Not just toast," she said. "Loving toast, cooked by my husband, whom I love and adore."

He leaned over and kissed her. "I'm gonna miss you."

She finished her breakfast in silence and took a long lazy shower.

"I'll try not to be gone for too long," she said as she got dressed.

"Promise you'll come and get Ayanna and me if anything happens."

"I promise." She kissed him. One last hug, and she was gone.

"May the Blessed Ancestors be with you," whispered Mika.

***

"Shaylae is coming," said Nashota.

"Yes," said Niyol. "It is time."

"She must soon face Istas, and we must help her to prepare."

"What has become of Istas? Have you been able to find her after the last encounter she had with Shaylae on the planet Sanostee?"

"No, and that concerns me. We know so little about her, what her intentions are."

"You think Shaylae can defeat her?"

"Nothing is known to me about the outcome of this."

Part Three
Istas, the White Stone

CHAPTER 30

The woman gradually returned to wakefulness and propped herself up on one elbow. She rubbed her tired eyes and shook her weary head. As if lost in a dream, she could not bring her consciousness completely to the surface; all she felt was disoriented confusion. She didn't know where she was, or even who she was; couldn't remember her own name. Memories hung nearby, just out of reach, tantalizing her, but just as she thought she could reach and take hold of one, like a dandelion seed in a gust of wind, it was gone.

She sat up and tried to take in her surroundings. She was sitting on a grassy bank next to a gently flowing river. Trees provided a restful canopy, shielding her from the sun which shone through their leaves, making pleasant dancing patterns on the ground. "Grass, river, trees, sun," she said slowly. Yes, she knew what they were, she knew the words for them, but no matter how hard she concentrated she could not recall her own name.

Kneeling on the river bank, she dipped one hand into the cool clear water and scooped up a mouthful to her dried lips. It tasted wonderful, almost divine. Divine? What is divine? A word she had remembered, but one for which she did not know the meaning. She dipped both hands into the water and took a longer draft, letting out a huge, contented sigh. Her stomach growled, announcing its need for food. Tentatively she tried to stand, but her legs were weak, unable to support her. I need food; the thought came to her, but not with urgency or insistence. Above her she saw fruit hanging from the branches of one of the trees. I wonder if it's edible, she thought. Not that it mattered; even if she could stand she would not be able to reach it. She reached heavenward, as if pleading for the fruit to come to her. There was a faint crack as the stem broke free of the branch and the fruit fell into her hand, but even this did not strike her as strange, as if this were the proper order of things. She held the fruit to her nose in both hands and breathed deeply of its fresh clean fragrance. Tentatively she bit into the crisp flesh, its juice filling her mouth, trickling across her lips, and down her chin. It was exquisite. Nothing she had ever eaten before had ever tasted this good. But then, how would she know that? She couldn't even remember her own name.

She felt a stirring within her, a distinct kick. She lowered her hand to her womb and smiled. I'm pregnant, she thought, and quite a few months, though how she knew that mystified her.

A soft rustling in the grass behind her made her turn her head. There before her stood a beautiful young woman, hair yellow as the sun, holding a bowl in both hands before her, a towel draped across her arm.

"Oh, you're awake," she said, with a voice that sounded musical and pure.

"Who are you?" asked the woman.

She shrugged.

"How long have I been here?"

"I found you this morning." She pointed to the spot where the woman sat. "Right there. You were lying right there, fast asleep."

"I was unconscious?"

She nodded. "Yes. When I found you I was quite worried. I just left to fetch water to bathe your head."

The woman raised her hand to her head. "I was injured?"

"Oh, no, but you had a fever, and I thought that if I bathed your head it would help."

She tried to stand, but found she still did not have the strength. "Who am I? Do you know who I am?"

"No, but I found something in your pocket."

"Something? What kind of something?"

"I don't know. I've never seen anything like it before."

"Where is it?"

"Back at my cabin. Should I go and get it?"

She tried to stand, but her left leg almost failed her. "Yes, please. I think that would be a good idea."

The blonde woman turned and ran back into the woods.

She felt reassured. Perhaps it would be something that would help her remember who she was, and how she came to be lying by this river.

She turned as the other woman ran back to her. "Here," she said, handing her a plastic device of some kind. She took it and looked at it strangely. It had some sort of screen on one side and was about ten centimeters by six. It fit neatly into her hand, and felt somehow familiar as she turned it over and over, looking at it intently.

"Please identify," it said.

"Identify?"

"Speak your name and place your thumb on the pad."

"I don't know my name."

"Identify through retinal scan."

She shrugged. "Retinal scan?"

"Hold the screen to your eye."

It seemed an odd request, but she complied.

"Welcome, Shaylae Lucero."

"Shaylae Lucero?"

"That must be your name."

I suppose so, she thought. Shaylae; a pleasant sounding name.

"But what is this?" she asked, holding out the device.

"I am your Personal Interface Device."

"Personal Interface Device?" She was beginning to feel foolish, repeating everything the device was saying.

"PID for short," it said. "How can I help you?"

"Where am I?"

"Unknown."

"How long have I been here?"

"Unknown."

"Where is my home?"

"Millcreek Canyon, Salt Lake County, Utah, United States of America, Earth."

Earth. That sounded familiar, but the rest… meant nothing. "Earth? You mean the planet Earth?"

"Yes."

"Then this is not Earth?"

"No. You are currently on an unknown and uncharted planet."

Shaylae was silent for a moment, trying to digest what that could possibly mean.

"Do I have a family?"

"Yes, you have a husband and two children."

"Can you show them to me?"

Immediately a holographic image of a young man appeared above the device.

"Your husband," said the PID.

The man was strikingly handsome, beautiful. His image stood thirty centimeters. He was naked except for a leather apron of some sort around his waist. His dark skin shone, and his back and legs rippled with powerful muscles. Long dark hair hung to his shoulders, held in place by a yellow headband with a feather in it. The image rotated slowly, his face filled with an oh-so enticing smile. She gasped as her heart fluttered.

"What's his name?" she asked breathlessly.

"Mika Hale."

"You must love each other a lot. I can tell by the look in your eyes," said the woman.

Shaylae smiled, her skin tingling as she looked at him. "Show me the children."

The holograph was replaced by the image of a family. Mika was dressed more conventionally, his hair gathered into a neat ponytail, and was carrying a girl about eight years old on his shoulders. Standing next to him was a dark-haired woman holding a three-year old little girl in her arms.

"Is that me?" asked Shaylae.

"Yes," said the PID and the woman together.

"You're quite beautiful. You have a beautiful family."

"But I don't remember any of them. I don't even know their names."

"Asdza is eight years, nine months, and three days; Halona is two years, eleven months and eighteen days," spoke the metallic voice of the PID.

"Mika, Asdza, Halona," said Shaylae repeating the names wistfully. "No, I can't remember anything about them."

"Perhaps this thing has more information about you; a history of some sort."

"Is there a personal journal in your memory?"

"Yes." The device sprang open like a book, exposing a small keypad. Please enter the pass-code to access."

"Pass-code? But you have already identified me through the retinal scan. Why do I need a pass-code to access my journal?"

"Your strict instructions, Shaylae Lucero."

"Now why would I do that?"

She looked at the woman, who had become very quiet, a tear or two rolling down her cheeks. "Oh I'm sorry. This has been all about me. I haven't asked anything about you."

The woman lowered her head. "There's not much I can tell you. I don't know who I am either."

"Oh, I'm sorry; I had no idea…"

"It's OK," she said, brushing aside Shaylae's concern. "I woke up right here too." She smiled. "At least you know you have a family. I have no idea who I am."

"I'm so sorry. How long have you been here?"

She shrugged. "I haven't been keeping count, but it's been at least fourteen days, maybe more."

"And did you have anything with you? Something like this that told you who you are," she said, holding up her PID.

"No, nothing. But the Spirit has been teaching me things."

"Spirit?" Inexplicably, Shaylae felt a shiver run down her spine.

"Yes, he's been teaching me about things."

"Can't he tell you who you are?"

"He won't."

"Won't? Why not?"

"He says that finding out who I am, or about my past would spoil things."

Shaylae was beginning to feel quite uncomfortable. There was a hint of something in her eyes which looked a lot older than her apparent twenty-five years.

"Can I see this spirit?"

She shrugged again.

"What's his name?"

"Rolling Darkness."

"That's an odd name." A sinister name, she added to herself. "What kinds of things has he been teaching you?"

"All kinds of things. He showed me where to find my cabin. He tells me what to eat. He's taught me about this planet and all the other planets in the universe."

"That's quite a wide range of subjects."

"I'm hungry. Do you want to come back to my cabin? I have all kinds of food to eat there."

Why did she change the subject? There was something distinctly odd about all of this. Even though she wasn't sure what *right* was, it didn't seem right.

"Would you mind if I bathed in the river first?"

She seemed shocked, almost frightened by the suggestion. "If you must, but I won't be joining you."

"No, it's OK. I'll pass. Let me see if I can stand." She pushed herself up to a kneeling position, and then one foot at a time, she was able to stand, but her left leg felt as if it might give way.

"Here," she said extending her arm. "Lean on me."

"Thank you." As she grasped her forearm a vague shadowy feeling crept into her mind, and she almost stumbled.

"What's the matter?"

"Oh, nothing," she said, forcing a smile.

They wound their way through the woods in silence for about a hundred meters.

"Here it is," she said. A small one-roomed log cabin with no windows stood in a clearing. She held aside the tarp covering the doorway.

"Who built this?" asked Shaylae.

"No idea. I found it. Well, the spirit showed me where to find it."

"And there was food here."

"Yes."

It was sparsely furnished; two stools, two cots, a low table and a pot of something steaming on a wood-burning stove. The woman picked up a wooden decanter and poured water into two roughly carved wooden cups. "Here, you must be thirsty."

"Yes," said Shaylae. "Hungry too." She tried to smile but she was still feeling uneasy.

She dipped a cup into the pot and passed it to Shaylae. "It doesn't look much, but it tastes OK."

"Thanks," said Shaylae, lifting the cup to her nose. It certainly smelled OK. "What is it?"

"It's a soup made from roots and other vegetables. The spirit told me which ones were edible."

Shaylae hesitated.

"Go ahead. It's not gonna poison you," she said with a giggle.

Why not, thought Shaylae. She was famished. She raised the cup to her lips and drank the soup tentatively. Mmm. It was good.

The woman was sipping from her cup. "See, I told you it was good."

Shaylae nodded, and took a drink of water. It was cool and refreshing. She gulped down the whole cup.

"Good, Shaylae. You like it?"

The uneasiness Shaylae had been feeling the last fifteen minutes deepened. There was something deeply sinister about the way she spoke her last question. Was that a smirk, or was it just a smile?

"Yes. It's fine." She put her hand to her forehead. "That is… I feel…"

"What, Shaylae? What is it?"

Shaylae didn't respond, instead she spun around and fell to the floor.

Istas waved something beneath Shaylae's nose and she recoiled from the smell.

"That's good. Sit here," she said, helping her to the cot. "Now, let's try again."

"Try again," said Shaylae, her voice a low monotone, a million kilometers away.

"Who created the universe, Shaylae?"

"The Holy Ones," she said, staring blankly ahead of her.

"Yes, but why?"

"To give us life; to give their children life."

Istas raised her hands and shouted. "No, you fool. We've been over this. This is the fifteenth time, and still you give me the same stupid answers." A burst of energy leapt from her hands to Shaylae's chest. Shaylae screamed and fell backwards. "They created this Universe to see us suffer."

Shaylae's face contorted with pain. "No, they allow us to feel sorrow so we can appreciate the joy, to feel sickness to enjoy the health…"

"Why would any parent enjoy seeing their children suffer?"

"So we could grow, and become like them."

Istas stood, walked over to Shaylae, and put her hand on her shoulder. "No, Shaylae, you have been fooled. They never wanted us to become like them. They want us for playthings, toys they can torture and make suffer. That's how they fill their evil minds."

"They are not evil, they are the Holy Ones."

"They are evil, Shaylae, they are. Only Rolling Darkness, their first born, son can save us. Only he can defeat their evil plan."

"Rolling Darkness?"

"Yes, you know of him?"

"He is the evil one, and he is not their first born son."

"He is not? And how do you know?"

"I don't know, only that I'm sure he is not."

"Don't you see, he is the only one who can save us? He will end suffering. He wants…"

"He only wants the power and glory for himself. He cares nothing for us." Shaylae turned her head and looked at Istas.

"Shaylae, Shaylae. You've been taught all your life about the Holy Ones, and your head has been filled with only half-truths. Yes, they feed you truth, but they don't want you to know the whole story. If you knew the fullness of their plan you would join me, join him."

"Never," said Shaylae. "I will never turn against them, never join you and your evil…"

A bolt of energy from Istas' hands silenced her, knocked her against the wall and into unconsciousness.

The spirit who had been skulking in a corner of the room sneered. "You've been at this for fifteen days, and for fifteen days the conversation has hardly changed. She'll never come around."

"You idiot," said Istas, shaking her head disdainfully. "That's your problem, you never learned patience. Even before the Holy Ones cast you out, if you'd had more patience then perhaps you would have defeated them, but instead, look at you; now you're a nothing. Even a weak Earth-girl can defeat you without breaking a sweat." She turned to him. "I have patience with her, and one day she will come around. It may take months, or even years, I don't care, I can wait. But for you my patience running out. Be careful I don't send you back where I found you; where the witch Shaylae sent you ten years ago." She curled her lip and with a voice dripping with sarcasm she added, "Rolling Darkness."

With a look of abject fear on his face, he bowed. "I'm sorry mistress, forgive me."

"Get out of my sight."

The woman awoke lying on a bank, next to a peacefully flowing river. She rubbed her tired eyes and shook her weary head. As if lost in a dream, she could not bring her consciousness completely to the surface; all she felt was disoriented confusion. She couldn't remember her own name, but looking down at her belly, she knew at once that she was more than a few months pregnant. Memories hung nearby, just out of reach, tantalizing her with unfulfilled promise, but just as she thought she could reach and take hold of one a gust of wind wafted it away...

"Who created the universe, Shaylae?"

"The Holy Ones," she said, staring blankly ahead of her.

"Yes, but why?"

"To give us life. To give their children life."

"But they let us suffer. Why?"

"They want us to grow, to become like them."

"You have children, Shaylae. You want them to become like you?"

"Yes. Well, I suppose I would like them to become more than I am."

"Exactly. You want what's best for them. But tell me, would you let them suffer?"

Shaylae stopped breathing and sat motionless. "I... I don't know."

"Of course you wouldn't. You would protect them, nurture them. You would teach them, raise them and make sure you didn't lose them to the world, and you would do this without allowing them suffer."

"Yes..."

"But the Holy Ones, what do they do?"

Shaylae was silent.

"They allow their children to fall, to fail and to suffer. Why is that?"

Shaylae hesitated, as if not quite sure of her answer. "To allow us to grow, to develop."

"No! Don't you see, you're simply repeating things you have been taught all your life? Things you've always accepted without question. How many of their children lived their worthless lives in suffering, pain, hunger, living as slaves and worse? How many of their children have they allowed to fail, and to be doomed in the eternities? Millions, Shaylae, perhaps billions. Think about it. You said you would not let that happen to your own children. You wouldn't want to lose any."

"No, I wouldn't…"

"Neither would Rolling Darkness. In the beginning, he tried to persuade the Holy Ones to protect their children, to keep them from harm. Rather than being hailed as a hero, they cast him out, along with those who agreed with him."

Shaylae turned to her, a look of understanding growing in her eyes, as if her consciousness was about to resurface. "No, you're wrong. He is evil; the Holy Ones love us…"

"Fool!" shouted Istas, a bolt of energy hitting Shaylae in the chest, driving her back against the wall. She fell to the cot senseless.

"See, I am making progress and it's only been twenty-three days. She will come around in time."

"So it would appear," said the spirit with a sigh.

"Do not patronize me. That is the last warning I will give you."

CHAPTER 31

For weeks Mika worried himself sick, not saying anything to anyone about his fears. Shaylae was... well, she was Shaylae. She could take care of herself. But the nagging thoughts would not leave him; why hadn't she contacted him at least? Well, Tal'el'Dine'h was a special place, perhaps she couldn't. But why hadn't she tried to let him know how she was? Finally, fed up with arguing with himself, he called Ayanna.

"She went to Tal'el'Dine'h?"

"Yes."

"And you haven't heard from her?"

"No."

In typical Ayanna fashion she was immediately galvanized into action. "Fine, then that's where we're going."

"To Tal'el'Dine'h?"

"Yes, to Tal'el'Dine'h"

"And how do you expect to get that kind of authorization?"

"Me? Authorization? You've got to be kidding. This is Shaylae we're talking about."

"Yes, but..."

"Yes but nothing. I'm going to file a return to Sanostee right now."

Mika immediately understood where she was going with this plan. She didn't give a second thought to the consequences, only that she had to go after Shaylae. "Should we tell Harley what we're really planning?" he asked.

"Why? Why risk his career as well as ours?"

As soon as Ayanna and her crew had returned to earth, Harley had formalized Ayanna and Sigmun's commissions in the ISA, making them permanent, and promoted Ayanna to full Commander. Ayanna asked for, and received the go ahead to promote Martin to Lieutenant JG, and Hansen to double-bar Lieutenant. She offered Chief Olsen a commission, but he refused.

"I enjoy working with the enlisted men. My goal is to be Master Chief Petty Officer of the Fleet one day."

"Then let me at least put you one step closer, Senior Chief Petty Officer Olsen."

He saluted. "Thank you ma'am, just so long as you keep calling me Chief."

"Deal," she had said.

She smiled, thinking about her incredible crew, but wasn't quite sure how they would take the news of their latest flight.

"Commander Hale, Captain, you appear to be off course." The flight officer at the other end of the hyper-transmission looked worried. "Please return to the approved flight plan."

Ayanna turned to Mika. "Well, now they know we're not returning to Delta Pavonis."

Mika shrugged. "Not that it makes any difference, they can't stop us now. We have to find Shaylae."

"Even if it costs me my commission," agreed Ayanna. She hit the transmit key. "There's been a change of plan, lieutenant."

"I was not notified. Has the ISA approved this change?"

"No, lieutenant, the ISA has not approved."

"Commander, I have to insist that you…"

Ayanna killed the transmission. "He was beginning to bore me." She flipped on the intra-ship communicator. "All hands, report to the bridge."

"Now we see how loyal the crew is to you," said Sigmun.

One by one, the crew came to the bridge. Lieutenant Hansen was holding her PID, looking worried. "Um, Dr. Hale, there seems to be an error in our first jump," she began tactfully. Out of respect for the leading hyper-analytical mathematician in the world, Jane had deferred to Mika and allowed him to compute the first jump.

"No mistake Jane. We're on a rescue mission," said Ayanna.

"Rescue mission?" said Mark.

"Yes, Chief," said Mika stepping forward. "Shaylae Lucero has been missing for almost four weeks."

"We're not going back to Sanostee?"

The revelation seemed to stun the crew.

"She shifted to Tal'el'Dine'h over three weeks ago, and has not been heard from since."

"What is Tal'el'Dine'h?" asked Tyler.

"It's a planet; the planet Shaylae's ancestors come from."

"What? You mean she's not… human?"

"As human as you, Steve," said Ayanna.

"In fact, all Navajo are descendants of the people of Tal'el'Dine'h," said Sigmun.

The crew's jaws dropped in unison.

"Tal'el'Dine'h is the third planet involved in the struggle against the Dark Ones," said Ayanna. "They were instrumental in defeating the assembly aboard *Revenge*."

"How come we've never heard of them?" asked Tyler.

"It's a long story, and I'll give you the history in a moment," said Ayanna. "In the meantime, I want to give you all a chance to abort the mission."

"Abort the mission?" said Mark. "We're with you, captain."

"Think about what you're saying. Think about what I'm asking you to do. You could all lose your careers."

"You don't have to ask any of us," said Steve. The rest of the crew nodded. "We're with you wherever you go, whatever you decide to do."

"The only thing that bothers me," said Mark slowly, "is why you didn't tell us before you made the first jump."

"I'm sorry, Chief," said Ayanna. "I wanted to take the responsibility myself. If they court martial me, I wanted to be able to say it was all my decision, not to implicate any of you."

"You know we all would have agreed to come with you, no matter what," said Ryan.

"That's what I was afraid of," said Ayanna. "This way at least, you may be able to ride out the consequences when we return."

"I would have rather been a part of the decision up front," said Mark.

"I know, Chief, and I'm sorry, but I was thinking of what was best for you."

"Well," said Jane, consulting her PID, "Looks like we're headed for Beta Canum Venaticorum."

"Yes, also called Chara, to the fourth planet," said Mika. "Known as Tal'el'Dine'h by its inhabitants."

"Pull up a seat everyone. Let me fill you in on the last five thousand years of history..."

Mika watched Ayanna tell her crew what only a handful of people so far knew. He was not in the least surprised how well Ayanna filled the role of commanding officer; how confident and at ease she was with her crew; how well she related to them; and more, how obviously devoted they were to her, even Sigmun. He had not always wanted to admit it, growing up as her cousin, but Ayanna was the most impressive person he knew, aside from Shaylae of course; decent, honest, strong-willed, unshakeable, and a hundred other superlatives he could have used.

He was relieved to have her at his side. He thought back to the time aboard *Revenge* when Shaylae had fallen, and he was about to be consumed by the power of the Dark Ones. Ayanna had been able to resist their onslaught and reached out for him, taking his hand, saving him from certain destruction. He knew that he was a strong willed person, but Ayanna had something extra. No wonder Shaylae had chosen her as her companion.

CHAPTER 32

"Let's try again, Shaylae," said Istas. Her voice was full of syrupy warmth. "Why do the Holy Ones allow their children to suffer?"

"I... I don't know."

"You do, Shaylae, but it's hard for you to let go of the lies you were told growing up."

"I know."

"I mean, you've already agreed that you would never let your own children suffer. Not that you would spoil them..."

"No, of course not."

"You would make them work hard at school, do chores around the house, but you would do all of this with love, and be very protective."

"Yes."

"If you think about it, only two possibilities exist: either the Holy Ones are all powerful, and they choose to let their children suffer, in which case they are evil and don't love them; or they are simply unable to stop the suffering, which makes them weak. Either way, they are not worthy of your worship, of anyone's worship."

Shaylae was silent. Is this the day I will break her, thought Istas? The anticipation was almost unbearable.

"What if there's another possibility?"

"Shaylae!" she shouted. "How can there be another possibility?"

"What if we just don't see things from their perspective? What if we simply don't have the long view? What if there are things that are just simply beyond our ability to understand?"

"It's really very simple..."

"Is it," said Shaylae interrupting her. "You say there are only two possible choices, and yes, it seems logical, but what if you have simply created a false dichotomy?"

False dichotomy! Istas was astounded that Shaylae had been able to come to this reasoning, in spite of the drugs. A look of understanding came to Shaylae's face. Istas was about to speak, but before she could Shaylae spoke again. "What about that time Halona fell and cut herself when we were out riding. We didn't have any medical equipment with us, so I had to put alcohol on the wound. I had to…"

"It's not the same thing," shouted Istas, becoming more impatient.

"Did Mika have the power to stop me but didn't because he doesn't love Halona, or did he not have the power, and therefore he's not a good parent. Of course not. And while she may not have understood that that at the time, as she grows older she will understand that there weren't just the two possibilities."

"Fool!" Istas was screaming now. A bolt of energy hit Shaylae in the chest; she fell to the cot senseless.

"I'm impressed, mistress. I think you are making progress."

"You're patronizing me again," she said. He cowered. "It concerns me that she remembered that incident involving her child." She took a lock of hair and twirled it between her thumb and fingers. "And despite the drugs, she can still reason." A dark expression filled her childlike face. "I may have to kill her after all."

***

"I don't get it," said Tyler. "I've checked it five times, and there's no mistake; the fourth planet is a gas giant."

"That just can't be," said Ayanna, a sickening feeling growing in her gut.

They had completed their penultimate jump twelve hours earlier, and were now only one-point-five billion kilometers from Tal'el'Dine'h, or at least where Tal'el'Dine'h should have been. But Ayanna's elation was shattered when Tyler announced his disturbing discovery about the fourth planet. Ayanna had insisted he check it again. Now, after his fifth go around, things hadn't changed. There simply wasn't a Tal'el'Dine'h.

"OK, like I explained earlier, the planetary system doesn't conform to the models that cosmology has developed over the last two centuries."

"Yes," said Mika. "Can you go over your reasoning again?"

Tyler pulled up a graphic on the main display, Chara in the center, surrounded by concentric circles, indicating the planetary orbits. He pointed to the first. "OK, this is obviously not to scale; this planet is rock, like Mercury. The second, also rock, but bigger than the first. The third planet is an out-of-control greenhouse, much like Venus. Then there's this gap…"

"Yes, that is a large gap between the third and fourth planets."

"The formula for predicting planetary orbits would put another planet here," he said, pointing at a spot in between the third and fourth orbits.

"So where is it?" asked Ayanna.

"At first I thought that the formula might be plain wrong; I mean, up until ten years ago we've only had one planetary system to verify it against. Now in the last few years we've got three."

"Earth, Yurob and Delta Pavonis," said Ayanna.

"Exactly. Both the Yurob and Delta Pavonis systems conform to the predictions of the formula within a hundred thousand kilometers for each planetary orbit."

"So why doesn't Chara?"

"Well, it's possible the planet was there, but some catastrophic cosmological accident destroyed it."

"How likely is this possibility?"

"It could happen," he said. "However, even if such a catastrophe occurred a hundred million years ago, there would still be debris."

"So, what other possibilities are there?"

"It's something else," said Tyler, taking his time over each word.

Ayanna, Sigmun, and Mika looked at each other. "Something else?"

"Yes. In science we were taught that even if we can't explain something with our current knowledge, doesn't mean that there isn't an explanation, only that we haven't figured it out yet."

"So, you don't have any possible explanation yet?"

"No, not yet."

"But there has to be another possibility?"

"Yes. Here's what we're doing. We're going on the assumption that there is a planet but we just can't find it. So we've got the computers doing three different searches. One: they're looking for any occluded stellar object, or an occlusion of one of the other planets."

"That's a long shot though?" asked Ayanna.

"Yes, it could take weeks, months, until we found anything; but who knows, we might get lucky."

"What's the second search?" asked Mika.

"We are looking at the other planets for any gravitational anomalies in their orbits that would point to another planet."

"Another long shot?" asked Sigmun.

"Yes, in fact, this could take up to a year before anything measurable was detected."

"And the third?"

"We're doing a massive sweep of space looking for any light distortion?"

"You mean relativistic effects?" asked Mika.

"Yes. The computer has already catalogued the position of approximately fifteen thousand stars within a hundred light years," said Tyler. "Now it's performing sweeps to check any fluctuation in these positions. Any discrepancy between any two calibrations could only be explained by the presence of a gravity well."

"How often is the complete calibration made?" asked Mika.

"Once every ten minutes. It takes that long to sweep."

"This sounds even more of a long shot than the other two methods," said Ayanna.

"Actually it's not. Unless we're really unlucky, I expect to have some results within a couple of days."

"Thanks, Tyler," said Ayanna.

Once they were alone, Sigmun turned to Ayanna and Mika and said, "Are you worried?"

"About Shay, yes, but not about the fact we can't find Tal'el'Dine'h. I was at first, but now I'm starting to feel better. It's some of the things Shay said about Tal'el'Dine'h."

"Such as?"

"Nashota told her it was a very special place, and that it had the protection of the Holy Ones."

"That's odd."

"Yes, I can't imagine what that means."

"Have you ever thought that we might not be meant to find it?" asked Sigmun.

"Yes, but like that's going to stop us," said Mika with a snort.

"Sigmun may have a point; maybe they have it so well hidden that none of our searches will find it."

Tyler burst into the room. "We've found it."

He'd only been gone about ten minutes. They said nothing, just stared at him.

"Oh, I'm sorry. Did I disturb something? You want me to come back later?" he asked with a huge grin on his face, turning back to the door.

"Lieutenant..." said Ayanna threateningly.

"No," said Mika. "It's just you caught us by surprise. We weren't expecting you back so..."

"I know. I can't believe it myself."

"So, tell us. What have you found?"

Tyler spoke a few commands to the computer. "OK, this is Chara 5." Chara 5 was in the center of the display. Just discernable as a disk, it had four moons visible from this distance. "At least we're assuming it's number 5. And you can see that we arrived pretty well on the plane of the elliptic. Just to orient you, if we are at twelve o'clock then Chara 5 is at about six-thirty. Let me replay you the feed we've been getting for the last hour." He spoke to the computer again, giving it a sensor and a time index. "Magnify."

"It's just over one arc second at this distance, approximately 2.5 billion kilometers. Now, watch."

They watched for a couple of minutes, but nothing happened.

"Did you see it?"

"See what?"

"Sorry, I am just playing with you. Actually, you can't see anything."

"Tyler!" said Ayanna, beginning to sound a little impatient.

"OK, bear with me. If there was a planet occluding the gas giant, and let's just say for argument's sake, it is one billion kilometers closer to us, and also let's assume it's approximately the size of Earth, with a diameter of say, twelve thousand kilometers."

"Then we should be able to see it. It would have an angle of about three arc seconds. It would cover the gas giant completely."

"Exactly. If it was exactly in the same elliptical plane, that is."

"So this video shows us nothing?" said Sigmun.

"Not if we are looking for an occlusion, but, if we are looking for a relativistic shift in the light coming from 5..."

"OK, Tyler, enough," said Mika. "What have you found?"

"Well, not me, the computers found it. No human could possibly have noticed any light bending, but the computers can, and did." He rewound the feed. "Right about... here..." he stopped the feed, "there's a shift of two ten-thousands of an arc second in the light."

"Wow, that's significant."

"Yes. We asked the computers to project the position, size, mass of a planet that could cause such a shift."

"And..."

"And, get this. If the computer is right, we've got a planet at 1.3 AU, with a mass of 0.95 Earth."

"And the computer is still tracking it, knows where it is?"

"Yep," said Tyler triumphantly, beaming all over his face. "What I don't understand though, is how it can be so well hidden that it doesn't occlude the gas giant, even though by all calculations it just passed directly in front of it."

"Then let's head on over and find out," said Ayanna.

"You're not worried the computer will glitch up like it did last time we tried to get within a million kilometers of a planet?" asked Tyler.

"Not a chance," said Mika. "Let's get Jane on it. Calculate the jump."

CHAPTER 33

The woman opened her eyes. Still sleepy, she was lying on her back looking up through a beautiful canopy of some kind of fruit trees. How did I get here, she thought; more to the point, as she became fully awake, she realized she didn't even know her own name. Memories hovered, just out of reach, but try as she might, she could not capture one.

She was sitting on a grassy bank next to a gently flowing river, and though she couldn't remember who she was, or how she got here, there was something distinctly familiar about the place. The child within her womb stirred as she lovingly caressed her belly. Even before the soft rustling in the grass behind her announced her arrival, she knew the woman was there, a beautiful young woman, hair yellow as the sun, carrying a cup and a towel.

"Oh, you're awake," she said, with a voice that sounded musical and pure.

"Who are you?" asked the woman.

She shrugged.

"How long have I been here?"

"I found you this morning." She pointed to the spot where the woman sat. "Right there. You were lying right there, fast asleep."

"I was unconscious?"

"Yes."

The woman tried to swallow, but her mouth and throat were too dry. "I'm thirsty."

"Here, drink this." She took two steps toward her, holding the cup before her but she stumbled. The woman was barely able to catch her before she fell into the river. The blonde woman screamed; a horrific, animal scream.

"Are you OK?"

The blonde woman was shaking violently and the already pale skin of her face was white. It took a moment but she quickly composed herself. "Yes, it's nothing. Just a scare, that's all."

"Here, let me help you." The woman tried to stand, but found she still did not have the strength. "Who am I? Do you know who I am?"

"No, but I found something in your pocket."

"Something? What kind of something?"

"I don't know. I've never seen anything like it before."

"Where is it?"

"Back at my cabin. Should I go and get it?"

She tried to stand, but her left leg almost failed her. "Yes, please. I think that would be a good idea."

The blonde woman turned and ran back into the woods...

"So, Shaylae, I think we're making great progress." Istas looked directly into Shaylae's eyes. They were somewhat misted over, but she looked a little more aware than she had on the previous times she had tried this. She knew she couldn't give her any more of the drug without killing her, but, she wasn't ready to give up yet, she would give it a few more days. "Shaylae, have you ever wondered why your Holy Ones created the Universe?"

"Not really, I..."

"Did it ever occur to you that they didn't."

"You mean didn't create the Universe?"

"What if they are simply products of the existence of the Universe, just like us?"

"How could that be?"

"Many scientists believe that all of this, the Universe, time, space, energy, matter, everything, is just here by accident."

"I've heard that before but I don't believe it."

"Why not? Just because the only explanation you've ever heard about its existence is that it was created, does that mean you have to accept it? What if there are other explanations we just don't see yet, because we don't have the long view?"

"I suppose that's logically possible."

"Not just possible, Shaylae. I'm telling you it's the truth."

"I don't believe it."

"Believe? So, it's a matter of faith then, not logic or science?"

"I suppose it is."

"Then, just follow me along this logical path. For a moment let's just suppose that the Universe is an accident. Have you ever heard that more than a hundred years ago a brilliant Earth statistician created a sophisticated proof that 'something' is more statistically probable than 'nothing'."

"Yes, I've heard that…"

"Then, let's suppose that the Universe did come into existence simply as a result of a statistical probability."

"OK…"

Istas was pleased. Shaylae could be persuaded; she was sure of it. "Then, the Holy Ones, Rolling Darkness, you, me, all life, is the natural result of such a probability."

"Logically, I suppose, it makes sense."

"Then, why assume that the Holy Ones are your parents. What if they're simply a higher, more evolved, life form manipulating and using you, all of us, just for their own amusement?"

"I don't know…"

"Think about it; humans evolved on Earth, Tal'el'Dine'h, Procyon 6, and Delta Pavonis 4, over a period of four billion years, right?"

"Yes, I suppose…"

"And how old is the Universe?"

"Thirteen-point-seven-five-eight billion years; approximately."

How did she know that, thought Istas? "And at what point did second generation stars first appear?"

"Not long after the first blue giants all went supernova creating the heavier elements, and the dense clouds of the big bang started to disperse."

"So, even conservatively, how long ago would that have been?"

"Very close to the beginning of the universe, certainly not more than three hundred million years after the Universe came into existence, possibly less."

"Then why did intelligent life take another thirteen billion years to appear? Doesn't it seem likely that we're not the first; that the Holy Ones, as you call them, evolved a long time ago and have simply been here longer than us?"

"I've never even considered that…"

"But, you accept the possibility; that it is possible that the Holy Ones could be nothing more than a manipulative and cruel race, more advanced than us, not the omnipotent creators you have always assumed them to be."

Shaylae was silent. I've got her, thought Istas. And with her at my side I cannot fail. She drove her point home. "And if that's the case, can't we, shouldn't we, do everything in our power to take that power from them?"

"I don't know…"

"Shaylae. You and I, together we can rule the Universe."

"But why would I want to?"

Istas immediately backed off, realizing that was probably not the best thing to say to this wimpy do-gooder. "Well, I didn't mean it that way. What I meant to say was…"

"Wait a minute, what was it you said before?"

"What?"

"You said it took four billion years for humans to evolve? Thirteen Billion years after the Universe began?"

"Yes. Suggesting, I think, that it is highly unlikely that we are the first intelligent beings…"

"Humans on Earth, Tal'el'Dine'h, Procyon 6, and Delta Pavonis 4?"

"Yes," said Istas slowly. She wasn't sure where Shaylae was going with this, but she was beginning to get the feeling she had just lost her.

"Why would intelligent life, on the only four planets we have investigated so far all be human? I mean, all the same species; exactly the same. And not mule-producing inter-related species either. Ayanna and Sigmun are from two different planets and have children of their own."

She had lost her! Could she recover from this huge mistake she had made, planting that thought in Shaylae's mind. And how was she able to remember Ayanna and Sigmun?

"Statistically, if the first four planets we have discovered all have human life, isn't it logical to assume that intelligent life on all planets will be the same?" she said, emphasizing the 'all'.

"Well, yes…"

"But, again, statistically speaking, if the only force involved was evolution – natural selection – wouldn't there be four different forms of intelligent life? We're not just similar, Istas, we have the exact same DNA. How likely is that?"

"Coincidence..."

Shaylae almost snorted. "That's the most ridiculous thing I've ever heard you say. The only possible explanation is that we have the same Holy Parents..."

Frantically she tried to regroup. "Don't you think it's a lot more logical that in any environment, in any solar system that has a terrestrial planet life would evolve in parallel..."

"That's even more ridiculous. And another thing, why do all of the habitable terrestrial planets we have found each have an oversized moon, unless it was by design? Without such a moon they would wobble, causing horrendous climate changes not allowing civilization to develop ..."

The bolt of electricity from Istas's hands ended Shaylae's comment abruptly as she hit the wall, and fell onto the cot like a rag doll. "Oh, you just signed your own death warrant!"

Rolling Darkness appeared from the shadows. "Can you defeat the Holy Ones without her?"

"Perhaps, perhaps not. But I can certainly destroy the four worlds."

"Then what?"

"I don't know."

"Maybe you should give it more time, mistress. You said yourself that you're not in any hurry."

Istas shook her head in disgust.

CHAPTER 34

Shaylae looked down upon her limp body lying on the cot. Sitting next to her was Istas, and in the background, cowering against the wall, was the spirit she had come to know as Denab, Rolling Darkness. Her memory was intact; she knew who she was. She knew her family and friends, and she knew what this evil woman before her was trying to do. She remembered vividly the conversations she had had with Istas over the last twenty-six days. She had been a convincing interrogator and she certainly had raised some questions for which Shaylae did not know the answers, but it didn't matter, her faith went beyond her reason.

Her spirit began to withdraw. She felt herself moving upward, looking down on the little cabin where Istas had kept her prisoner the last four weeks. Soon she could no longer see the cabin as she rose higher and higher. A few seconds later she was looking down on an unknown planet from space, and then even the planet's star shrank before her eyes. Where was she going? She didn't know, but felt no fear or anxiety. Somehow she knew she was safe in the arms of the Holy Ones. The stars which comprised the local cluster soon melted into a bright nebula, the cluster in which the stars Sol, Procyon, and Delta Pavonis all existed. Faster and faster she flew. The local star cluster disappeared from sight as she looked down on the spiral arm of the Milky Way galaxy, and soon, that was lost as she receded from the Galaxy, until it too was a small disc. Other galaxies, including Andromeda, the Milky Way's sister, began to gather into a discernable cluster, and then they too, hundreds of Galaxies, were only discernable as a small diffuse nebula.

Why are they showing me this, wondered Shaylae, but she was too overcome by the magnificence of the sight to care. The clusters of Galaxies became super clusters as she receded even further. Millions of such super clusters hung in space, perhaps billions. She had always known, intellectually, that there were literally more stars in the universe than there were grains of sand on the whole Earth, but now this was no longer an intellectual stretch – she was seeing it for herself.

Suddenly, without warning, she was in a place, a huge brilliant white place. She couldn't see walls, roof or ceiling, but she knew instinctively she was in some kind of room. Hovering in front of her was an elliptical cloud of some sort, perhaps twenty-five centimeters across, about the size and shape of a football.

"What is it?" she said to no one in particular.

"It is your home."

She turned to see two People, a Man and a Woman, whose countenance was so bright and glorious she could hardly look at them. "My home?" she asked, holding her hands in front of her eyes.

"Yes."

"This is the Universe?"

"It is a Universe; your Universe."

"Then where am I?"

"We are your Holy Parents, Shaylae," said the Woman. "You are in our plane of existence, our Universe."

"But where are we? For me there is no outside of the Universe. How can I be outside of my Universe?"

"Physically you cannot; you cannot leave your Universe. Only your spirit is here with us."

"You've speculated this yourself, not long ago as I recall," said the Man.

"It's an infinite chain, Shaylae," said the Woman.

"An infinite chain? What does that mean?" She looked down and saw she was no longer pregnant. "My baby…" she began.

The woman smiled. "Your baby is fine. She's healthy and strong."

Shaylae felt the vision slipping away from her, like wakening from a dream.

"This is all, Shaylae," said the man. "Now, you must return."

"No, let me stay."

"You cannot stay. You are needed there," he said, pointing to the cloud.

"But can you help me?"

"We will be with you, beloved daughter," said the Woman. "It is all we can promise."

Shaylae woke and tried to move, but every muscle in her body ached, agony in every joint. Was it a dream? Had she really traveled outside of the Universe? Did she really see the Holy Ones in their Universe? It didn't matter. Dream or not, she knew now that it was the truth. An infinite chain the Woman had said. The Woman, her Holy Mother. In spite of the pain, Shaylae smiled. No matter what happened, to her or her husband or children, she knew that one day she would be like her Holy Mother, and that she and her family would be together through the eternities.

"What do you have to smile about?" sneered Istas. Shaylae looked up. Istas stood at the doorway. "Soon all those you love will be dead, horribly, painfully. Then you; then I will kill you."

"It doesn't matter," said Shaylae. "All you can take from me and those I love is our lives, our physical bodies, you cannot have our spirits, and you never will."

A bolt of electricity from Istas's hands slammed her against the wall.

"And that gets to you," croaked Shaylae through her pain. "Doesn't it?"

Another bolt rendered her unconscious.

It's a shame I have to kill her, thought Istas. Now I have no choice but to battle the Holy Ones on my own. No other person has reached the level which would allow them to join me; no other human has gained her level of knowledge of the Holy Ones… She stopped dead in her tracks. "Wait," she spoke aloud as a spark of realization hit her. "Shaylae is not the only one who has reached that level of knowledge of the Holy Ones that she needs in order to reach my state. There is a whole planet of them… and I'm already here. I just need to find those who are susceptible and teach them."

"Perhaps the children …"

Istas raised her eyebrows. "On Tal'el'Dine'h?"

"Exactly."

Istas smiled. "Yes, perhaps. Your first useful suggestion."

CHAPTER 35

"There has to be a planet," said Tyler, shaking his head. "The only way we can be traveling in space in our current trajectory is if we're in orbit around an object of planetary mass at a distance of just over of thirty-three thousand kilometers," said Tyler. "It should be taking up fifteen degrees of our field of vision."

"But we still can't see it?" said Ayanna.

"Not only can we not see it, but we can see stars through the space where everything says it should be."

Mika was frustrated. How could this be? "The only explanation I can come up with is that there is a black hole where the planet should be," he said.

"But everything we know about black hole formation contradicts that theory," said Tyler.

"I know," said Mika. "There is no cosmological event that can create a black hole of this small a mass."

"No cosmological event we know of," said Ayanna.

If it is a black hole, thought Mika, then where is Shaylae. There was only one way to find out. He took out his PID and tapped in a few commands. "It's the only theory we have right now, so let's either verify it, or eliminate it. The event horizon of a black hole of this mass would be less than two centimeters."

"Which at this distance is impossible to detect," said Tyler. "It would only subtend about one-thousandth of an arc second."

"Then, what if we moved to within, say two hundred kilometers above the surface of where a planet of this mass would be."

"Then what? The angle would still be little over three one-thousandths of an arc second."

"We fire a probe directly at the center of gravity," said Mika.

"Dr. Hale, you're not serious?" said Tyler.

"Deadly," said Ayanna, nodding her head. "We need answers." She turned to the intercom. "Ryan, fire up the fusion drive, we're going in closer." She turned back to Tyler. "Plot us a course to put us into an orbit sixty-five-hundred klicks above that center of gravity."

"Ayanna, Mika, there is no need to fire a probe. Besides, sixty-five-hundred klicks will not be enough. The radius of Tal'el'Dine'h is sixty-seven-hundred."

"Matriarch Nashota," said Ayanna as she whirled around to face the man and woman dressed in green and gold robes who had appeared on her bridge.

"And this is my husband, Niyol," she said. She gracefully waved her arms in the air. There was a shimmering in space, and a beautiful blue and white planet appeared before them taking up twenty degrees of the sky. Not too far distant a beautiful yellow Sister Moon kept her company.

"What…" said Tyler, lost for words.

"Tal'el'Dine'h has been in a space-time shift for almost five hundred years."

"Why did you return it to normal space?" asked Mika.

"I didn't," said Nashota. "I shifted your ship."

Mika's curiosity was not even piqued by what Nashota had just told them; all he wanted to know was where his wife was. "Is she here?" asked Mika.

"We don't know."

"What?" said Ayanna.

Mika was stunned. Shaylae had always told him that Nashota was more powerful than her. "How can you not know where she is?" he asked.

Nashota gave a gentle, but sad smile. "We don't know everything, Mika. We're not that different from you."

"You're significantly different from us."

"No," said Nashota, shaking her head.

Mika, Sigmun and Ayanna looked at each other questioningly.

"Perhaps it would help if we told you what has happened to us since we arrived here."

"But what about Shaylae? Shouldn't we be…"

"There's nothing we can do at the moment, except trust the Holy Ones."

"I think we should listen to what she has to say," said Ayanna.

Mika's heart was racing. The last thing he needed right now was a history lesson; he had to be doing something. But when Nashota put her hand on Mika's arm, it reassured him. This woman, who looked no older than Shaylae, calmed his breathing soul.

"When we arrived here, we lived just as we had done on Earth, just as if we had decided to set up a new village in Dinetah. The only difference was that it was more beautiful than anything we had seen on Earth. The grass was greener, the sky bluer, and the climate kinder. Even after being here for a year, a Tal'el'Dine'h year, we had not experienced any extremes of temperature; no major storms; no droughts; no floods. It was perfect. We did notice that Father Sun did not retreat as far in the winter as he had on Earth even though at the height of summer he was as about as high in the sky as back on Earth. Now of course we know that Tal'el'Dine'h's axial tilt is less than Earth's."

"We didn't think much of it at first," continued Niyol "We were too busy building our Hogans, planting our crops, and tending to our children." He smiled at Nashota. "We were the first to have a child, not long after we arrived; and within the first year we had twenty-three babies among us. That's when we started noticing things."

"What sort of things?" asked Ayanna.

"Well, for one thing," said Nashota, "all of our babies were still alive."

Mika was shocked that she would say such a thing, but then he realized that back in the early part of the eighteenth century the mortality rate for babies could reach ten to fifteen percent among the tribes; even higher in the civilized countries of Europe and the eastern United States.

"And another strange thing," she continued, "none of our people had become sick; none had been injured. Even then, we didn't think much of it; we simply put it down to providence and good fortune. But after two or three years, it was obvious that this was more than providence. Everyone was asking questions; why had no one suffered a broken bone, or even a cut?"

"There was no illness among you at all?" asked Ayanna.

"None."

"We decided to have a prayer celebration," said Niyol. "We gathered around our fires, sang songs of the Blessingway, and danced dances of thanks and praise. For three days we did no work; we feasted and prayed. It was the most glorious celebration. And then, the greatest miracle of all; at the end of the three days, Nashota had a vision."

"It was more like a dream really. I saw a young man. His skin was dark like ours, but he did not look like one of us, or like any of the Spanish or Europeans we had seen. His hair was dark also, and it hung down to his shoulders. But in spite of this he shone with exquisite glory. He said that the blessings that we had received were just the natural consequences of the way we lived."

"No, there's got to be more than that to it," said Ayanna. "We've always been told that Tal'el'Dine'h was special."

"It is – now. It hasn't always been this way. It wasn't when Asdzáán Nádleehé lived here else they would have been protected from the Dark Ones."

"So, none of this… this strangeness with Tal'el'Dine'h was planned out or directed by the Holy Ones?"

"Who can tell what the Holy Ones plan, or intend; or even if they don't, how much they can see the outcome."

"If it is just a result of natural law, then why had this never happened on Earth before?" asked Mika.

"It has happened," said Niyol, "many times. It's just never been made known, except to a few."

Ayanna shook her head, as if trying to clear her thoughts. "So what was so different about the way you lived here, from the way you had lived on Earth?"

"We lived in complete harmony; not only with each other, but with the land, with Tal'el'Dine'h herself," said Nashota. "The Elders of Dinetah chose wisely when they chose the couples and families who would return to Tal'el'Dine'h. There were times during this selection process that we were confused. Couples whose names we had put forward were rejected, and there were couples chosen who we did not expect. But when we arrived here, it became obvious that their choice had been led by the Holy Ones. Each person filled a vital role in our new society. There was no jealousy, no competition; we felt a bond, united in our quest to make a new home for ourselves. In my vision the Holy One, who called himself the Firstborn, told us that when a society lives together like this they become a little less than the angels; and not just them, but the land on which they live. It's an eternal law that was framed when time began."

"Not long after Nashota had her vision our minds were opened. We learned the true nature of the Universe, the true nature of the Holy Ones, and of our relationship to them."

"And what is that relationship?" asked Mika.

"That is a truth that cannot be taught," said Nashota. "It can only be learned and experienced."

"And so, are you immortal?" asked Ayanna.

"No, not exactly," said Niyol. "In order for us to..." he paused as if searching for the right words, "In order for us to progress to our full potential, we will have to pass through death, like all mortals. But until that time comes, we cannot die."

"Are your children born this way?" asked Mika

"Not exactly, but like all children, they are born innocent, pure. Things like hate, envy, and prejudice all have to be learned, and since there was no one on Tal'el'Dine'h who had those feelings to teach them their purity remained. But as they grow, they too must come to the knowledge of the Holy Ones by themselves"

"You mean faith?"

"It begins that way, but it's more than faith, it becomes pure knowledge."

"And you have lived this way for five hundred years?" asked Mika.

"Doesn't it get boring?" asked Ayanna.

Even in his anxious state Mika had to chuckle. It was just the kind of response he would have expected from her. Even Nashota laughed. "Far from it, it was a time of great learning, wonderful art, and unimaginable love between us; between all of the people."

"So how come your world isn't over populated?" Another typically practical question from Ayanna.

"Most couples have kept themselves to two or three children, so our population doubled about every thirty years. By the time we sensed the Dark Ones preparing to return to Earth, we numbered less than two million souls."

"And that's when you sent White Cloud to Earth; to teach Shaylae?"

Nashota and Niyol looked at each other sadly, and then nodded.

CHAPTER 36

Shaylae stirred on her cot. She was in terrible pain. She opened her eyes and the small dark room came gradually into focus. Istas was sitting in a chair, staring at her, as if she had never moved. Shaylae groaned as she tried to prop herself up on one elbow. "Where are you from?" she asked her.

"Your husband is here."

"Did you bring him?"

"No, he came here all by himself; him and that insufferable Ayanna and her husband."

"They're all here?"

"Not all. Now I must bring your children."

"Leave them alone," said Shaylae through her gritted teeth. "Hurt them and I will see that you suffer."

Istas laughed, the way one might dismiss a child. Changing the subject she responded to Shaylae's earlier question. "I'm from Tal'el'Dine'h. But you probably already guessed that too."

"No, it's the last place I would have imagined."

"Really?"

"Yes. For one thing, your skin and hair are the wrong color. Besides, you tried to destroy Nashota five hundred years before you were born? You..."

"Oh, how quaint," she said, laughing cruelly. "The time paradox has you confused. If I'd have destroyed Nashota before I was born, then I wouldn't have been born to destroy Nashota." She laughed again. "How your mind is trapped, Shaylae."

Istas waived her arms, and suddenly standing before her were Asdza and Halona. Shaylae's heart leapt into her throat.

"Mommy," said Halona. She looked scared and didn't move.

Asdza looked around the room with a questioning, almost knowing look on her face.

"I'm not going to kill them now. I think Mika should see that, don't you?"

Shaylae wasn't the least bit relieved by the stay, in fact it heightened her anger, but she had already discovered she was no match for Istas.

"Mom, what's happening?" asked Asdza. Then, as she looked at Istas she said, "She is the woman who came to my room." She reached forward and put her arms around her mom's waist. Immediately Shaylae felt warmth and strength flow into her body from Asdza, and with it came a renewed confidence.

"Istas has no knowledge or understanding of the power within the covenant of the family, Shaylae."

"White Cloud," she exclaimed. But it was not just him whose spirit had touched her; Asdza's spirit filled her with a strength that almost consumed her. "Come, Halona,' she said, opening her arms for her younger daughter, "we're leaving."

Istas laughed, but Shaylae, Asdza, and Halona were already gone.

"What happens if one of your children does not come to that knowledge?" asked Ayanna.

"They always do, but what we couldn't even imagine was that one of our children would begin to question the plan of the Holy Ones."

Right away Mika knew, but it was still unbelievable. "Istas!"

Nashota nodded. "She was different from the beginning. Her blonde hair and blue eyes were a surprise, but aside from that she grew normally. More than that, she was the fastest learner we had ever seen and she was a lovely child. By the time she was ten years old, she had already progressed to the full knowledge of the Holy Ones. By twelve she had seen them."

"And then she turned against them," said Mika.

"Not right away. It happened in stages. As we watched events unfolding on Earth she questioned how the Holy Ones could let their children suffer, how they could allow them to hurt each other so. She couldn't understand why they didn't stop it. We tried to teach her of agency and growth, but of course, she had seen how we lived here and felt it was a huge contradiction. I suppose it is… or could appear that way. Then she asked why the Holy Ones didn't destroy the Dark Ones. The final step in her fall was when Rolling

Darkness managed to convince her that the Holy Ones' plan was flawed. He convinced her that he could save everyone; that no one had to suffer. At first she was Rolling Darkness's slave, but soon she became the master."

"It was not until two years ago that her fall was complete," said Niyol.

"What did you do?" asked Ayanna.

"Nothing. What could we do?"

"Can she be… I don't know… reclaimed?"

A tear came to Niyol's eyes. "Once someone has turned against the Holy Ones, after coming to a complete knowledge of them, there is no turning back."

"Then she has nothing to lose?"

"Nothing."

"What does she want? What does she hope to accomplish?"

"The same thing Rolling Darkness wanted when he rebelled."

"She wants to conquer them?" said Ayanna incredulously.

"Surely that's not possible…" began Mika.

Nashota was shaking her head. "I don't know, Mika, I just don't know any more."

"She has great power," said Niyol.

"And that power grows daily. So, I …"

"Where is she now?" asked Mika.

"We don't know."

"Then she has Shaylae," said Ayanna.

"I'm afraid she must."

"Not anymore."

They all whirled round to see Shaylae, Asdza, and Halona. Shaylae's clothes were ragged and filthy, her dirty skin covered in scars and dried blood, her hair a tangled mess, but her eyes shone with a brilliant glory; she was the most beautiful sight Mika had ever seen. He quickly took her and his children in his arms and hugged them, but she had something to say, and she wasn't going to be interrupted. "Nashota, Niyol, take back those words. I give my solemn oath that she cannot defeat the Holy Ones. I have seen them. They do not belong to our Universe, they are outside – I've seen where they live. They control everything, at least they can control anything that they want to. Even if we lose, even if we are all killed, Istas will not prevail."

Everyone was stunned. "You've been there?" asked Nashota incredulously. "Never in the history of the Universe has anyone been to the home of the Holy Ones."

Shaylae smiled weakly. "That you know of…"

"Shaylae, you truly are the most incredible person…"

She brushed her off. "I wasn't there in body, only in spirit."

"Shaylae," said Mika, pulling her closer to his chest. "What happened? How did Asdza and Halona…"

"Shh." Stretching up on her tip-toes she kissed him. Tears fell from his eyes, making little rivulets on her dirty cheeks.

"How? How did you escape her?" asked Nashota.

"White Cloud spoke to me; he said the covenant of the family…"

Nashota quickly brought her hand to her mouth.

Shaylae's eyes widened, and then it hit her. "You're his parents aren't you?"

A tear came to Nashota's eyes.

"About a hundred years ago," said Niyol, "we discovered that Nashota was to have another child. It was a huge surprise to us, to all of us. It was the first time since we had returned that a couple had had another child after so long."

"And from what you've been telling us, he would still be alive if he had stayed here?" said Mika.

"You sacrificed your own son's life – he gave his own life – in order for him to come to Earth and teach Shaylae," said Ayanna.

"An act not without precedent," said Niyol.

"It was his choice," said Nashota, wiping her eyes, but smiling nevertheless. "He knew exactly what he was doing."

"His name is doubly blessed," said Mika in a whisper.

"As it is here, Mika," she said, lowering her eyes, "as it is here."

For a moment the room was silent as each person cherished their own memories of White Cloud.

"Well, would you like to see my home?" asked Nashota finally.

"Give me the coordinates and I'll plant this baby on the surface," said Ayanna.

"There'll be no spacecraft landing on Tal'el'Dine'h, Ayanna," said Niyol. "Leave her here, parked in orbit. We'll get you down to the surface."

"Give me a few moments to freshen up," said Shaylae.

Thirty minutes later the whole crew was down on the planet surface, in the same impressive building Shaylae had seen when White Cloud first showed her his home. It seemed as if all of the ruling council of Tal'el'Dine'h were there to greet them. It was like reuniting with old friends; Shaylae felt like she knew each one of them. They certainly knew her.

"Shaylae, what an honor to meet you," said one.

"I've watched you since you were a baby," said another.

"You are truly an amazing young woman," said a third.

Nashota must have sensed Shaylae's discomfort because she held up her hands and spoke. "Friends, I think you are overwhelming our guests. Come, let's eat."

The food, though unusual, was delicious. Shaylae was not surprised to discover there was no meat, only hundreds of varieties of fruit, vegetables, and herbs. The beverages were delicious; fruit juices, vegetable juices, and of course water, the purest, cleanest tasting water Shaylae had ever drunk. Some things tasted a little strange, at least new to her, but everything was delicious.

Asdza and Halona were having fun, playing with the other kids. Shaylae was concerned that they might be overshadowed by the unusually talented children of Tal'el'Dine'h, but she had nothing to worry about. Asdza had already shown signs of developing the power, and both were brilliant beyond their years. They played as if they had been friends for years.

Shaylae felt more relaxed than she had for a long time. After her grueling experience with Istas it was if she was in paradise. "I am in paradise," she said to herself, beaming, feasting her eyes and her breathing soul with this beautiful world. Even the knowledge that the storm was about to come upon her with full vengeance could not dispel her mood. She looked into Mika's eyes and sensed he felt the same too.

"You must be tired," said Nashota, appearing out of nowhere. "Let me show you to your rooms."

"Now you're talking," said Ayanna, hanging on to Sigmun.

It was still dark when she awoke, and the feeling of wellbeing had stayed with her throughout the night. Mika's steady breathing next to her brought a smile to her face, reassured her, and strengthened her. She snuggled up closer to him, put her arms around his warm body, and laid her head on his chest as the strong beating of his heart quickened hers. It was the first time she had slept next to him for what felt like a lifetime. He stirred and kissed her forehead, but she raised her head and kissed him lovingly on his lips.

"Oh how I love you, Shaylae of the Gentle Heart."

"And I love you too, my husband."

She nestled back onto his shoulder, safe in his arms. Together they lay like that until Chara brought the first slivers of dawn to the black sky. She carefully extricated herself from his embrace and headed toward the shower. The warm water and soap felt wonderful against her skin as she closed her eyes and indulged herself under the pulsating flow. She let her hands wander across her belly, now six months great with child.

"You are truly beautiful, Shaylae," said Mika, whistling under his breath.

"Help, there's a strange man in my bathroom," she said, whirling around in mock distress, covering herself as best she could with her hands. Even after ten years of marriage she was still a little uncomfortable standing in front of him like this, but still she tingled all over at the thought of him looking at her. "And how could you say I look beautiful," she said, putting her hands over her belly.

"Oh, Shaylae, you look more beautiful now than ever; the flower of womanhood." He slipped off his robe and climbed into the shower with her.

"The kids will be awake any minute," she protested, but Mika ignored her, kissing her passionately.

Still glowing, thirty minutes later Shaylae wandered into the girls' bedroom. "Come on, sleepy heads; time to…" she stopped dead in her tracks. Halona was sitting on her bed, eyes wide in terror, and Asdza's bed was empty.

Mika, who had walked in behind her must have sensed Shaylae's panic. "She probably just went to start breakfast," he said.

But Shaylae knew better. What she couldn't understand was how she had not sensed that something terrible had happened. Why had she not sensed her daughter's danger? Not only had she not sensed anything, she had actually been feeling relaxed and calm. She immediately sent a thought to Nashota. *"Asdza's missing."*

"Fifteen of our children missing too," replied Nashota. *"All about Asdza's age, or a little older."*

"Mika…"

"I heard," he said, taking Shaylae in his arms. "But why the children?"

"Shaylae, can you meet me in the council chamber," said Nashota.

"I'm coming too," said Mika.

She kissed him. "Not this time. You stay and take care of Halona."

CHAPTER 37

Asdza awoke to a pounding headache and intense light which hurt her eyes. She buried her head in her palms and applied pressure to her eyes with the heels of her hands, hoping to relieve the pain. She stopped. Through squeezed eyelids she saw that she was not in her bedroom. She wasn't even in the apartment that Nashota had put them in.

"Where am I?" came the plaintive cry of another kid.

Asdza's eyes were barely accustomed to the light as she strained to look around the around the stark, brilliantly lit room in which she and fifteen other children were just lifting themselves up from simple cots. Other voices joined adding their own questions. Asdza sensed an overwhelming feeling of confusion coming from those other kids which was quickly turning to fear, fueling her own.

A boy, maybe a year older than her, stood up, and trying unsuccessfully to shield his eyes from the light which seemed to emanate from every surface of the room, began walking its perimeter. The room was nearly square, approximately a ten meter square, and although it was difficult to see the ceiling, Asdza thought it was about ten meters high.

"No doors," he announced. "No windows either."

"Where are we?" asked a girl, also about the same age as the boy.

"It would appear we're in a ten meter square box," said the boy.

By now, all of the other kids were up and walking around; eleven girls, twelve including her, and four boys.

"And what are we doing here?" asked another girl.

The room suddenly became pitch black, and even though she knew it was impossible, it felt as if the temperature had dropped ten degrees. A couple of kids screamed.

"Hey, it's OK. Don't be afraid," said the boy, although there was a definite edge of fear in his voice too. "Everyone come to me, hold hands."

That sounded like a good idea to Asdza. She needed not only human comfort, but warmth. The temperature still seemed to be falling, but maybe it was just her reaction to this strange situation.

"Keep talking then so we can find you," said a girl.

"I'm over here," he said.

Asdza started carefully making her way toward the sound of his voice, bumping into other kids as they eased their way toward his voice. She lifted her hand to her face; she couldn't see it; inches in front of her eyes she saw nothing.

"That's it, keep coming. Let's hold hands, and keep each other warm."

"Maybe we can combine our power and contact our parents," said another boy.

"Good idea," said the first. "They're sure to be looking for us, and once we contact them this – whatever it is – will all be over."

Asdza reached the boy and touched his arm. "That's right," he said, as he put his arm around her shoulder. She felt nothing. Usually when she touched someone she could feel their soul, just barely, but enough to know she had connected with another person. This was definitely weird. Gradually the others all joined in, huddled together in the middle of the pitch black room. Asdza felt other pairs of hands and arms around but again, she felt nothing.

"OK," he said. "Let's sit down and form up into a circle."

There was a little unintentional jostling, but soon they managed to arrange themselves into a circle on the floor, all holding hands.

"Now, let's join together."

Yes, thought Asdza, that's what we need, soul-sharing. Whenever she was frightened or confused, soul-sharing with her mother brought her almost infinite comfort and warmth. But as Asdza held hands with the two either side of her, all she felt was hands getting colder.

"I don't feel anything," said a girl, verbalizing what Asdza imagined everyone in the circle was feeling.

"Give it a chance," said the boy. "Let's face it, this is an unusual situation for us, and I for one am a little... scared..."

"Me too," said a few of the other kids.

"But if we stay calm, and lean towards each other's strength, I'm sure we will find each other's souls soon."

He was probably right, thought Asdza. This was like nothing she had ever felt before… except… a dark thought came to her mind… this was exactly how she felt each time that Istas woman had come to her. "Istas," she said, almost involuntarily.

"Who?" said the boy.

"This is Istas' doing," she said.

"Who is Istas?" repeated the boy.

"An evil woman who has tried a few times to destroy my mother."

"You're Shaylae's daughter," said the boy. "Asdza."

"Yes, that's right."

"I've never heard of this Istas. Who is she?"

Without warning the light was back on, and each kid immediately broke the circle, shielding their eyes with their hands. A low noise began, seeming to come from all around them; from the floor, the walls, and from above them. It was a combination of a very low pitched droning and nerve-wracking grinding noise. It terrified Asdza so much that she felt she would lose control of her body. "Stop it, please make it stop," she said, but knew at once that the sound of her voice did not even travel a centimeter from her mouth, cancelled out, eaten up somehow, by the awful din. She managed to open her eyes a tiny crack, and saw fifteen other children all, like her, trying to block out the noise. Their lips moved, but no sound came out. Some of them looked to be screaming, but Asdza heard nothing but the reverberations of the droning.

On and on went the noise. Was it minutes or hours? Asdza hardly knew, only that she felt she was losing her mind, and then as abruptly as it had started it was over. Her ears were ringing, and she realized her whole body was shaking. The other kids seemed to be in a similarly disoriented state. Even the boy who had tried to rally them before looked as if he was in a state of complete panic.

She held out her hands. "Let's come together again," she said, trying to sound calm, but her voice trembled and had no conviction. "Come on. We can't let this defeat us."

"How long have we been here?" asked a girl, tears streaming down her face.

No one responded, each one looking at the others.

Finally the boy coughed and spoke again. "Asdza's right. We should come together again."

Asdza managed a weak smile as she held her hand out to him. He reached out and took it. Again she felt nothing, just his cold clammy hand. Gradually the others joined them until they were once again standing in a circle. She closed her eyes, and raising her head upward she spoke. "Holy Ones, help us. Help us to share each other's strength, to feel each other's warmth." Nothing, only emptiness.

"How old are you Asdza?" said the boy.

"Nearly nine," she replied. "You?"

"Earth years?"

She nodded.

"I'm almost eleven of your years; Ten-and-a-half Tal'el'Dine'h years."

"So, a Tal'el'Dine'h year is about four hundred days?" It seemed silly to be talking about the geology of Tal'el'Dine'h, given their circumstances, but her interest was piqued.

"Earth days, yes, but a Tal'el'Dine'h day is 25.9 Earth-hours, making a Tal'el'Dine'h year 370 of our days."

"Are you two crazy?" asked one girl in disbelief. "We have no idea where we are, what is happening to us, where our parents are… and you're having a science lesson."

Asdza shrugged. It had taken her mind off their predicament for a while, and she felt at least an intellectual bonding with this boy. She squeezed his hand harder, and tried to concentrate, willing herself to touch his soul, but there was still nothing.

"I'm thirsty," said one kid.

"And hungry," added another.

"I need a bathroom," wailed a third.

Once again, and without warning, they were plunged into the absolute blackness they had experienced earlier. A fine rain, like a mild drizzle fell upon them.

"Water," said Gren.

Asdza raised up her head and opened her mouth, grateful for the moisture.

"AGH!" she shouted, spitting it out. "It's awful."

Apparently other children had also tried to drink, with the same result. Asdza heard one kid vomiting. She barely held back her own gagging from the foul tasting rain. Gradually it increased, until soon it was a downpour, cold and painful against her skin. Like the sounds which had assaulted them earlier, the rain seemingly had no end. All she could do was to bury her head in her chest and squeeze her arms around herself in a vain attempt to keep warm and dry. She had no way of knowing exactly how long it rained, but her best guess was that after an hour it stopped, and the light gradually returned.

The kids looked even more confused than ever.

"How long have we been here?" said the boy.

"Hmm," said Asdza, rubbing her tummy. "Based on how hungry and thirsty I am, I would guess it's around lunch time."

"And if she took us first thing this morning, then we've been here maybe six hours."

Asdza nodded, as did the other kids. It made sense.

"I'm Gren, by the way," he said.

"And I'm Asdza, but you already knew that."

One by one, the rest of the kids introduced themselves, beginning with the boys.

"I'm Derian."

"Pelias..."

"Wahkan..."

Then the girls.

"Aponi..."

"Suleta..."

"Quanna..."

"Luyu..."

"Magena..."

"Doli..."

"Elu..."

"Hurit..."

"Tiva..."

"Takala..."

"Kanti..."

"And do any of you know anyone else here?"

They looked around at each other, and one-by-one they shook their heads.

"Then we have all been taken from different parts of the city," said Gren.

"Why don't we try to get to know one another?" suggested Kanti. "I love music. I have always wanted to be a musician."

"I love animals," said Doli.

The mood in the room lightened as each kid told the group something about themselves.

"I like girls," said Derian, a mischievous smile on his face. Everyone laughed.

"You like me, Derian?" asked Suleta flirtatiously, prompting even louder laughter. She was an extremely cute girl, probably the same age as Asdza.

A humming sound made them all turn around. It was not like the horrific sounds they had endured earlier, more like a subdued electric motor. In the middle of one of the walls a door appeared and slid open. Istas strode into the room; most of the kids cowered.

"It's Istas, isn't it?" whispered Gren.

"Uh huh," said Asdza.

"Well, children, how did you enjoy this morning's lesson?"

"Lesson?" said Gren.

"Yes, lesson. You'll realize how important it was as we spend some time together."

"But..." began Asdza.

"No questions for now. Now, let's take care of some practical things." She held up her hands and the white room gradually faded, morphed into a beautiful common area. Everything was made of rich, brown wood; the walls, the floor, the beams and the ceiling they held up. Around the room were a dozen bamboo couches and chairs, all with pale green cushions, arranged in groups of three around bamboo coffee tables. Woven bamboo screens sectioned the room into comfortably small areas were groups of people could chat and socialize without disturbing their neighbors. Along the almost the full length of one wall was a bar, complete with bar stools, and rows and rows of liquor and wine bottles. The other three walls had windows along their complete length, beginning a meter and a half from the floor and reaching to the ceiling; the views were spectacular. To the west, reflecting the setting sun was a beautiful lake with lush trees and plants along its shore. To the north and south hundreds of brightly colored birds flew in and out of the dense green forest.

"Where are we?" asked Kanti. "I don't recognize this at all."

"We're not on Tal'el'Dine'h, are we?" asked Gren, rhetorically.

Istas waved them off. "It doesn't matter where we are, only that we hope to accomplish great things over the next few months."

"Months?" said Asdza. "What about our parents?"

"Ah, if isn't Shaylae's daughter. Asdza, isn't it? Yes. You're really going to enjoy our time together."

"Without our parents..."

"Enough. Now, let me see. Oh yes," she said, walking to the left of the bar. "Follow me." The kids followed her through a door into a long corridor, ten or twelve doors along each side. "The lodge has twenty five rooms, but only eight are open, each with two beds and a private bathroom. You'll find everything you need; clothes, food, toiletries, linens... find yourself a room and a roommate," she said, waving her arm in the air. She walked through the door at the end of the corridor. "Through here we have kitchen, library, recreation, and an exercise room, everything you need..."

"Everything except our homes and our parents," said Kanti.

She turned around to face them, a kind but disappointed half-smile on her face. "Look, I know you're upset, but give it a few days. You'll hardly miss them by then, because believe me we have some exciting times ahead of us. You will learn so much; much more than your parents and teachers would ever have told you. You'll learn of the Universe, its beginning and its future. You'll learn of the origin and destiny of the Holy Ones; your own origins and destinies."

"But why us?" asked Asdza with slow determination. "And what will you gain from all of this?"

"It's not about me," she said. "It's about the ultimate truth, and the emergence of fairness and equity in the Universe."

"But the Holy Ones..." began Doli.

Istas held up her hands. "That's enough for today. We can continue these discussions tomorrow. In the meantime, why don't you freshen up and have something to eat. Change into some more comfortable clothes." She turned as if to leave. "Take the rest of the evening to get to know each other, and your new home, then get a good night's rest; we'll be busy in the morning." Istas simply disappeared again.

For a moment the kids just looked at one another. A hundred questions flooded into Asdza's mind, none of which seemed to jump to the front of the queue, so she asked none of them.

"Well, there's nothing we can do right now," said Gren. "Maybe we should get acquainted with our new home. And I for one could do with a shower, a change of clothes, and then something to eat."

That seemed like a good idea to Asdza, and apparently to everyone else. Asdza headed toward one of the bedrooms, the same one chosen by Suleta. The others easily split into twos and went into their bedrooms.

Asdza opened the door. The room was sparse, but quaint, and certainly adequate. Like the common room it had a rich brown wood floor. A bunk bed stood against one wall, and against the opposite wall two nightstands, one with a candle, the other a flask of water and two glasses. The far wall had a thick green curtain across its full width. Asdza walked over to it, opened it and looked out over the same tranquil lake. Their small bathroom had a toilet, a washbasin, and a shower. The closet though was not small; it was almost the size of their room. Along each side hung dresses, shirts, pants, and robes. Under the hangers she found shoes and slippers. She pulled out a drawer and found socks and underwear. It was then she noticed her own name in English above the clothes rail. She looked to the other side of the closet where Suleta was discovering a similar array of clothing, but the writing above hers was in a language totally foreign to her; she assumed it said "Suleta."

Suleta stepped forward, mouth open, and ran her hands through the clothes. She pulled a shirt from its hanger and held it against her. "These are mine? This is weird; just my size. How did she know?"

Asdza shook her head, and grabbed a towel, soap and shampoo. "Well, it certainly is a mystery. Regardless, unless you'd like to go first, I'd like to take shower."

"Sure, go ahead."

An hour later everyone had freshened up and had gathered in the kitchen. The boys were ready first and were busily cooking up dinner.

"Smell's good," said Kanti.

"Lots of vegetables, but not like any I've seen on Tal'el'Dine'h." He stuck his nose a little closer to the pot. "They smell delicious."

"Those are called potatoes," said Asdza. "And that's broccoli, carrots, cauliflower, tomatoes, peppers…" she added, pointing to the others.

"I guess it's official then," said Doli. "We're definitely not on Tal'el'Dine'h."

Gren laid out plates and cups on the table while Pelias and Derian shared out the food. Kanti picked up a pitcher of water and started to fill the glasses. Suleta joined in, starting at the opposite end of the table. Soon they were all sitting down, eating and drinking, socializing as if they had been friends for years.

It's amazing what good food and clean clothes will do for your mood, thought Asdza. She wasn't sure if she should suggest that they not become too comfortable or trusting of their new environment. Istas was obviously up to something, and have them relaxed like this could only help her. But she decided against it. The food tasted too good, and the company of these fifteen other extremely bright and good humored kids was far too intoxicating to allow herself the luxury of worrying.

Istas looked on at the scene of domestic tranquility with a satisfied smile. "See," she said. "See how they have already fallen into my trap. Already they are woefully underestimating their plight." She turned to Rolling Darkness. "Just as you underestimated Shaylae, fool, now these children underestimate me."

"But you don't know what they're capable of. Shaylae's girl worries me the most. Are you sure it's not you who is underestimating them?"

Istas's face tightened, her teeth clenched, as she raised her hands toward him, ready to deliver a punishing bolt, but she laughed as Rolling Darkness cowered in abject fear. She sneered at him. "Soon I will not need you, but I may let you stay and bask in my glory." She raised her voice and seared him with her gaze. "That is of course, unless you continue to defy and doubt me."

Rolling Darkness fell back, bowing his head. "Forgive me mistress," he said.

"Of course, my little pet," she said, patting his head.

CHAPTER 38

With Shaylae and Nashota as the only occupants, the council chamber felt empty, like Shaylae's heart. Not once had she entertained the possibility of any of her children being in danger – it was not something a parent could begin to imagine – but now it had hit her full force. Fear for her own life was nothing to the fear that now totally consumed her. Even facing situations in which Mika or Ayanna's lives were in danger could not compare to how she was feeling at the moment. She couldn't think straight, and her mind was in such a state of panic that she couldn't even commune with the Holy Wind, and that made her emptiness all the more profound.

"Shaylae, I'm sorry," said Nashota. "I wish there was some comfort I could give you. But I don't know where Istas has taken our children, or what she intends to do with them."

"I think I know what she intends."

"You do? What?"

"It's been staring me in the face. Why does she have power over Rolling Darkness? Why didn't the Dark Ones, particularly the First Prophet have similar power over him?"

"I don't know. Because they weren't as evil, I suppose."

"No, that's not it. Having a physical body gives me power of him, but the Dark Ones all had physical bodies, and yet they were his servants."

"So..."

"So, what do Istas and I have in common?"

"Not much..."

"A lot more than you think."

Nashota shrugged.

210

"You too, Nashota. You know the answer," said Shaylae. "Both of us have gone beyond faith; we both know without any doubt that the Holy Ones are real. And I believe very few reach that level of knowledge. The Dark Ones themselves only had 'faith' in Rolling Darkness, the same way that most people have 'faith' in the Holy Ones. They didn't know for sure."

"Shaylae, that must be it. Knowing the Holy Ones, and then turning away from them must somehow give her power even over the legions of hell."

"There's a religion on Earth that has a similar concept. As I recall it, their version of hell is only temporary, eventually even the most evil will be redeemed from hell, but there is another place, a place they call perdition, from which there is no escape."

"Of course," said Nashota. "And I think they have another name for the children of perdition – the Gadiantons. And these Gadiantons don't go to hell; they go to perdition where they rule over Rolling Darkness and his legions for the rest of eternity"

"And they rule over them because they have bodies?"

"Yes."

Shaylae could not even begin to fathom such a fate. "And you think that Istas has reached this point?"

"Yes."

"This point of no return?"

"Yes."

For a moment Shaylae felt utter hopeless sorrow and pity for Istas. "And there is no hope for her."

"None."

"And this is the fate she intends for our children."

"Yes, but our children are not there yet. They have not yet reached this point of knowledge that you and I and Istas have reached."

"That's why she wants them now. She wants to catch them just when they are on the verge."

"And if she is able to persuade any to join her cause."

Shaylae shuddered. "Then I think they'd be as lost as she is."

"Lost?"

"Yes. Lost for all eternity." The possibility that Asdza could be so lost was infinitely worse than thinking about her losing her life. The pity she had felt for Istas just a few moments earlier faded away. "So, we have to find them. There has to be a way."

"But how?"

"Well, first, we should be able to either verify they are on Tal'el'Dine'h, or eliminate it from our search."

"How?"

"When I was looking for Mika and Ayanna ten years ago, there was a place on Yurob where my mind could not penetrate. Somehow Denab had shielded it from me. We need to determine if there is anywhere on Tal'el'Dine'h that is closed to us."

"But, Shaylae, you were looking in a very small location, the imperial palace; and I'm assuming it is a sort of process of elimination to find such an inaccessible place. You're talking about combing an entire planet?"

"Yes. But what other choice do we have. And it doesn't matter how long it takes, since we have no other plan."

"If we use every adult…"

"Yes," said Shaylae. "Yes, but how would you coordinate such a search?"

Nashota barely smiled. "Ah, I see you've never experienced living among a whole planet of people with the power. I'll get Niyol to organize it; no one can organize things like Niyol."

CHAPTER 39

Asdza awoke feeling refreshed and relaxed. She had slept well, and so it seemed had her roommates. She heard restful music in the background, and wondered if it was another of Istas' tricks to relax them.

"Time for a first day of school, children." It was Istas' voice, calm and soothing. "One hour from now we'll meet in the common area, and I'll explain what it is you will be learning over the next few months."

Asdza's first reaction was to resist, not show up, somehow find a way to reel against Istas, but she was at a loss as to where to begin. She shrugged. "Might as well get ready," she said.

Suleta nodded but didn't say anything.

An hour later all sixteen of them were gathered in the common room. Some were looking out of the windows at the glorious scenery. A few were simply sitting on the bamboo couches, staring into space. Asdza found herself at the center of the room with Gren, Pelias, Kanti and Suleta.

"Any ideas?" asked Suleta.

"Why she wants us? What she intends to teach us?" said Gren. "None whatsoever."

"All I know is that it can't be good." Shaylae had not told Asdza much about her time with Istas, but it was enough for Asdza to realize that Istas wanted to recruit her mom, and that she had failed. "Somehow she needs us."

"But we're kids," said Pelias.

"Yes, but not like kids anywhere else in the universe," said Gren.

"Yes, for one thing, you are all much more intelligent and advanced…" began Asdza.

"Don't leave yourself out," said Gren with a wry smile.

"I'm not as advanced as you guys," she said with a shrug. "And we need to be extremely careful. She is a genius and knows exactly how to manipulate us. We must not be persuaded by her."

"Not be persuaded to do what?" asked Kanti.

"I have no idea. Only like I said, it can't be good."

"Well, children, gather round."

Istas had materialized in the middle of the room.

"Where are we?" asked Gren.

"And where are our parents?" asked Kanti.

"Why are we here?" asked Suleta.

"I can't answer the first two questions… yet, but as to the third, the answer is simple. You are here to expand your minds. Expand them in ways you never thought possible. You're embarking on a journey of knowledge."

"More than we would have gained back on Tal'el'Dine'h?"

Istas laughed. "Oh yes, infinitely more. Unfortunately your parents, all of the adults on Tal'el'Dine'h, are only concerned with imparting as much knowledge to you that will keep you captive."

"Captive? What are you talking about?" said Pelias.

"Yes, captive, I'm afraid. Your minds were being filled with a terribly one-sided view of the Holy Ones and the universe they created. You think you are free? You are not. You think you are open-minded? Not at all. In fact, your minds, and unfortunately the minds of most of the adults on your world are closed entirely to some of the universe's most exciting possibilities. In order to be truly free you have to see both sides of the situation and then make up your mind for yourself. How can you be free when you are only told one point of view? That's why we're here."

"But…"

"Enough questions. Why don't we begin; I think you'll find your questions being answered as we go along." She motioned her arms in a circle around her. "Come, sit."

Reluctantly the children began to gather around Istas.

"Come on. These are going to be the most fascinating moments of your lives so far. Don't dawdle."

As the children sat, comfortable cushions appeared for them to relax on. The room morphed back into the same clinical white room they had originally found themselves. The light dimmed, but not entirely black as there was a dim light hovering in the center of the room, in which waved diaphanous clouds, almost like silk cloths wafting in a gentle breeze.

"What are we looking at? Anyone know?"

There were a lot of blank stares.

"You're looking at eternity. I would say that you are looking into the past, but words like past, present and future have no meaning in eternity. Neither do words like distance or volume; anything to do with time or space is a non sequitur in eternity. The only truth about this eternity that in it your universe, my universe, doesn't exist."

"I don't understand," said Gren.

"Think about it. You believe that our universe was created. So, where was it created?"

There was a brief silence, and then Asdza spoke up. "The Holy Ones somehow exist in eternity, and they created our universe here."

Istas clapped her hands together. "Very good, Asdza."

Asdza felt a burst of pride. But then, wait, what am I doing, she thought. It's only been a few minutes and already she is getting to me. Asdza realized she had to be a lot more guarded than this.

"But it's not completely correct," she said, holding up a finger, a benevolent frown on her face. "The Holy Ones exist in a universe, like ours in fact. And our universe is a part of theirs." She held her hands up. "But I don't expect you to understand that, and it's not important. What is important is that as Holy Ones they can move between their universe and eternity; and between their universe and ours."

"Can they move between their universe and any other universe?"

"A very good question, Suleta. No, they cannot, but to explain that would take us on a diversion I don't want to explore right now. I will only say that you can think of it organized like a family and they can only travel to universes that are part of their posterity."

"Posterity?"

"Yes, their creations, and the creations of those they created. They cannot travel upward, if you like, only downward."

"Then there are universes above them?" asked Pelias.

"'Above' may not be the best word, Pelias, but essentially what you're saying is true."

Asdza recalled what her mom had told, only two nights ago. Was it only two nights? She had told her she had traveled in spirit to the Holy Ones, and they had said eternity was an infinite, unbroken chain. She had no idea what her mom was getting at, but it didn't matter.

"Wait a minute," said Gren, his face all screwed up, his forehead furrowed. "Are you saying that we can create our own universe? We can become Holy Ones."

"Have our own creations?" said Kanti.

"And our own children, as we are children to the Holy Ones?" said Pelias.

"Yes," said Istas. "You can become as the Holy Ones." She smiled, as if beaming with pride. "You kids, you're amazing. I had thought it would take us days to get to this point, but look at you. You're way ahead of what I expected."

Asdza had to admit she was good, very charismatic. She seemed genuinely pleased and proud, and it was all Asdza could do to stop herself from being drawn into the enthusiasm. Some of the others were not so cautious, hanging on to Istas' every word as if she was a superstar. Gren and some of the others looked a little less trusting but Asdza was afraid that if Istas could be this persuasive in less than an hour, what could she accomplish in a month?

"Why haven't we ever been taught this?" asked Wahkan. Wahkan did not look so taken in.

"Your elders and your parents have decided that this truth can only be taught once you have reached a particular level of knowledge."

"And what level is that exactly?"

"Ask Asdza, Wahkan. She knows," said Istas, turning toward her. There was an edge to Istas' voice, which Asdza was sure was designed to plant seeds of distrust of her in the other kid's minds. "Why don't you tell us?" She paused, then added caustically, "daughter of Yanaba."

Her mother had hinted at it; hinted that until a person reached a perfect knowledge of the Holy Ones, much more than a belief or faith, the knowledge of her true destiny would mean nothing. But how would she explain this to the others? She hadn't reached that level herself yet, so she said nothing. It was awkward.

Fortunately Wahkan was still not satisfied either, and he broke the silence. "Well, if we're not supposed to have this knowledge yet, why are you telling us?"

"Oh, Wahkan," she said, her voice dripping with sadness and concern. She walked over to him and touched his shoulder. "I didn't say you weren't supposed to have it, only that your parents don't want you to tell you."

"And why would our parents hold anything back from us, unless they thought it was for our own good?"

"Now that, Kanti," she said, pointing her finger at her, "is the real question." She paused, adding to the tension and drama in the room. "And it's the reason we're here."

How clever, thought Asdza. We're like chicks being led by their mother hen. Well, not all of us. She could see that there were others, like Wahkan, who were not satisfied.

"Then what is the reason?" asked Gren.

"Gren, what I want is for you to answer that question yourself. I think as we get to know each other better, and as you learn more, the answer will become obvious. But, I do think it's important that you find the answer, rather than me giving it to you."

There were a few audible sighs.

"Hey, you guys; give me a break," she said with a friendly laugh. "All will become clear; trust me."

The light in the room faded, the diaphanous cloud dissipated and one of the walls seemed to melt away. What appeared in its place was an image of a huge compound, surrounded by tall wire fences topped with barbs. Dark clouds hung in the sky, not allowing even a hint of sunshine to show through. Smoke filled the air above the compound, huge clouds of it billowing from an enormous chimney in the distance. Rows and rows of huts, hundreds of them, stood like gravestones in an endless cemetery.

Istas sucked her breath through her clenched teeth. "I'm sorry kids, but what I have to show you now is going to be very unpleasant," she said apologetically. "I've seen it before, and to be honest, I'm not sure I could stomach seeing it again. But I'm afraid you have to see it."

"What is this?" asked Kanti.

"We are in Poland, Earth, in the year 1943. It's summer, although you'd never know it, and it's about 5 am in the morning. In a while the occupants of those huts will begin to appear, along with those who have captured and subjected them. I warn you, it's not pleasant, and there is no way you can shield your eyes from what you're about to see. Only trust me, that it is necessary for you to understand your true destiny."

"How can you force us to look?"

Istas didn't bother to elaborate. "I'm going to leave you here for a while, and after you have seen enough I'm taking you to Yurob, fourteen years ago, when the Dark Ones ruled there. Later, perhaps, I will take you to Asdza's home, to see how some of her ancestors, your kinsmen, were treated by the invaders from Europe."

"You will take us?' questioned Asdza. "You mean we are actually in Poland, a hundred-and-eighty-five years ago?"

Istas merely cocked her head wistfully. "I'll be back in a few hours, or days, however long it takes" she said, and disappeared. Suddenly they were no longer looking at the compound, it surrounded them; they were in it.

CHAPTER 40

Mika sat watching Shaylae helplessly. There was nothing he could do to help her as she scoured Tal'el'Dine'h with her mind, reaching out to every square meter of the planet, hoping to find a blind spot. Mika knew that so far she had found nothing; neither had anyone else who was searching. Nashota and Niyol were looking; so were the parents of the other children, and like Shaylae they had not slept or even rested for two days. Every adult on Tal'el'Dine'h was helping as best they could but of course they could not devote anything like the same amount of time as Shaylae and the other parents. At least she was doing something to find their daughter, but there was nothing he could do; so he sat and watched her.

"She has to eat," said Ayanna. She was carrying two plates of food, and Sigmun was behind her with a pitcher of water and glasses.

Mika shrugged. "You could try..." he said, gesturing toward her.

"Shay, you have to eat," she said, putting the food on the table, and walking over to her. "Supposing you do find where Istas has her, what condition will you be in to help her?"

Shaylae's visibly relaxed and breathed a huge sigh. "I suppose you're right." She stood up looking tired and worried. She came and sat at the table where Ayanna had placed the food and began nibbling at a sandwich.

"I'm assuming you've not found anything yet," said Ayanna.

"Nothing. So far no one has found any blind spots."

"How much of the planet have you covered?" asked Mika.

Shaylae shook her head. "So far we've covered less than ten percent."

"At that rate it's going to take another eighteen days," said Sigmun.

"That's assuming that we can keep this pace up..."

"Which I don't think you can, Shay. Look at you; you're worn out."

"I have to. What else can I do?"

"Then at least get some sleep."

She looked up at the clock on the wall. "OK, but make sure I don't sleep more than an hour." She left the room, almost stumbling from exhaustion, and headed to her bedroom.

Ayanna's gaze followed her, and when she was sure she was out of hearing range she turned to Mika. "Mik, I've got an idea."

"Something we can do to help?"

"Maybe, but if nothing else it will make give us something to do instead of just sitting moping around."

"OK, what is it?"

"It's just a hunch, but I think she has the kids back on Earth."

"Why Earth?"

"Well, I'm hoping she at least has them on one of the four planets; even that we cannot know for sure. But, if she does, then I'm betting on Earth."

"Yes, but why Earth?" he repeated.

"Lots of reasons." She held her hand up, extending her index finger. "First, it's the most developed of all of the four planets; it would be easier to hide a structure, or compound, or whatever, where she might have them."

"Well, that makes sense; I suppose," agreed Mika reluctantly, but he was still skeptical.

Her middle finger joined her index finger. "How about this – think of the irony of it. Back on Shaylae's home planet; the last place she'd expect us to look."

Mika thought about this. It made sense, well, just a little. Istas did seem to have a penchant for irony. "And searching on Earth should be a lot easier, considering the thousands of satellites covering the planet."

Ayanna extended her ring finger. "That's my third point," she said. "But here's the kicker." Her little finger finally completed the four. "There's a gazillion people on Earth who can help us."

Ayanna was making sense, practical sense, just like she always did. Mika felt a little ashamed. Here he had sat for two days, helpless, worrying, doing nothing, watching his wife. Ayanna had offered at least some action, and who knew, perhaps it would lead them to his daughter.

"Let's do it," he said, balling his hands into fists. "We should get the rest of the crew in here; go over the plan with them."

Ayanna had already walked over to the door and opened it; in walked her crew, looking ready to go.

"I've already briefed them, and they're all on board."

"Great," said Mika. "Ok, let's make some plans. How long to fire up the engines on Enterprise, and get her ready for flight."

"Once we get back on board, maybe two hours," said Jane.

"Come to think of it," said Steve. "How will we get back on board?"

"I can put you back on your ship." Unnoticed, Nashota had joined them.

"Nashota. Then you think this is a good idea?"

She shrugged. "It's an idea, which is better than no idea."

"Exactly what I was telling him," said Ayanna.

"So, let's get you back on your ship."

"Great," said Mark. He turned to Jane. "How long to get back to Earth?"

"With the recent improvements in the hyperspace generators we can do it in three jumps…" began Jane, but Nashota interrupted her.

"I can put you in orbit around Earth."

"Fantastic," said Mika. "Let's do it. What are we waiting for?"

"Mika, are you sure this is what you want to do?"

"Absolutely. I'm with Ayanna on this. I've a feeling her hunch is correct."

"Very well," said Nashota. She waved her arms and they were back on board Enterprise, standing on the bridge. Another wave of her arm and Tal'el'Dine'h disappeared. "You're back in normal space."

"Wait," said Mika. "Shouldn't we say goodbye to Shaylae; tell her what we're doing."

Nashota shook her head. "No, let her sleep. I'll tell her when she wakes."

Mika wasn't sure about this, but he felt he should trust Nashota. Perhaps she had another reason for not wanting to let Shaylae know before they left.

"Now, are you ready?"

"Ready as we'll ever be," said Steve.

Everyone nodded. There was a slight feeling of queasiness, but when they looked on the view screens, there was Earth, in its entire blue and white splendor.

CHAPTER 41

There was no way to describe what they had seen, what they had been forced to witness. While Asdza had read about this in history books, seen documentaries and fictional movies that focused on this horrific time, nothing could have prepared her for what she saw. The other kids looked equally stunned, horrified, and sickened; no one spoke for a long time. Even though the scene had long since been replaced by the view of the lake and the forest, Asdza could not get the image of those poor people, starved, half naked, frozen, living in those desperate conditions. Just when she thought it couldn't have gotten any worse, an old steam engine hauling fifty cattle cars had pulled into the compound. The train jolted to a halt and immediately soldiers unlocked the sliding doors and pushed them open. The smell that escaped those cars was foul. At least a hundred people were packed into each car, and as the doors slid opened they tumbled out, some falling and hurting themselves, some were already dead. Men, women and children poured out of those cars; some quite young, some crippled with age. Boys and girls milled aimlessly among them, as if looking for their parents. Many of the women held babies in their arms.

The soldiers began the sickening task of separating them into two groups. The first group was quite small and was made up of young men and women, and teenaged girls and boys. Perhaps one in ten was shepherded into this group, the lucky ones. They would make it to the huts; some might even live until the allies came to free them. The others, the very young and the elderly were methodically and quickly separated into another group. Babies were ripped from the arms of screaming mothers in the first group and handed to any in the larger group who would take them. The larger group was marched toward the showers... Asdza vomited many times watching this horror unfold. The thought came to her mind: how could the Holy Ones allow this, until she realized with revulsion that this was exactly the question Istas wanted them to ask.

Finally Gren spoke. "Did that really happen," he asked, his voice barely a whisper.

"It couldn't have," said Suleta.

"I'm afraid it did," said Asdza. "And it wasn't just in Nazi Germany that these things happened. The Soviet Union, Cambodia, Rwanda, Sudan, Iraq, and many other countries have seen horrors equal to this, perhaps worse."

"Why?" asked Kanti. "And how can people do this to each other."

"And why do the Holy Ones not stop it?"

There. Pelias had voiced the question that had to be on everyone's mind. Istas looked very pleased with herself.

"Children, you should eat and rest before I take you to Yurob."

"I don't want to eat," said one.

"I couldn't eat even if I wanted to," said another.

"Very well," said Istas. "Let's go back to Yurob."

The scenes they witnessed on Yurob were as sickening as those they had seen in Poland, except here it was not just within a few compounds, it was the whole planet. An elite few used the rest of the population as slaves. Hundred of millions of men, women and children worked in appalling conditions, dying at thirty of crippling, painful illnesses. Those teenagers cursed with beauty had a worse fate: they were shipped off to the various regional and imperial palaces where they would be forced to entertain the ruling class in unthinkable ways. Again, Asdza had heard of this period of Yurob's history, her mom had even alluded to it, but nothing could have prepared her for this.

For hours, they were forced to watch these inhuman scenes, but Istas wasn't finished with them. After they had a short rest she took them to nineteenth century America, where they watched soldiers destroy native villages, burn them to the ground, rape innocent women and girls. She took them to Acoma, the Sky City, where they watched Spanish soldiers throw men, women and children from the cliffs of the mesa a hundred meters to their deaths and then chop of the right feet of the men who survived.

Asdza had lost track of time, but she was sure that it was days before Istas finally left them alone. Everyone was subdued, and not much was said about the things they had witnessed. All were in a state of shock. No one, especially kids like themselves, should be forced to watch such horrors. But in a perverted sort of way, Asdza had to give credit to Istas; by now everyone had to be asking the same question: how could the Holy Ones allow such things to happen? It was a question that was certainly on her mind, and one for which she didn't have an answer.

CHAPTER 42

Three days, and still nothing. Not one square inch of the planet that they had so far combed with their minds was closed off to them. She was beginning to wonder if Istas was still on Tal'el'Dine'h. It had been her first thought that she would have remained here, but now she was having her doubts. What if she was on Earth as Ayanna suspected? What if she was on Yurob or Sanostee? What if she was on a totally different planet, somewhere not yet discovered? And then another, even scarier thought hit her: what if she wasn't even in the present time? What if she had taken them to the past, or to the future? Yes, that was also a possibility. She could be absolutely anywhere in time or space. What hope did she have of finding her? The despair that had been building in her the last few days reached a critical point. Was she ever going to see Asdza again?

"Shaylae, we think we may have found something."

She jumped and whirled around. "Nashota, you startled me."

"I'm sorry, but we think we may have found a dead spot, over on the other side of the planet."

Her despair changed into hope. "Where?"

Nashota brought a picture to her mind of a lush, green forest, a slow moving river meandering through it. She moved along the river, until her mind could penetrate no further. "You're right. Let's go over the there now, right now."

"Let me get some of the other parents…"

"No, just you and me. We can come back and get them once we have a better idea of what we might be up against."

"I think it might be dangerous."

"You coming or not?" she asked almost impatiently.

"OK, OK, I'm coming."

In an instant they were standing by the river, at the edge of the lush forest. "Here. This is where the dead spot begins," said Shaylae. "I say we go right in. Our minds may not be able to penetrate this shield, or whatever it is, but we can walk right through it."

Nashota made as if to stop her, but Shaylae was already walking along the river bank. She came to a stop. "OK, we're inside of the barrier, but I'm not sensing anything here." Her mind could now explore the whole area, but to her acute disappointment, she found nothing. No sign of Istas or the kids. Once again her heart fell. She had been sure that they had found them, built up her hope, and now that hope was dashed.

"Shaylae, I'm sorry. We have to keep looking, I guess…"

"Wait, I think I recognize this place." She walked into the forest. "Yes, a little further along this way there is a hut."

They followed the path, and soon came to a clearing, and just as Shaylae had said, there was a small hut.

"This is where she held me captive. All that time and I had no idea where we were. Even after I escaped, I was never sure what planet we had been on."

Nashota brightened. "But now we're sure she held you in the present, not the past or the future."

"Yes, so it's a fairly safe bet she has our children in the present." Shaylae sounded reinvigorated. "And if she kept me on Tal'el'Dine'h, why wouldn't she keep the children here. We will find them; I know we will."

"Then let's get back to our search."

***

"I think we can get the resources you need," said Harley.

"Thanks, Admiral," said Mika.

"How far back do you think we should go?" asked Anne.

"Hard to say, but let's start by going back a month."

"And you say we're looking for anything unusual that wasn't there a month ago," she said with a chuckle. "That's gonna be hard to explain to the analysts."

"Yeah, I suppose. Let's just tell them we're looking for new structures; structures which appeared out of nowhere. No, wait, that doesn't sound right either." He thought for a moment. "Can they compare the data to all building permits issued, and look for either a new permit which resulted in a completed building in a very short time, or better still, a building for which no permit was issued."

"Yes, I think that would be better," said Harley. "Anything else?"

"Let's start with that. If that doesn't yield anything, we'll expand the search."

"OK, I'll get right on it."

"How long does that kind of analysis take?"

"Not as long as you think. Of course, all the satellite images are processed digitally, so we're looking for 0's and 1's that weren't there a month ago. We're still talking about millions of terabytes of data, so it may take twenty-four hours or so. Then we've got to cross-reference those findings with the permit data… I'm guessing we could be looking at a couple of days, total."

"Sounds good to me."

"I'll let you know as soon as we have any news. What are you doing in the mean time?"

"We're staying in orbit. I think I want to steer clear of the ISA. They've probably got too many questions about our last little trip."

"Nothing to worry about there," said Harley. "The folks at the Pentagon were furious at first, but someone had the insight to pass it on to the President at which point he stifled all investigations. Would you believe we were called to the White House? After all these years only a handful of people really know what happened aboard Revenge, or on Yurob, and one of them is the sitting president. Once we explained that Shaylae was in trouble he was able to smooth things over with the ISA. They demanded an answer; he refused to give it."

"Also, Shaylae is still one of Director McLaughlin's pet projects," said Anne. "He follows her every move." McLaughlin, the current Director of the FBI, had been second in command fourteen years earlier and had originally assigned Shaylae's case to Anne. "I think he has a special place in his heart for her. I'm sure he had something to do with hushing up your last escapade."

"Either way, I think we'll stay in orbit. It will be easier to get to anywhere on earth in a hurry – that is if we find anything."

"OK, I'll let you know as soon as we have any leads."

***

"That was horrible," said Gren. It was early morning, and everyone was getting out of bed, taking showers, and grabbing breakfast. "I hardly slept at all."

"Me neither," said Suleta. "I could never have imagined..."

Asdza was still feeling sick to her stomach at what they had been forced to witness, although witness was hardly the right word; Istas had put them right in the middle of those horrible scenes. There was nowhere to hide, no way to look away. And even if they had looked away, the sounds, the smells, the very atmosphere of those awful events would have filled their whole beings. Apparently none of the other kids had slept very well either. Everyone looked worn out, and perhaps a little older than they had just a few days ago.

Istas appeared in the middle of the common room, looking almost contrite and conciliatory. "I'm sorry I had to put you through that," she said. "But believe me, it was necessary. And I promise you there will be nothing like that for the rest of your stay here."

"We don't want to stay," said Pelias. "We want to go home now."

Istas held up her hands. "I'm sorry," she said, apologizing for the second time. "But that's not possible. Not until we've had a chance to talk about what you have seen."

"Where are we?" asked Asdza.

Istas waved her off. "It doesn't matter where we are. What matters is that you come to understand a little more of the history of our universe."

"Oh, please," moaned Kanti. "I couldn't take more history lessons like the last one."

"No more first-hand experiences. I want to go over what you already know, perhaps help you to fill in some of the gaps in your knowledge. But more importantly, I think you're ready to ask some of the questions which your parents have never asked, and certainly never wanted you to ask." She motioned in a semi-circle in front of her. "Come, sit down and let's begin."

Slowly, reluctantly, the kids sat on the floor in front of Istas. Asdza wasn't sure what to expect. She seemed very friendly, even loving; not what she had expected from the stories her mom had told her.

"Ok, let's just start with the short version. Before the Holy Ones created the Universe, they showed to us their plan, their Eternal Plan, they called it. At the time we were so happy that according to one writer we all jumped for joy; all of us except one. He had a few questions. He wanted to know why there would be suffering. Apparently no one else seemed to care that some of them would spend their whole lives in misery and suffering, just as you witnessed."

For a moment there was silence while Istas let this sink in. Pelias was the first to speak up, to ask the question that Asdza figured was probably on everyone's mind. "What did the Holy Ones say? How did they answer him?"

"They gave him the same line that your parents give you: that it's all about free will and growth."

"And isn't that important?" asked Asdza.

"You tell me. Is it important for you Asdza? For someone like you who has never had to face suffering. How have you exercised your free will in life so far? Everything has been handed to you on a silver platter has it not? How is that a result of your free will?"

It was a good question. Asdza had to admit she didn't really have a good answer to it.

"And what about those children who were taken to those horrible camps, gassed, and their frail little bodies burned? What about those girls and boys, some not much older than you, who were forced to become sexual slaves for the perverted rulers of Yurob? What chance did they ever have to fulfill their destiny as children of the Holy Ones? How did the fact that they had free will help them?"

An even better question, but Asdza was curious about what point Istas was trying to make. "Why are you telling us this?"

"Because I want you to know why Rolling Darkness was cast out. I want you to know what he had to say about this awful plan, and truly, I think it is an awful plan, and what he suggested to improve it."

"How could the plan not be perfect?" asked Suleta. "If the Holy Ones are perfect, then wouldn't their plan be perfect?"

"You've all assumed that the Holy Ones are perfect?" She paused for a moment looking around the room. "Well, let's have a show of hands. Who thinks the Holy Ones are perfect, omnipotent, all powerful, all knowing, possessing infinite love for all of their children?"

Asdza's hand shot up, as did a few of the others, but some of the kids, including Gren, took their time raising their hands.

"So, I see, there is some doubt, at least with some of you. But let me ask you this: how do you know the Holy Ones are omnipotent? Who told you? Did they?" No one volunteered an answer. "Asdza, why don't you answer for those of you who are sure that they are all that you believe them to be."

Asdza was flustered, and she had to admit to herself that she really didn't have a good answer. "It's something I've always believed." It was the worst thing she could have said, but it was too late; the words had already left her mouth.

"Exactly," said Istas.

"But…" she stammered, trying to recover. "Surely it makes sense that they are perfect. How else could they have created the Universe?"

"Now that," said Istas, "is a good question. Let's think about that for a while." She stood up and slowly walked around the group of kids, their gazes fixed surely upon her. "Let's list the things that are indisputable about the Holy Ones," she said. She held up her hand in a fist, and then flipped up her index finger. "Number one: they created the Universe. Everyone agree?" Everyone nodded. "OK, someone else. What else do we know for sure about the Holy Ones?"

"Wait a minute," said Asdza. "All of us, you too apparently, agree that the Holy Ones created the Universe. But that doesn't make it a fact, does it? Millions people on Earth who believe that everything was an accident, maybe billions. They don't even believe the Holy Ones exist. Isn't it a matter of faith?"

"Asdza, you wonderful child," she said, clapping her hands together and smiling broadly. Asdza had the horrible feeling she had just walked into a trap. "No it doesn't make it a fact." She turned to Gren. "Gren let me ask you; do you believe your parents know the Holy Ones are real, or do they have faith?"

"They know for sure," he said confidently.

"As do all of the adults who live on Tal'el'Dine'h." She turned to Asdza again. "As do some of the inhabitants of Earth; Shaylae Lucero being one of them. They've all had experiences, which while very personal to each of them, have assured them beyond any doubt that the Holy Ones exist."

Asdza knew this to be true. And while she hadn't had such an experience, her mom assured her that one day she would.

"So, can we agree that it is a fact?" Reluctantly Asdza had to admit she had led them like puppies on a leash. Istas held her hand up again, with her index finder extended. "So, who can tell me something else we know for sure about the Holy Ones? Gren?"

"They more than just created us, they are our parents."

"OK, let's pursue that one for a moment. How can they be our parents? We have parents here don't we." Istas was really starting to reel the kids in, like catching fish in a net.

"Yes," said Luyu. "But the Holy Ones are the parents of our spirits."

Istas nodded. "Everyone agree?" Lots of nodding heads. "And that this physical life," she said passing her hands over her body, "is just temporary. We will one day return to the Holy Ones. Certainly there's a lot more to that," she added. "But for now with our limited understanding we all accept that the Holy Ones are our parents?" She extended her middle finger. "What else?"

Magena put up her hand. "They are old. They must have existed before the creation of the Universe."

"We won't discuss the theoretical difficulties that the concept of 'before the universe was created' introduces, but essentially you're right." She extended her middle finger.

"They are omnipotent," chimed in Asdza.

"Asdza, Asdza," she said, wagging her finger at her, and with an almost friendly grin on her face. "This is where we're trying to get to. Let's not jump ahead."

"Why not? I believe it to be a fact." She turned to the other kids. "Who else believes this to be a fact?"

"Wait, before you answer, let's go back to the awful things I made you experience. Would you have stepped in to save those poor children being led to their deaths?"

"Well I would have," said Doli.

"What about those poor young men and women forced to perform for the Dark Ones?"

Most of the kids shuddered. "I would have," said Elu.

"And what about all the terrible diseases that take the lives of young children, tearing them away from their parents? Or the young parents who are killed leaving behind little children with no one to take care of them?

Would you change that if you could?" Most of the kids nodded their heads. Suleta, Kanti and she were the only ones who seemed skeptical but Gren seemed almost enthusiastic. "Yes, of course you would." She took a deep breath. "And so would the spirit whom you call Rolling Darkness, who is known to some as Lucifer, a name by the way that mean light bearer. He tried to convince the Holy Ones to change their plan. He wanted there to be no suffering for any of their children." She smiled smugly. "He basically wanted everyone to live just as you have, as has everyone who was lucky enough to have been born on Tal'el'Dine'h. And for that he was cast out. All he wanted was for all of his brothers and sisters to have the same kind of life as you have here on Tal'el'Dine'h."

Asdza was stunned. She had nothing to say. Istas had led them to this terrible point, comparing a caring human being to Rolling Darkness. It was unthinkable. But thankfully Kanti was not so speechless; she stood up and spoke in a loud voice. "I will not let you make such an awful claim. I'm not sure how to answer you, but there is a fundamental flaw in your logic."

"Really why don't you tell us what that is, Kanti."

"I'll tell you," said Suleta, standing up. "The assumption you are making is that we have all of the facts, but we don't. We don't know everything. The Holy Ones must have had their reasons for casting Rolling Darkness out, and just because we don't understand those reasons doesn't give us the right to question the motives of the Holy Ones."

Asdza stood up and joined Kanti and Suleta. "They are right," she said defiantly. "We don't always agree with our parents, but we trust them to act in our best interests. I believe it is just like that with the Holy Ones."

"Really? And do you think your parents would ever allow you to suffer? Even if you don't always understand them, you know without a doubt that they would keep you from harm. So, granted, we don't know everything about the plans the Holy Ones have for us, but wouldn't it be safe to assume that if they loved us as much as you say they do, that they would not let us suffer."

"It wasn't long ago on Earth that children were given needles to prevent disease," said Asdza. "Did those parents allow their children to be stuck with needles? Of course they did, because they had the complete picture, and while their children may have suffered, even if they thought it was the worst thing that ever happened to them, they are still better off. And their parents know that. Just as I believe the Holy Ones know what is best for us."

A look crossed Istas's face which frightened Asdza; she was still smiling, but there was a definite threatening look in her eyes. "OK, does anyone else have these doubts?" A few worried glances went between the rest of the kids, but perhaps they too had caught the change in Istas's mood and her implied threat. "Fine. And you three, you're not going to back down are you?"

Kanti, Suleta and Asdza looked at each other, and while Asdza could see genuine worry and concern in their eyes, they showed no sign of changing their minds. "No," said Asdza, trying to sound more confident than she felt.

"No," said Kanti.

"Me neither," said Suleta.

Istas sighed, and smiled again. "Then there's no point me keeping you here, is there? Why don't I let you go back to your parents? Come with me." Asdza didn't feel reassured by this; she was certain Istas did not intend to let them return home, but Kanti and Suleta brightened up.

Istas gestured with both arms in the air, and they were gone.

CHAPTER 43

"I found another dead spot," said Shaylae. She didn't sound too excited; it was the fifth they had found since their initial discovery. "But it's probably just another decoy." It was obvious by now that Istas had deliberately mislead them, creating dead spots all over Tal'el'Dine'h to frustrate their search for the children. Nevertheless, they transported to it, and as expected, it indeed was a dead end.

"Should we keep trying?" asked Nashota.

"What other choice do we have," said Shaylae, refusing to give up searching for her daughter.

***

"Mika, I think we have something." It was Harley, and he sounded excited.

"Go ahead, admiral," said Mika.

"OK, it's in South America, Peru to be exact."

"You found a new structure?" said Ayanna.

"No, not new at all, quite old in fact, a historic landmark."

"Then what makes you think it's what we're looking for?" asked Mika.

"Call it coincidence, if you like, although when it comes to situations involving Shaylae I'm not sure there is such a thing as a coincidence. The analyst who was assigned to that part of South America is a descendant of brazil nut farmers from the area."

"Brazil nuts?" exclaimed Ayanna. "What on earth does that have to do with..."

"Wait, let me finish. His family still administers the government conservation trust for Tambopata reserve, which includes Sandoval Lake.

There's a lodge there which used to be a hotel for tourists, but it's been abandoned for fifty or more years."

"And…"

"Well, since he was analyzing data from the trust land, he decided to check in on the lodge; and guess what? According to the heat signatures, as many as twenty people are in that building."

Mika perked up. "But that could mean anything, right?"

"That's what he thought at first; poachers perhaps, since as I said the place has been closed for fifty years. But further investigation indicated that no one has left the property, not even to walk around the perimeter of the lodge, or skip stones on the lake, for the last three days. That's not all. Now he was suspicious, so he checked the local records. It's fairly remote, even for twenty-second century Earth. No records exist of anyone passing through Puerto Maldonado, which is really the only possible starting point for anyone headed to Sandoval."

Mika's hope rose; this did sound promising. "Can you send us the relevant data?"

"Right away. And our contact there will arrange for everything you need to get you there."

"Where's a good place for us to touch down?" asked Jane.

"I'm afraid the closest space port where you could land a craft like yours is Lima, which is eight-hundred-and-fifty klicks from Puerto Maldonado. In a pinch you could possibly land at La Paz, which is only four-hundred-and-fifty, but I don't have anyone there who can assist you."

"Lima it is then."

"Colonel Martin and a small group of marines will meet you there with suitable equipment."

"And they can fly us to Sandoval?" asked Ayanna.

"Sorry, even I can't pull those kinds of strings. Closest we can get is Maldonado. After that it's canoe down the Madre de Dios river, followed by a forty-five minute hike."

"But…"

"The conservation movement would be all over us if we tried to fly into the reserve. We could get away with it, I suppose, but the international press would bury us."

"Fine." Mika turned to Jane. "How long 'till touch down?"

"About two hours."

"Martin should arrive about the same time."

"Thanks, Harley," said Ayanna.

"Do you think we should let Shaylae know?" asked Ayanna, after they had closed the connection.

Mika thought for a moment, and then decided he should probably not distract her from her search on Tal'el'Dine'h. "No, let's wait until we have something more concrete."

"I dunno, Mika. I feel pretty confident about this."

He smiled. "Me too actually. And I feel better that now we are doing something." He shrugged. "But I still think we should wait."

***

"Mika and Ayanna think they might be on to something on Earth," said Shaylae.

"Really," said Nashota. "What did they say?"

"Nothing," she said with a smile. It was the first time she had smiled in days. "He still thinks he can hide things from me."

Nashota smiled too. "So, what is it that they're on to."

Shaylae filled Nashota in on what Harley had discovered. Nashota shrugged. "Could be something, I suppose."

"I think it sounds just like something she would do."

"So are you going there too?"

"No. I think it more likely that if I went there it could possibly alert her. A traditional reconnaissance team might be able to get more information undiscovered."

"But you'll be watching closely..."

CHAPTER 44

The place had an awful stench – blood, sweat, fear, death, and a strong animal odor. It was dark, cold and damp. In the distance she heard sounds of fighting, shouts and screams.

"Where are we?" said Suleta.

Asdza's eyes gradually became accustomed to the light. They were in a cell of some kind, perhaps no more than five meters square, and they were not the only inhabitants. A dozen other girls lay on filthy smelly straw, huddled together. They had been sleeping, but the arrival of the three girls woke them up.

"Who are you?" asked one of them. She could have been no older than twelve.

Asdza, Suleta and Kanti looked at each other, blank stares.

"How did you get here? Are you Christians too?"

Asdza heard an evil, disembodied laugh. "Ancient Greece, the year 305 AD. The city is Smyrna at the time of the Emperor Diocletian, a time of the last, and perhaps worst of the persecutions of the Christians. And yes, you're really here. They can see and hear you, and you can see and hear them and to make things easier, you can understand and speak their language."

"Why have you brought us here?" asked Suleta. Her voice trembled, and her whole body shook. Kanti seemed too terrified to even move.

"What?" said the girl.

"But they can't hear me," said Istas, laughing again. "As to why you're here, that will become obvious momentarily."

"We're here to die," said another of the girls, weeping profusely.

"Die? What for?"

"You're Christians too, else why would you be here with us. This is where they bring us to kill us."

Asdza felt a knot of terror beginning in her stomach, and spreading over her whole body. She could hardly breathe. This was another period of Earth history she was familiar with. She didn't even want to bring the thoughts to her mind, but they came anyway. "We're in an arena."

"What's an arena," asked Kanti, her voice shaking uncontrollably too.

"It's where the people of the Roman Empire came for entertainment."

"What kind of entertainment?"

"I'm afraid we're the entertainment."

"You there! You three. Where did you get those clothes?" A soldier, perhaps no more than twenty years old was standing just outside of their cage. Asdza looked down at herself. She, Kanti, and Suleta were wearing the clothes they had been wearing earlier; the other girls wore simple shifts made of some kind of crude gray linen. "Take those clothes of, now." He commanded. The girls looked at each other, but didn't move. The soldier gave an evil grin. "Or, if you'd prefer, I can come in there and rip those clothes off you."

"Do as he says," said the girl. "You don't want him coming in here."

Shaking uncontrollably Asdza quickly started undressing. Suleta and Kanti did the same.

"Here," said another soldier almost kindly. He was perhaps ten years older than the first. "Put these on." He pushed three shifts, similar to the ones the other girls were wearing, through the bars. He turned to the younger soldier and backhanded him across the face so forcefully he knocked him down. "It's bad enough these girls have to die, and you want to humiliate and degrade them. You make me sick." He leaned over and spat on the other, then walked away.

The younger soldier stood up glaring into the cell and wiping blood from the corner of his mouth. "Get those clothes on," he said, and he too walked away.

"Asdza, what's happening?" asked Suleta.

Asdza couldn't bring herself to answer. Fear gripped her whole body, down to her toes, knotting every muscle in-between. She prayed that this was an awful nightmare from which she would soon wake, but she knew this was no bad dream. One of the other girls spoke the words for her.

"They've finished the chariot races, the gladiators will fight until only one remains alive, and then some of us will be the main event."

"What main event?"

The girls in the cell looked at each other, their eyes full of primal fear. "We will be fed to wild animals, probably lions," said one of them through her hysterical tears.

Suleta stumbled and fell back onto the floor. Kanti screamed and tried to stuff her fist in her mouth. Asdza said nothing, and tried to imagine what it would feel like to be torn apart by lions and eaten. For Kanti and Suleta, who had never eaten meat before, the image was probably even more horrifying.

From the arena the screaming and clashing of swords was dying down. Surely now only a few gladiators remained. Soon there would only be the victor. She sat on the floor, hugging her knees, trying her hardest not to scream. Would she be one of the ones picked?

The noise of the crowd reached its climax as cries of "Kill him! Kill him!" assaulted her ears. A final cheer, and she assumed it was all over. The victor had slain the only other surviving gladiator. A few minutes later the sound of grating metal announced the heavy gate being raised and Asdza's eyes were forced to look upon the hero – a poor young man who looked more dead than alive, covered in wounds and blood, much of it his own, hardly even grateful for the fact that he was the sole survivor. Perhaps he knew that tomorrow, in his weakened condition, he would be one of the first to die.

"Get three of the girls ready; they're next," came a cry from the arena.

The young soldier stormed to their cell. "You three," he said, pointing to Asdza, Suleta, and Kanti. "Time to entertain the crowds." He opened the door and three other soldiers came and roughly pulled the three girls to their feet. Suleta and Kanti tried to back away, screaming and blubbering with fear, but the soldiers were too quick and strong. "Oh, I'm going to enjoy this," said the young one.

As they were dragged into the arena Asdza could no longer hold back her primal fear. "Yana, Yana! Help us," she screamed.

CHAPTER 45

The journey down the Madre de Dios was spectacular. Hundreds of birds, blue, yellow, red, purple and green, flew in and out of the enormous, broad-leafed trees which lined the banks. Huge dragon flies buzzed all around them while monkeys screamed at them from the canopy, clearly not happy with this invasion into their territory. If Mika had not been so focused on his mission, had not been so worried about where his precious daughter was, he probably would have enjoyed it, but now, his attention was focused on paddling as fast as he could. Colonel Martin, ever the cautious one, had insisted on a small group to reconnoiter the lodge. In addition to himself he had handpicked a group of the best marines; three women and five men. The only ones from the Enterprise he had chosen were Mika, Ayanna, the Chief, and his son. In fact when he had announced Ayanna's name one of the marines had questioned him.

"Are you certain she won't hold us back, sir?" she had asked.

"You questioning my judgment, Ensign?" he replied angrily.

Ayanna was about to say something but Ensign Wilson didn't look a day over twenty-two; probably quite new to Martin's company, so she let it slide.

And so, sixteen in total, they had crammed themselves and their minimal gear into three canoes. Mika doubted that any one of the marines had been in the Amazon, let alone down this particular river, but they all seemed at home as they silently and efficiently paddled toward Sandoval. Soon they had gone as far as the river would take them. The rest of the journey would be on foot through the dense jungle.

Martin beached the lead canoe. "Tie them up here," he said, pointing to a sturdy tree. "We don't want them being washed away in a river surge."

While the others secured the canoes, Martin searched around for the trail. "Here it is," he said, kicking aside the dense undergrowth. The trail had been well maintained when the lodge had been open, but for the last ten years had been allowed to deteriorate. Underneath the carpet of grasses and shrubs was the original pathway, constructed from mahogany trees, washed down from the Manu National Park. Mika was amazed he had been able to find it so easily. "Machetes out, we'll be hacking our way through this the rest of the way."

"What kind of speed you think we'll make?" asked Ayanna.

He shook his head. "We'll be lucky to make five klicks an hour; forty-five minutes if we're lucky; no more than an hour though I'd imagine."

"Then let's get going," said Mika.

***

Shaylae stumbled, almost falling to her knees when she heard the faint call from her daughter.

"What is it?" asked Nashota.

"It's Asdza," said Shaylae. "And she's in trouble."

"You've found them!" Nashota exclaimed with enthusiastic joy.

Shaylae held up her hand, asking for silence. She strained her extra senses as hard as she knew how, hoping to hear her daughter's cries again. There it was! "I can hear her, but I have no idea where they are."

"They? Then you've found all of the children?"

Shaylae concentrated again. "No," she said slowly. "There's Asdza plus two others."

"Only three of them?" Nashota's excitement had quickly turned to disappointment. "But, Asdza is with them? Where are they?"

"I can't quite…" she paused, screwing up her face. "I think they're on earth… but not in the present." The she caught the full seriousness of her daughter's plight. "Oh no, Blessed Ancestors, no."

"What is it?"

Shaylae's hand was covering her mouth, her eyes wide with horror and fear. "They're in…" she gulped, hardly able to say the words. "They're in an arena; ancient Rome, or perhaps Greece."

"You mean…"

Shaylae nodded.

Nashota reached out and took Shaylae's hands in hers. "Let me join with you. Let me see what you're seeing." As the connection was made Nashota's face turned white. "Suleta and Kanti; they're the other two. I think somehow that they have not met with Istas's expectations, and knowing those two, and knowing your daughter, I'm not surprised."

On the one hand Shaylae was relieved. Whatever plans Istas had had for the kids surely involved swaying them to her side, possibly causing them to lose their eternal souls. Asdza, Suleta and Kanti had been rejected, at least that's what Nashota was thinking, and it made sense. All Istas could take from them was their lives. "But not like this," she said out loud. "Not devoured by wild animals."

"Can you reach her?"

Shaylae concentrated even harder. But she could not communicate with Asdza. All she could feel was her terror. She withdrew her hands.

"No, Shaylae, hold on; let me connect with the other elders; let them see and feel what you're seeing and feeling. Perhaps together we can narrow down where, and when, they are."

Shaylae took Nashota's hand again. Yes, that made sense. If she could only find where and when her daughter was in time to save her...

***

The iron gate rose slowly, making a horrible grating noise, as a slave operated the capstan. The soldiers smirked. "Give us a good show, girls," said one of them.

"You should try running," said another. "Who knows, you might be able to outrun them." All of the soldiers laughed at this.

"Besides," said the third. "They won't be hungry. They only ate yesterday."

"And those girls were fatter than you three. No, I wouldn't worry if I were you."

By now all of the soldiers were laughing, almost hysterically; Kanti and Suleta were weeping uncontrollably. She reached a hand toward Suleta and Kanti and smiled. "If we are to meet the Holy Ones today, let us do it not with screams and tears, nor fear and trembling; let us do it with dignity and joy befitting three of their daughters."

Suleta and Kanti looked at her, and for a moment she was worried they might not be able to compose themselves. But as their hands touched

Asdza felt their minds touch, and as their minds touched she felt their spirits touch. She gasped, almost unable to breathe. The feeling defied description. To this point in her life she had only joined this way with her mother, but now, two strangers, girls she had known for only a few days, were joined with her in the most intimate union humans can experience. Immediately she knew both of them, deeply, closely. She sensed their strengths, their intelligence, their fun-loving personalities, but most of all she sensed their faith in the Holy Ones, faith even stronger than her own. She felt their souls calm, their minds return to reason, and their bodies to full control.

Kanti smiled. She spoke out loud, although Suleta and Kanti could feel the words blossom from her spirit. "But, today is not our time," she said. The transformation was swift and complete.

"These animals are our brothers," said Suleta.

"And like Nashota and Shaylae, our mothers before us, we can speak to them," said Asdza.

They turned to look at the soldiers, who had fallen silent, and whose faces were full of confusion.

"They are beyond fear," said one, not sounding too sure of himself.

"Push them in," shouted the officer, "and lower that gate."

The soldiers reached out to throw them into the arena, but Asdza, Suleta and Kanti were already five steps beyond the gate which closed noisily behind them. The crowd went wild, cheering and shouting, but as the three girls walked calmly into of the arena the noise died down. Asdza knew very little about this awful period of Earth's history but she suspected that even though the Christians went willingly to their deaths rather than deny their faith, she doubted that they went calmly. A gate, directly opposite them opened, and immediately ten or twelve animals bolted toward them.

"They're not lions," said Asdza, momentarily disoriented.

"They're hyenas," shouted a soldier from behind them. "Unlike lions, who kill their prey before they feed, hyenas are impatient and greedy; they'll start eating you before you are dead; it could take a long time."

Asdza felt her resolve fade.

"They will not harm us," assured Suleta with her mind.

The hyenas slowed to a trot, and stopped their cold-blooded yapping. Rather than attack the girls they circled around them, crouched down, growling deep within their throats, the hair on their backs standing rigid.

"Be still, brothers," said Kanti.

"Calm, my friends," said Suleta.

The hyenas relaxed; some of them flopped to the ground, heads laid on their paws. Kanti stepped forward. "No," said Asdza fearfully. But there was no need to be concerned. One of the animals, a male and the largest of the group raised his head as she approached. She reached down and stroked him behind the ear. He slobbered his tongue over her arms and hands, and then reached up to lick her face.

The crowd bean to jeer; quietly at first, but building quickly into a cacophony of catcalls and boos.

"Get out there and kill one of them; kill one of the hyenas too. Perhaps the smell of blood will arouse them."

Asdza turned to see the gate being raised. "Can we control the soldiers?" she asked.

Kanti shrugged, a touch of fear working its way back into her eyes.

"I don't know," said Suleta. "Perhaps not, but let's try."

Four soldiers ran toward them, brandishing spears. "The younger one, kill her," same the shout from behind them.

Asdza gasped again. They mean me, she thought. Once again she felt Kanti and Suleta's hands as they took hold of hers. "Stay calm, Asdza. Remember, you are a daughter of the Holy Ones, creators of the Universe; you have nothing in common with these feeble minded men."

They directed their thoughts at the soldiers who did falter momentarily, but the screaming and threats from behind them seemed to be stronger than the girls' combined willpower. The one in the lead raised his spear, pointed it at Asdza's chest and charged. She closed her eyes, shrinking from the cruel weapon about to pierce her body and take her life. She held her breath, but nothing happened. Instead, their soul-sharing was joined by a hundred others; others who were stronger, kinder, infinitely more powerful than the three girls on their own. She opened her eyes again and looked upon a hundred elders of Tal'el'Dine'h; most beautiful of all was her own mother, standing at their head, looking like a she-bear guarding her cub.

Above her and all around her she heard a hellish scream which she immediately recognized as Istas. "Then you will all die!"

A fireball thirty meters across materialized in the middle of the arena and hurtled toward the group. The elders stretched forth their hands and slowed it, but did not stop it. "We're not fighting you, Istas," shouted Shaylae. "We're leaving you."

"But you will never find your other children. They are lost to you forever. They are mine." She did not sound defeated; she sounded victorious.

CHAPTER 46

Martin turned and gave a downward motion of his hand, meaning stop and remain silent. Everyone crouched down. He put his finger to his lips, and lay down on his belly. Slowly and without a sound, he inched forward until they could no longer see him; his camouflage was perfect.

The minutes ticked by. "Where is he?" whispered Ayanna. "Is he OK?"

Ensign Wilson let out a barely audible sigh; a sigh of derision. "He's fine," she said caustically. Ayanna was shocked. She couldn't remember the last time anyone had spoken to her like that. It was all she could do to stop herself from protesting, but the barest of sounds in the underbrush announced the return of Colonel Martin. He stood and beckoned them back along the path they had come. After thirty meters or so he stopped, and signaled them to gather round.

"OK, the lodge is just there, beyond that line of vegetation. There's no sign of a grown woman…" He must mean Istas, thought Ayanna, "… but there are at least fifty guards, and would you believe they are armed with clubs and spears."

"What are they wearing?" asked Mika.

"It sounds crazy, but it looks like they're wearing loin cloths."

"She's brought some of the natives of Sanostee with her," said Ayanna.

"The planet Sanostee?" asked one of the marines. "Delta Pavonis IV?"

"Yes. They're still in their stone age, so are probably quite pliable and able to understand simple but direct orders."

"Which is all she needs," said Mika. "I doubt they are being used to guard the kids. 'Kill anyone who comes close' is probably the standing order."

"My thought precisely," said Martin. "Which is what one of them did when he surprised me, or at least tried to do."

"What did you do?" asked Ayanna. The same derisive sigh escaped Wilson's lips. "So help me, Ensign," said Ayanna glaring at her, "if you do that once more..."

"You'll have both me and the Commander to deal with," said the chief.

"And me," said Mika.

"OK, OK," said Colonel Martin. "That's enough." He put both his hands up in a cupping shape, and gave a quick twist in the air leaving Ayanna in no doubt as to the fate of the poor man. At least he had died quickly and in no pain. "There're only thirteen kids though."

"Thirteen? But she kidnapped sixteen. Are you sure you counted them all?"

"Thirteen is how many are in that lodge, and yes, I'm sure of it."

"What's the plan, Colonel?" asked Tyler.

"Well, a head-on assault is out of the question. Any ideas?" He asked.

Mika was impressed. Having seen the Colonel in action, Mika knew him to be a decisive leader, and an excellent tactician, but always ready to listen to his troops.

"What about gas?" said one.

"I thought about that, but I'm afraid of the effect it would have on the kids."

"What about picking them off, one-by-one," said another.

"You mean kill them? All of them?"

"I guess..."

"No, I don't think so. It would be impossible to get them all before we were discovered, and who knows what they would do. For all we know they might have orders to kill the kids rather than let them be rescued. Besides, I don't think there's any need for more of them to die."

"Perhaps if you describe the lodge to us, Colonel, it may help us formulate a plan," said the chief.

"OK," he said, picking up a stick and drawing on the ground. "There're three buildings, all crudely constructed of wood on raised pylons, maybe one meter off the ground. Roofs are some kind of thatching, again, fairly crude. Only one of them is being used. It's about fifty meters long, thirty-five wide, single story. These three walls," he said as he pointed to his drawing, "beginning about halfway along this side, here, are all windows and enclose a common room and dining room. From here to the back are twelve rooms this side, thirteen this side. It looks like only eight of the rooms have been used, two kids in each, so I grant until recently there were probably sixteen kids being kept here."

"And here," said the chief, pointing to the end of the corridor, "is this wall the outside wall?"

"Yes."

"OK, here's an idea," continued the chief. "We set up ultra low frequency sound generators here and here which will create an area here into which the guards will not want to proceed." He drew a triangle from the end of the building fanning outward, "They won't know why, and hopefully won't get suspicious; they'll simply turn around and go back the way they came."

"Good, I like it," said the Colonel.

"And how do we get the kids out?" asked one of the marines.

"We go under the building and cut a hole in the floor."

"Hmm," said the colonel. "I'm not sure. What if the placed is wired?"

Mark shrugged. "If it's wired we're screwed whatever we do. But there are three possibilities: one, it's not wired at all; two, it's completely wired; and three, only the doors, walls and windows are wired."

"Why wouldn't they wire the whole thing?"

"Why would they?" said Mika. "They've got guards patrolling twenty-four hours. My guess is they didn't wire at all."

"Either way it's a gamble," said Tyler.

"Agreed, but it's our best plan," said the Colonel. "OK, let me put in a call for the sound generators and the canceling devices we'll need."

Mark patted his pack. "Right here, Colonel."

"Why would you bring sound generators?" asked Tyler.

The Colonel laughed. "We've used these once before when I was a Lieutenant and he my staff sergeant."

"Another jungle operation, as I recall. They also keep unfriendly animals at bay."

"Indeed."

"How many frequency canceling devices?"

"Only four," said Mark.

"Then, how do we get the kids out?"

"We only use the generators when the guards approach. We coordinate taking the kids out during the times when we can leave them off."

A few looks went between them, but with shrugs and nods they all soon acknowledged that the plan was workable and for the next thirty minutes they drew out detailed plans, choreographed the whole operation.

***

"Ok, Mom," said Asdza. "You can let go of me now."

Shaylae smiled for the first time in three days. It was true, she had hardly let go of her daughter since they had arrived back on Tal'el'Dine'h, hugging her, holding her hand, kissing her, and just fussing over her. Kanti and Suleta's parents were equally relieved, doting over their daughters. One thing Shaylae couldn't help but notice was that her daughter had grown up. Suleta and Kanti also both seemed to have matured, not only intellectually but spiritually. Certainly their experience of soul-sharing amongst themselves and talking to the hyenas' minds was ahead of their age. Shaylae was fourteen when she had spoken to the snake, and even Nashota was eleven when she had spoken to the cougar.

But then a darker thought flooded into her mind. "Mika, Ayanna! I can't find them." She had been so preoccupied with her daughter's safety it had never occurred to her that Mika and Ayanna were somewhere beyond her reach.

"What?" said Nashota. "You can't find them?"

"No." Shaylae went right back into her panic.

"Wait, Shaylae. If they're inside of one of Istas's protected zones it means they've found the other children. And since we know where they went we can find them."

"Well, we only know they went to Earth. We have no idea where on earth."

"We could start a sweep of the planet, looking for dead spots, just as we did on Tal'el'Dine'h."

"No," said Shaylae. "That won't be necessary. They would have spoken to Anne and Harley for sure. They will know where they went."

"Then what are we waiting for? Let's go."

Shaylae sent her thoughts back to earth, and very quickly she found Anne.

"Shaylae, where are you?"

"I'm on Tal'el'Dine'h."

"I don't think I'll ever get used to the fact that we can talk instantly across twenty-eight light years."

Shaylae wasn't pausing to marvel at the wonder of thought. She got right down to business. "Do you know where Mika and Ayanna went?"

***

So far things had gone according to plan. They had set up the low frequency sound zone and Mark, Colonel Martin, Ayanna and Mika had been the ones designated to contact the children. It was 10:00 pm, local time, but all thirteen of the children were still up, relaxing in the common room.

"We'll get through the floor as close to the wall as we can," said Colonel Martin. He held up his scanner to the floor above his head, moving it around to find the best spot to cut through to the corridor. "Here," he said. "There's a cupboard of some kind against the wall, and a rug that comes almost all the way up to it."

"Perfect," said Mika. "The rug might be able to disguise the hole."

Martin took out his laser drill, set it to cut through the wood, but not the carpet, and quickly cut a circle, large enough for him to get through. He straightened up and raised his head through the hole. "No sign of any guards," he said, pulling himself up into the building. "All clear," he whispered helping the other three up.

They covered the hole as best they could with the rug. Quickly they made their way down the corridor into the common room. The children were startled.

"Who are you?" asked one of the boys.

"Wait," said another. "I think I know them. Aren't you Ayanna Hale, and you're Mika, Shaylae's husband?"

"Yes, and we've come to rescue you."

"Rescue us?" said another. "From what? We're in no danger."

"What is your name?" asked Ayanna.

"Gren," he replied.

"Gren, your parents and the Elders of Tal'el'Dine'h have sent us to find you and bring you home."

"But we're learning so much from Istas; things we never would have learned on Tal'el'Dine'h," he said.

"But I miss my mom and dad," said a girl.

"What is your name?" asked Mika

"I'm Doli."

"Doli, do you know what happened to Asdza? And there were another two also."

"Suleta and Kanti," she said. "Istas said she was taking them home; said they couldn't be taught."

That didn't sound good, thought Ayanna. It was extremely unlikely that she would have taken them home.

"Doli, your parents miss you too. Come with us, please."

"I don't trust you," said another. "You're exactly like she described you. You want us to stay ignorant. You don't want us to learn."

Ayanna was worried, she hadn't been expecting this. Istas had obviously been doing a great job of winning these kids over. Blessed Ancestors! What if they were too late? What if she had already turned them? She concentrated as hard as she could, hoping to be able to connect with them, but there was nothing. Shaylae, where are you?

"I'm afraid you don't have any choice," said Mark. "We've come to take you home."

"He's right," said the Colonel. "Besides, once you get home you'll feel a lot better. Once you're back with your parents you'll be fine. Come on; let's go while we still have the chance."

It must have been the authority in the voices of the Chief and the Colonel, because the kids looked around at one another and slowly began to stand up.

"That's good," said Martin. "Now, be quiet and follow us." Once they got to the hole he radioed his team. "We're coming out. Is the coast clear and the generators off?" Nothing but static. "We're coming out. Is the coast clear and the generators off?" he repeated. Again nothing.

There was a commotion behind them. The main doors of the lodge flung open and in walked Istas, followed by the rest of the team, guarded by about thirty men, although they didn't seem to need guarding; every one of them looked to be in a trance. Outside the lodge the other guards jostled each other trying to get into the already cramped common room. Istas looked angry, and Ayanna felt an inexplicable flood of terror through her body.

"How did you find us? Even the witch Shaylae couldn't find us. How did you find us?"

"Old fashioned science," replied Mark.

"And some luck," said the Mika.

"We've got to move," she said, beckoning the children. "It won't be long before Shaylae comes looking for her sidekicks." The children obeyed, gathering around her. She turned to her stone-aged guards. "Once we've gone, kill them. Kill them all." She waved her hands in the air, and the marines came out of their trance. "You surely don't want to sleep through your own deaths," she said with a smirk.

Gren looked at her, confused. "You're going to have them killed?" he asked incredulously.

Istas glared at him but said nothing, then she and the children disappeared.

Before anyone had a chance to react, the guards raised their weapons. One of them plunged his spear into Wilson's stomach. That was all the others needed. Ayanna was not sure what Istas could have been thinking; how would even a hundred of these cavemen been able to fight sixteen accomplished martial arts fighters. But she supposed that Istas didn't rate physical fighting skills too highly. As fast as the guards outside rushed into the common room, the marines rendered them unconscious; it didn't take the marines long at all. Even with Ensign Wilson down all of the guards were quickly overcome.

Ayanna rushed over to where Wilson had fallen, lying on her side in a fetal position. Her face was contorted in agony as she clutched at the crude spear which had been thrust completely through her. "Hold on, Wilson," she said. "You're gonna make it."

Mark and the Colonel had joined Ayanna at her side. Mark looked at Ayanna and sadly shook his head.

"No," said Ayanna. "She's not going to die. What's her name?"

Wilson managed the barest of smiles. "It's Evelyn. But even I know when it's over, Commander."

"Call me Ayanna," she said softly. Now, more than ever, she needed to call upon her power. As little as it was compared to Shaylae's, it had been enough to heal Shaylae fourteen years earlier. She closed her eyes. "Blessed Ancestors, come to my aid, help me save this young woman." She put her hands on Evelyn's stomach, around the spear. Focusing her entire will she felt herself connect with Evelyn's spirit. Evelyn gasped as Ayanna filled her with comfort and peace.

Her face relaxed. "What's happening," she said looking intently into Ayanna's eyes. "There's no pain."

"It's the Holy Wind," she said. "If only I was stronger I could heal you."

"I should already be dead. How are you doing this?" She smiled again. "Unless I'm already past the pain and sinking into the next life."

Ayanna tried again to feel Evelyn's wound, and while was able to stop the internal bleeding she could not repair the damage to her vital organs. She felt tears coming to her eyes. "I can't do this."

She felt a familiar presence fill the room, then a hand upon her shoulder. "Ayanna, let me take it from here," said Shaylae.

As Shaylae knelt over Evelyn, Ayanna turned around to see at least twenty elders from Tal'el'Dine'h filling the room with goodness, driving out the feelings of evil that Istas had left behind. By the time she turned back around the spear was on the ground and she was helping Evelyn up. She looked at Shaylae, hardly able to speak, then walked over to Ayanna, her head bowed. "Commander, what can I say... I'm sorry... Thank you."

Ayanna reached over to her and took her in her arms. "I told you, it's Ayanna, and no apology or thanks are necessary."

Nashota stepped forward. "Where are the other children?"

"You missed them by about ten minutes," said Mika, who by now had taken Shaylae into a warm embrace. "It's our fault," he continued. "If we had not alerted her, you could have surprised her."

"But it was you who found them," said Niyol.

"Yes, but we were too eager," said Colonel Martin. "If we'd have reconnoitered as we had originally planned we could have let you know we had found them."

"No one could possibly blame you for what you did, Colonel," said Nashota. "But now, where would she have taken them? And could you give us a sense of their state of mind."

"At first I thought they might have already been turned. She's definitely had a deep impression on them but I think Istas's command to have us killed shocked them."

"Yes, I can imagine that would be a mistake," said Nashota. "They're so unfamiliar with death. Convincing them that the Holy Ones are not our loving parents is one thing, but having people killed could have set her plan back significantly."

CHAPTER 47

Gren wasn't sure what to think anymore. He had to admit Istas had been very persuasive, almost convincing him that the Holy Ones' plan was flawed, but when Ayanna had tried to connect with them, even though he had only felt her soul for a second, he felt her intrinsic goodness and superior intelligence. Clearly Istas was not telling them the whole truth, and equally clearly she had an agenda, something he had never sensed from any of his elders on Tal'el'Dine'h.

It was already dark when they had arrived at a crude village. Simple wooden huts sat in a circle around a clearing in the center of which burned a large fire. A few natives, dressed in smelly animal skins, milled around, not quite knowing how to react to their new guests. Istas divided them up into twos and assigned them to huts. Gren grimaced and screwed up his nose; the smell in the hut was worse than outside. Pelias, who was to be his roommate, seemed similarly disturbed by the unpleasantness of their new accommodations.

Istas had brightened up again, as if nothing had happened at the place they had come from. He thought he had her figured out; she was a great actress, nothing more. All of her pleasantness, her positive encouragement, her sense of humor; all of it was just a scheme to achieve whatever purpose she had kidnapped them for.

"She almost had me fooled," he said to Pelias.

"What do you mean, fooled?"

"You know, convinced that we were being led like mindless slaves by our elders."

"You mean you've changed your mind again? Weren't you one of the first to come around to her side?"

"Well, yes, but…"

"In fact, it was you who convinced me that she was right."

"Well, now I'm not sure anymore."

"What made you change your mind?"

"A lot of things really, things that didn't make sense, but when she told her guards to kill those people, I think that's what shocked me back to reality."

"Reality. Whose reality, Gren?"

"There is only one reality, and I intend to find out what it is. Apparently Suleta, Kanti, and Asdza weren't persuaded; perhaps they already understand reality."

"Or they were further along in their indoctrination."

"Pelias, how can you say such a thing? You got to know them over the last few days, just as we all did, and one thing I can definitely say about any of them is that they've not been brainwashed."

"Ok, then how do you explain the suffering we saw? How can you explain the fact that through nothing but bad luck people suffer unimaginable horror, while others through nothing but good luck live happy productive lives? What about us? Born and raised on Tal'el'Dine'h we will never suffer anything. We won't even suffer death, at least not in the same way regular mortals do."

"I admit that I don't know the answers to those questions, but just because I don't know the answers, doesn't mean I have to listen to the first answer that comes along. There are some things that maybe we won't find the answers for until after this life, and maybe suffering is one of them."

Pelias shrugged and Gren thought that perhaps he too had his doubts. "So, I wonder what the three girls have told their parents about what happened, what they've told our parents about us?"

"I have a bad feeling that Istas didn't take them home at all."

"What do you mean?"

"You think she would just let them go?"

Shaylae and Nashota were alone again, back to square one in their search for the missing children. "Now what do we do?" said Nashota.

"Let's see if we can get into her mind."

"What do you mean?"

"From what the kids said, it seems she was surprised to have been discovered. And let's face it, if we'd continued searching for her with our minds we'd almost certainly still be searching. She wasn't expecting anyone to search using traditional methods to find her; to actually use science."

"So you think she may have acted hastily in choosing her escape route."

"Yes, although I wouldn't call it an escape route. Obviously she has nothing to fear from us; no, I think she wants more time with the kids, which is a good thing; it probably means she hasn't yet turned them."

"Do you think her power has increased?"

Shaylae had not even considered this question, but now that Nashota had brought it up it did make sense. "Perhaps. It was only a few months ago that I was able to hold her while you escaped to Tal'el'Dine'h from Dinetah."

"A few months for you, but hundreds of years for me. We don't know how long it was for her."

"True. But something tells me she's on the same timeline as me."

"So what are her options?"

"You think it's safe to say she is on one of the four planets?"

"I would say it's likely, but not definite. So, let's consider what her options were, and see what we would have done in her position."

"Well, I would put Tal'el'Dine'h as the last of her options," said Nashota.

"Why?"

"With no time to prepare, where would she take them?"

"To one of the regions she has closed off to our thoughts."

"Yes, but the whole planet is roused, especially since now everyone knows what she tried to do to Asdza, Suleta and Kanti. With that many million minds looking for her, how long do you think she could remain undiscovered?"

"OK, I'll grant you that, so let's say that Tal'el'Dine'h is not likely, but not ruled out."

"Agreed," said Nashota. "What about Earth?"

"First of all, I'm guessing she chose the location in Peru very carefully. In many ways it was ideal: a beautiful location to relax the kids, and remote enough that she would not have any uninvited or unexpected guests."

"So we put Earth as an unlikely location too. What about Yurob?"

"From what we know of Istas, she's never been to Yurob, and so is the most unfamiliar with it."

"You want to rule out Yurob without even a discussion?" said Nashota with a smile.

"Nothing is ruled out," said Shaylae. "Not even the opposite end of the Galaxy, but now I think about it, I think it's less likely she took them to Yurob than back here or to Earth."

"Which leaves us with Delta Pavonis 4."

Shaylae brightened up. "Yes, think about it. From the way the girls describe them, the guards had to be from Sanostee."

"You think she may have taken them back there."

"Yes, in fact I'm thinking of a specific place, a specific village; the one where she held the crew of the *Enterprise* after they crashed."

"Can you find that place?"

Shaylae stretched her mind across the forty-four light years that separated Tal'el'Dine'h from Sanostee, and soon found the crash site. Her heart leaped in her chest when she found one of Istas's thought barriers around the village. Nashota had made the journey with her. Surely, they had found her.

"Let me call the rest of the council."

The council Chamber was soon filled with elders and optimism. The only people in the room who were not elders of Tal'el'Dine'h were Shaylae, Mika and Ayanna. Shaylae had no idea what to expect, but she knew that whatever it was she needed her two most loyal companions by her side.

"Most of you know Istas; many of you taught her as she grew and watched in disbelief as she turned away from the Holy Ones. Some of you who have seen her recently may also be aware of how much power she has. In fact, we may have only seen a hint of her capabilities."

"What I still don't understand is why she has more power than us, more power than you Matriarch," asked one of the council members.

Nashota stood in their midst, speaking with assurance and authority. "Shaylae and I believe that as she turned away from the Holy Ones, she became totally free of them. They no longer look upon her as one of their children. She turned to Rolling Darkness from whom she learned of the powers of the Dark World. At first he was her master and teacher, but because of her physical body she soon realized that she had power over him. She is now the most powerful being in the Dark World, and as such perhaps in the entire Universe, only the Holy Ones have more power than her."

"Then how do we defeat her?"

"I don't think we can," said Shaylae. "For now our only goal is to rescue the children she stole from you. Perhaps Istas is now the Holy Ones' problem."

"I would doubt that," said another council member. "As I understand it they do not interfere in the affairs of their children, they expect us to deal with these problems."

Shaylae was afraid she was right. But how were they to conquer her? Even after the children were rescued, if in fact they could even rescue them, Istas would never give up. Her power would increase, her determination to defeat the Holy Ones would never abate, and her evil would surely fester and grow inside her. A terrible foreboding filled Shaylae's heart, a foreboding that, for the first time in her life, left her wondering if there was any solution, if there was a way she herself could escape Istas's wrath. She quickly put those thoughts behind her; instead, she told herself, she had to concentrate on getting the children back and worry about tomorrow when it came.

"So, what's the plan?"

"I'll let Shaylae give you her idea," said Nashota. "And then we can open it up for discussion."

Shaylae stepped forward. "I think we need to have three coordinated operations. First, we have to assume that she has the Sanostee natives guarding them. For this I suggest we ask Colonel Martin to lead a team of his marines to contain them. Second, we need a large group of Tal'el'Dine'h elders ready to transport the children away from Istas, that is if our third operation succeeds."

"And what is the third operation?"

Shaylae paused a moment and looked at Ayanna and Mika. She had not discussed anything with them yet, although she knew they would follow her, whatever the cost. She had never felt as unsure about the future as she did right now, and she suspected that they also felt her fears. Regardless, it was the only option open to her. "Mika, Ayanna and I face Istas and hopefully distract her long enough to allow you to rescue the children."

There were a few surprised looks among the elders. "You think that's wise?" asked one of them.

"Only three of you? She will surely defeat you easily."

They're probably right, thought Shaylae.

Nashota stepped forward again. "Perhaps, but I think they have the best chance, of at least distracting her. You've all watched these three remarkable people as they grew up, as they faced the Dark Ones aboard Revenge, and on Yurob; you watched as they each individually faced Rolling Darkness and defeated him. You've seen Shaylae manage to get the better of Istas on a number of occasions; when I was a young woman back on Earth she was able to defeat her, or at least distract her, allowing us to make the journey to Tal'el'Dine'h; and just recently she was able to escape Istas when she threatened Asdza, her daughter."

Shaylae felt the uncertainty in Nashota's thoughts and surely the elders of Tal'el'Dine'h felt it too, but they had heard the plan, and now it was up to them to approve or disapprove it.

CHAPTER 48

As Shaylae joined with Ayanna and Mika her heart was filled with love for them, friends who had been through so much with her, but for the first time she felt their doubt.

"You think we are being foolish?"

"Yes, but why let that stop us?" said Ayanna.

"You know we're with you whatever happens."

"Whatever happens, Mika my love?"

"Whatever happens," he said after a moment's hesitation.

The feelings of foreboding that had begun only a few hours earlier continued to grow inside her, but she knew Mika was right; they had to do what they had to do – whatever happened. Her heart quickened as she finally brought to the front of her mind the thought that had haunted her since the first day she had seen Istas: that her life was in desperate danger.

***

Evelyn Wilson's world had been turned upside down. Just a few weeks ago she understood the universe, at least she thought she did; it was an orderly place which followed fixed and well-known laws of physics and logic. At twenty three she was facing a long and hopefully distinguished career in the Marines. She knew she was a good marine, with almost blind loyalty to her commanding officer, to her fellow marines, and to the country which she served. She had no doubt that she would give her life in service of any of those loyalties. Six months earlier, when the legendary Lieutenant Colonel Martin had requested her as a platoon leader, she had hardly been able to contain her excitement. Yes, everything had been as it should: straightforward, uncomplicated, and certainly logical. But now she had met two people who had changed all of that. First there had been that insufferably confident Commander Ayanna Hale, so full of herself, so sure of herself. She had always thought she was a good judge of character, but she had certainly misjudged Commander Hale. And then there was Shaylae Lucero. Sure, she had heard rumors about her but in her practical mind she had put them down to exaggerated stories. Shaylae was not on the curriculum at the academy, and even the Colonel didn't talk much about her even though he had been on two or three missions with her, so she had been confident in her initial assessment of Shaylae's accomplishments as apocryphal myth. The only minor record of her in the Marine files was an incident in which she had returned to the scene of a desperate battle to bring back the bodies of two fallen marines, but that was it; nothing else.

Her mind went back to that incredible moment when she had looked into Shaylae's eyes as her life slipped away from her. The first feeling she got from this incredible person was peace; yes, she was about to die, but the pain left her, and was replaced by a certainty of the existence of God and her eternal life. To this point in her life her faith had been somewhat practical, something she managed to fit into her life, but not something that dominated it as it did now. Then she had felt Shaylae's mind take over her body, and watched with disbelief as she removed the spear from her gut and healed her. That Shaylae was in touch with God was beyond doubt, even though they both understood God very differently.

Colonel Martin had called for volunteers for this latest mission, and of course, everyone volunteered, but he limited the team to fifteen. Initially he had not included Chief Olsen, but pressure from him and Ayanna changed his mind. Evelyn had to admit he was certainly one of the finest fighters she had ever met. The Colonel's son was not included, and he made it quite clear there would be no arguments over this decision. Apparently they were going to Delta Pavonis 4, now called Sanostee, as one of two diversionary missions to rescue the kidnapped children from Tal'el'Dine'h. Their task was to take on the guards, who they were told would be the same guards as those who protected the lodge at Sandoval. The other diversionary mission was Shaylae Lucero, her husband Mika, and Commander Hale whose task it would be to distract the woman they had met at Sandoval, and who had ordered their death. The primary mission would be led by Nashota and

Niyol of Tal'el'Dine'h. They and up to a hundred of the other elders, they hadn't yet decided on how many, would concentrate on bringing back the children.

Shaylae Lucero would be transporting them to Sanostee. It would only be the second time she had experienced travel in such a bizarre way, the first time being when Shaylae had brought them all to Tal'el'Dine'h. Never in any part of her education had such a mode of transport even been up for speculative discussion. Hyperspace transport was new enough, and that seemed almost like magic to her, but to be transported by someone's thought was… well it was just plain bizarre.

After their final strategy meeting she had cornered Colonel Martin. "So, Colonel, what are our chances?"

"Not relevant, Ensign."

"Yes, sir, I understand, but I'm not talking about us personally, our fellow marines, I was wondering about your assessment of the success of bring home those children."

"To be honest I haven't really given it much thought. I know what is expected of us, and I know that each of us will perform our roles with honor, and that's all I can expect, all I can count on." He smiled warmly, something she had not seen before. "I have to admit that if she asked me to fly into the Sun, I would do it."

Evelyn knew of course he was talking about Shaylae Lucero, and wondered what had happened on their previous missions. She decided to ask him. "So, tell me about her, Colonel. She obviously has had a powerful impact on you. I've heard the rumors. Surely you can at least confirm or deny them."

"I'm sorry, I can't tell you. But I will tell you that Admiral Davidson told me once that she is the most important person alive today – on any of the four known worlds, and that the rumors are probably understatements."

"No, that's not possible."

The Colonel held up his hands. "I'm not saying any more, Lieutenant. Now, you'd better get your gear ready."

"But, Colonel…" but he had already left her standing with more questions than she had before.

***

Niyol sat facing his wife, staring into her lovely eyes. In the history of the four worlds no couple had loved as they did.

"I thought you had not even noticed me," she said, breaking their silence. He raised his eyebrows.

"When you first came to my village I thought you had not even noticed me. Right away I saw you and knew I wanted to be your wife, that I wanted you for my husband."

"And you think I felt any different?" He leaned forward and kissed her cheek.

"And when you got on that horse to ride away, I thought my young life had just ended."

He laughed. "And when you rescued me from the Spanish, I thought I had died and you had come to take me to the land of the dead. I thought that you were one of the Holy Ones."

"Niyol, a girl couldn't have asked for more in a husband."

"Nor you in a wife." He squeezed her hand tighter.

"It has been wonderful, hasn't it?"

Niyol felt his heart fall into his stomach. It was almost as if she was saying goodbye.

***

"Is everyone ready?" said Shaylae.

Twenty-one people surrounded her. There were twenty Tal'el'Dine'h elders. The council had been unanimous in their decision to not let the parents of the missing children accompany them, fearing that their worries may impair their abilities. Additionally they had agreed that a smaller group would have more chance to concentrate on rescuing the children. Then there were fourteen marines, including Colonel Martin and Ensign Wilson. In addition to their regular equipment each marine carried an m-wave rifle; one silent burst from that could deliver a microwave burst that would render the victim unconscious. Shaylae, Mika and Ayanna completed the group.

She was still not completely happy with the plan, but she didn't have any better ideas. The marines would be the first ones to transport. Their job would be to incapacitate the guards, as many as they could before Istas had time to react and take action. Shaylae was afraid what that action might be, knowing that Istas had no qualms about human life or dignity. She had expressed this reservation to Colonel Martin but he had waved her off.

"Promise me one thing," he had said. "Promise me that you will not come through until you see evidence of Istas' intervention. We can handle ourselves. Promise me." She had not promised him, although she knew he was right.

The second wave would be her, Mika and Ayanna. Shaylae would be watching very closely to determine the moment Istas began to intervene, at which time they would launch their attack against her. She doubted they could hold her for long, but hopefully long enough for the final wave of the plan, which was that Nashota and her group would transport across space, gather up the children and return to Tal'el'Dine'h as quickly as they could. The next part of the plan was what gave Shaylae the most concern. Even if they could pull off these first three waves, what would happen next? What would Istas do? They were of course working under the assumption that she would not be able to mount an attack on Tal'el'Dine'h, because every single adult was attuned to defending their planet and keeping her out, but even that Shaylae was not sure about.

"Is everyone ready?" she repeated. Everyone nodded. "Then, let me reconnoiter a moment before I send in the marines." She stretched her mind across space to Sanostee, and found the edge of the village. Nothing. No sign of life; no guards, no villagers, and certainly no sign of Istas. And then with more doubt than had ever filled her mind before a confrontation she transported the marines.

The second they arrived they were surrounded by hundreds of natives, already fighting with their crude weapons. In a matter of seconds three of the marines had already fallen and the situation looked grim for the rest of them. They were separated, each one surrounded by three or four natives, and unable to form up. Shaylae watched in horror as more marines fell.

"Shaylae, don't go yet," pleaded Nashota, but her appeal fell on deaf ears.

Shaylae was already joined with her friends as she transported, knowing that she didn't have to ask Mika or Ayanna for their opinions. Mika and Ayanna immediately joined the fight, struggling to reach the marines.

The whole world stopped, frozen in time. Behind her Shaylae heard laughing and a slow clapping.

"Shaylae, you are so predictable. You just don't learn do you?"

She turned around to see Istas standing above her in the air. Her whole body and face was filled with a radiance, but not the radiance she had seen that brief moment she had beheld the Holy Ones, it was an evil aura that surrounded her.

"I wanted to savor this moment," she said. "In just a few minutes everyone will die, but for now, why don't we talk."

Defeat filled Shaylae's heart, mind and soul. Never had she felt so helpless. "We have nothing to talk about," she said.

"Oh come now, Shaylae, hear me out." She waved her arms and before her stood Asdza and Halona, frozen just like the marines. "I have some interesting plans you may be interested in hearing about."

"Leave my children alone," she said through gritted teeth.

"Or what? You think you are capable of even causing me to stumble? I admit in the past I underestimated you. But each time we met I learned more about you, and my powers increased. You are not even a bug on my wall." Shaylae felt her muscles lose all their strength as she was encased in a force, gripping every inch of her body. She and Istas rose, until they were about ten meters off the ground. "You think you will be able to save yourself if you fell from here?"

"It doesn't matter."

"It doesn't?" she said. "I should tell you that your friends are not frozen in time, just in space. They can see and hear everything."

The force which had held Shaylae was released and she plummeted to the ground. As she hit she felt and heard her left knee break. She screamed in pain.

"You like the irony, Shaylae? Your left knee." Istas laughed again. "But the next part of the performance is not about you, it's about them," she said, pointing to the others. The Elders of Tal'el'Dine'h materialized, and for a brief moment hope returned to Shaylae's soul, but it died as she saw them caught in the same frozen state as the marines, Mika and Ayanna. "And them."

Shaylae could hardly move. Her left leg was folded under her body as she tried to support her weight with her arms. "You know you will ultimately lose, Istas. Why not try to make peace with the Holy Ones."

"Shaylae, even you know it's too late for that. Besides, I will not lose. I cannot lose." She clapped her hands together once, and from nowhere eleven children stood by her. They looked to be in a trance of some sorts. "Oh, yes, their training is not yet complete; I still have to control them just a little."

"There's only eleven," said Shaylae. "What about the other two?"

Istas turned around and looked at the children, almost absently. "Oh, you're right. I forgot about Gren and Pelias. I had to dispose of them. They were proving too difficult, not worth the effort. But these eleven—another fortuitous irony don't you think, my own Council of Eleven—are so close. Just a few more days and they will be mine for eternity."

"To be cast out for eternity like you."

"This is your last chance to join me, Shaylae."

Shaylae had been in this position before. Rolling Darkness, as Denab, had tried to make the same deal with her and this was not the first time Istas had tried to make this same deal, but on all of the previous occasions she had felt just the barest of hopes. Now, there was no hope within her, only the deepest, darkest despair. She didn't even feel the presence of her Blessed Ancestors, or the Holy Ones. "Why have you all left me?" she pleaded into emptiness.

"They have not left you, Shaylae. I have forbidden them to come near."

Could that be possible? Could she already have some kind of power over them?

"Well, let me tell you what I am going to do next, and believe me, it wasn't an easy decision. First, I'm going to tear that child from your womb, and then you are going to watch as your husband and children including the infant, are torn apart and devoured by animals before your eyes." She let that sink in for a moment. "Next, I think will be your precious Nashota." But Shaylae was barely listening. Istas grabbed her chin and forced her to look into her eyes. The evil emanating from her was overpowering, almost making Shaylae faint. How did she ever dream she could defeat her? "Fine, let me skip ahead. After everyone here is dead I'm going to destroy the three planets; Sanostee gets a reprieve, I can work with these people. You want to know how." Shaylae could not even answer her. "I'm going to fuse the core." Shaylae looked up at her, her interest piqued a little. "Aha, she is curious about how I'm going to fuse the iron core of three planets. Did you know there's water vapor and steam trapped in the core? Oh, not much, but enough. Once I fuse that there will be enough energy to fuse the iron. Can you figure out what will happen then, Shaylae?"

Surely it was not possible? It was awful. If what she was saying was true and she could fuse the iron, because the reaction was endothermic not exothermic, it would not give out energy it would consume energy. What would happen? Shaylae gasped as the realization hit her; the planet would collapse in on itself.

Istas's laugh was piercing, strident, almost hysterical. "Yes," she shouted. "And you, Shaylae of the Gentle Heart, get to witness it all. Almost anticlimactically she shrugged and finished describing her plan. "Then I kill you. I haven't decided how yet, I have so many options, but I will have picked an especially painful death for you by the time you are ready to die."

"Water." The thought which came into her mind was almost imperceptible; in fact she wasn't even sure it was a thought from outside of her own fear and horror. But it came again. "Water." What could it mean? Was it White Cloud, or one of her ancestors trying to tell her something? What could they possibly mean by 'water'? Certainly the communication wasn't clear, meaning it had probably taken a terrific effort to break through Istas's compulsions, which meant it had to be important. What were they trying to tell her? "Water." Now it was unmistakable. And it wasn't White Cloud, or any one of her ancestors, she had the distinct impression that somehow it was all of them. Water? Was it a weakness Istas had? And then it hit her. Yes, on a few occasions, when Istas was trying to indoctrinate her, she had shown fear, or at least strong distaste of water. She looked up. A few kilometers to the east was huge lake glistening in the sunlight and knew at once what she had to do.

"Ready, Shaylae?" said Istas. "It's time."

She felt a wrenching within her womb. Istas was trying to rip her baby from her. Summoning up what little strength she had left, she screamed "NO!" and launched herself at Istas, her left leg an agony of fiery pain. Istas laughed as Shaylae hit her, but for a moment Shaylae felt her guard waver. "NOW!" she screamed again, and calling upon all the power in her soul, all the power of her Blessed Ancestors, all the power of the Holy Wind, she transported herself and Istas to the bottom of the lake.

Immediately she felt the immense pressure of the water above them crushing her ear drums, compressing her eyeballs, and squeezing the breath from her lungs. The horror of her situation almost made her falter, but once she realized that Istas was in the grip of total all-consuming terror she managed to brace herself. Istas's eyes were wide open, her mouth also. Her panic must have been so great that her hold on Shaylae's mind disappeared completely. Her powers must have been totally overwhelmed by her physical fear. She was frantically shaking her head back and forth, pleading for Shaylae to let go of her. Her nails dug into Shaylae's arms, drawing blood which floated away into the water, as she gripped her with all of her strength. She no longer looked like an evil monster, more like a terrified child but Shaylae refused to waver.

Hold on, hold on, she told herself. She dared not let go of her for fear Istas would find the will to transport herself to safety. The pain in Shaylae's lungs was almost unbearable, begging her to take a breath, but she had to hold on a little longer. And then finally Istas's eyes widened even more as she finally accepted the inevitable and drew a deep breath of water into her lungs. The sight was horrific as her body thrashed around, trying to cough the water from her lungs, only succeeding in drawing in more. It only took a few seconds before Istas was finally still, but Shaylae held on, even after Istas's body went limp. Her lungs were screaming for air, screaming in pain, but she had to hold on just a few more seconds. She reached her mind back toward the village, and found that everyone had been released from the hold Istas had placed upon them. They looked confused, not knowing what had happened.

"Ayanna," she sent the thought to her friend. "You were a great friend, the greatest friend."

"No, Shaylae, what are you doing?"

"Mika, I'm sorry... I love you more than you will ever know."

He said nothing; all she could feel from him was intense panic.

"Nashota, I will see you on the other side."

Only Asdza seemed calm. "It's alright, mommy," she said. She could almost hear her tears, but then Asdza surprised her and said "I know, mommy, I understand."

At that moment Shaylae realized that one day Asdza would be a wonderful matriarch of the Gentle Heart Clan. She reached inside her own body and transported her baby to Asdza's waiting arms. "Take care of little Sonora for me."

She wrapped her arms and legs around Istas even tighter, still terrified to let her go, afraid that there may still be a spark of life in her. And then she almost gratefully drew a breath of water. There was no pain; it tasted sweet to her, and as her life faded peacefully away she saw her Holy Parents holding out their arms, waiting for her.

CHAPTER 49

"What just happened?" screamed Ayanna frantically. Mika had fallen to his knees apparently not even able to talk. Even Nashota looked stunned. Chief Olsen looked at Ayanna helplessly, as if he wanted to come and comfort her, but he was too busy taking care of the injured. Colonel Martin was down, as was Ensign Wilson and two other marines. Frantically Ayanna tried to search her mind for a sign of Shaylae but there was nothing. She wracked her brain for a plan of action, but nothing was coming. She ran to Nashota's side. "What just happened? Where's Shaylae? Where's Istas?"

"Ayanna... I don't... I could..." Nashota was totally lost for words.

Ayanna's panic was turning into anger now. This couldn't be. Her friend was OK, she had to be. "Nashota," she almost screamed. "Get a grip! Where's Shaylae?"

"I have to help..." she said absently and walked over to the marines, beckoning some of the other women from Tal'el'Dine'h to follow her. "They need my help." She sounded as if she was in a daze.

Ayanna started to feel dizzy and unsteady on her feet. She realized she was hyperventilating as she fell to her knees, lowered her head into her hands and began wailing. "NO, NO, NO. This can't be."

A hand touched her shoulder, and she turned around to see Asdza smiling at her, yet her face too was filled with sadness. She was holding a newborn infant in her arms "She's gone, Ayanna." She sounded more like an adult than a child.

"Gone? Gone where?" asked Ayanna almost foolishly.

"She's passed over to the land of the dead."

"No, that can't be possible. That's ridiculous. She's Shaylae!"

"Asdza, what happened?" Mika had joined them.

Asdza looked up into his eyes. "She gave me her baby just before she died, Daddy. Her name is Sonora."

Ayanna was dumfounded, he just seemed to accept the inevitability of what Asdza had said.

"Here, let me take her." His face was streaked with tears, but he didn't seem to be in the panic that had gripped Ayanna until but a few moments ago.

Nashota and the other elders had finished ministering to the Marines, and all were now on their feet but they too looked stunned. The Sanostee natives were still milling around them, not knowing what to do, and the children were being held and hugged by their elders. Ayanna couldn't help but think it looked like the scene you might expect just after a tornado had thundered through the group, and they were content to thank their good fortune they had survived it, and that it was over.

"This is NUTS!" shouted Ayanna. "It's not over! Someone, do something. We have to get Shaylae back. She's fine." But even as she said these words she knew it was not true. She had been connected to Shaylae as she had gone. The feeling had been unmistakable as Shaylae simply drifted away from her. She had felt no pain, panic, or regret from her, only determination. Finally, just before the connection was severed, she felt unbelievable peace, and she knew Shaylae was back with her Holy Parents. She buried her face in her hands and sobbed bitterly, "Shaylae, Shaylae, Shaylae!"

"I felt it too, Ayanna," said Mika. He too had been connected to her as she left them. "What will I do now?"

Ensign Wilson held out a clean bandage. "Well, for one thing you can take care of that precious little soul." Mika looked at her helplessly. "Here," she said kindly, "Let me take her, clean her and wrap her up."

Mika nodded his head and handed over his new baby. "Thank you, Ensign."

Nashota seemed to have regained her poise as she spoke. "I too was connected with her before she... I'm not sure how but somehow she realized that Istas was terrified of water – I think it might have something to do with her fallen state – and that if she could get them both...," she swallowed, and fought back a tear, "... to the bottom of the lake, Istas's panic would override her power." She waved her arms around her. "Apparently, she was correct."

"No," said Ayanna weeping. "Why didn't she just transport Istas to the bottom of the lake? Why did she have to go with her?"

"I think she was afraid Istas would find the strength to transport herself out," said Mika. "That's the thought I got from her."

Colonel Martin had finished checking the condition of his marines. "Did you hear what Istas was planning? What she intended to do with the three planets?"

Ayanna looked up at Nashota. "Could she have done that?"

Nashota nodded.

"Even to Tal'el'Dine'h? I thought the Holy Ones protected Tal'el'Dine'h."

"I'm not sure, Ayanna, but when it comes to Istas I think perhaps only Shaylae knew the true extent of her power, which is why she felt there was no other choice, why she…"

"… why she gave her life to save us all," completed Mark Olsen.

For a moment there was silence, and then Asdza spoke. "Blessed be her name," she said.

EPILOGUE

Sonora wiped the tears from her eyes as her father awakened from a fitful sleep. He had only slept for an hour, perhaps less; that was usually all he was able to manage these days. She, together with his family and friends had gathered around his bedside, refusing to accept what in her heart she knew to be true. He was almost ninety and ready to shed his weakened body, but she was not ready to let him go. It had been a long time for him to have been without his love, and Sonora knew it had been a struggle. Everyone, even Ayanna and his own children, had tried to persuade Mika to remarry, but he laughed, asking who in the universe could take Shaylae's place. But he did admit that she would also have wanted him to remarry if for no other reason than for the companionship but for him it was always out of the question. He never did show any interest in finding another to share his life; instead he shared his life in service of others. He had started many foundations; some to help build homes for the sick and neglected; some to further education in the inner cities; some to spread scientific knowledge around the world to benefit all mankind. He had received lots of recognition and many awards for his science and philanthropy, culminating in two Nobel prizes: one in physics for his work in hyperspace, the other the Peace Prize for his charitable work. He was one of the most well-known and well-loved men in the planetary commonwealth.

Over the last sixty-two years Shaylae's role in history had gradually been made known. It was inevitable really, there were just too many people who had first-hand experience of her incredible accomplishments, and even though they were under official-secrets-act compulsion not to reveal what they knew, the stories spread. The government finally made the Shaylae files public to squelch the more bizarre rumors. In addition to the official record, there had been five, or was it six, books written about her. Her favorite of course was her big sister Asdza's *The Heart of the People*. She must have read it a dozen times, each time sobbing when she reached the story of her birth and Shaylae's death, but each time she felt she knew her mother more, almost as if she was still with them.

Everyone told her she was the one who looked the most like Shaylae, even down to her blue eyes. Looking at the holos of her mom, she had to admit that there was a resemblance. Halona had only been three when Shaylae had died, and didn't really remember very much about her mom except for the feelings she had enjoyed being her little baby. Asdza stood watching Mika, tears of understanding in her eyes. Perhaps she was the only one who accepted that it was his time. She was dignified and graceful, and looked more like a CEO than a wonderful mother, grandmother and the matriarch of a thirty-eight member clan of The People, the Gentle Heart Clan.

"Come here, children," Mika said, barely able to get the words out. "Kiss me one last time, and say goodbye."

Sonora began weeping again. "Daddy, no."

Asdza reached her arm around her shoulder and hugged her. "It's OK, Sonny. Mom is waiting for him."

"Don't ever let the flame of your mom's life die. Promise me."

"I promise," said each of his daughters in turn as they kissed him.

His eyes closed and his head fell back against his pillow as his spirit left his body.

"Mika." The voice was strong and masculine, but it was also kind and loving. He opened his eyes and saw a young man by his bedside, holding out his hand. "It is time."

Even though his skin was olive, and his hair black, he shone like gold. He wore a white cloak, which flowed all the way to his feet which were bare. His eyes, penetrating and all-knowing, bored into Mika's heart and he knew at once that he was in the presence of one of the Holy Ones. As he took his hand he felt strength returning to his body. He raised himself up from the bed and stood. The Holy One took him a few steps from the bed, where his body lay. His daughters had their heads on his chest, and Sonora was still weeping. He made as if to turn back to her, but the Holy One shook his head kindly, took him by the hand and led him away from his hospital room which faded gradually until he could no longer see it. He turned and gestured behind him. "There's someone I would like you to meet," he said, his voice ringing, filling space. Mika's heart leapt as he beheld a vision more lovely, even than the Holy One who had led him here.

"Mika," she said, running to him, throwing herself into his arms and kissing his lips.

"Shaylae, I have missed you so much," he said, tears filling his eyes

"I too have missed you, but we will never be apart again, my love." She kissed the tears from his eyes and cheeks.

As he held her head against his shoulder he watched as hundreds of others began to gather, ready to welcome him: his own parents, Shaylae's parents and grandparents. White Cloud, and hundreds of others he did not know, and yet he recognized as part of his family. He had returned home from a journey in a strange land.

"Welcome to my Kingdom, Mika, welcome to your eternal reward, welcome home."

"But, Holy One, I don't deserve this."

He smiled kindly. "No one deserves it, Mika. It is my gift to you and to all of my faithful children," he said, spreading his arms out before him.

Mika looked at his beloved. She was no older than the day she had died, and looking at his own body, he saw he too was young again. Yes, this was his home and his life, his eternal life.

THE END

ABOUT THE AUTHOR

Miller was born and raised in a small town suburb of Liverpool, England. He attended Exeter University where he studied Maths and Psychology. He helped support himself through school singing and playing the guitar in local clubs.

In February 2002, for the first time in his life, he was out of work. The company he was with folded, taking most of hisretirement with it. Since job hunting isn't a full-time activity, he decided to try his hand at writing and began writing Shaylae of the Gentle Heart in February of that year. It wasn't until 10 years later that he finally decided to publish. He currently has two novels published, Shaylae of the Gentle Heart and Hauron of the Eleven, which is the second in the "Shaylae" trilogy

Miller has been happily married to Ellie, formerly Parry, for forty-five years and has 9 kids and 21 grand-kids (and counting)

Printed in the United States
By Bookmasters